and listen to the people and the music
on the radio.").

In Sitting Pretty, Al Young has created a funny, original, and altogether
human character whose predicament is
as universal as middle age.

Al Young is the author of two previous
novels, *Snakes* and *Who Is Angelina?*,
and three books of poetry, *Dancing*,
The Song Turning Back Into Itself,
and *Geography of the Near Past*. He
has received the Joseph Henry Jackson
Award, a National Endowment for the
Arts Fellowship, and was a Guggenheim Fellow. He currently teaches at
Stanford University and lives near San
Francisco.

SITTING PRETTY

SITTING PRETTY

PRETTY

A Novel by Al Young

Holt, Rinehart and Winston
New York

Copyright © 1976 by Al Young

All rights reserved, including the right to reproduce
this book or portions thereof in any form.

Published simultaneously in Canada by Holt, Rinehart
and Winston of Canada, Limited.

Library of Congress Cataloging in Publication Data
Young, Al, 1939–
    Sitting Pretty.

    I. Title.
PZ4.Y67Si [PS3575.068] 813'.5'4 75–21461
ISBN 0-03-015266-6

Printed in the United States of America

10 9 8 7 6 5 4 3 2 1

The author wishes to thank the John Simon Guggenheim Memorial Foundation whose Fellowship and encouraging support made possible the completion of this work.

To the memory of my father
Albert James Young, Sr.
1918–1974

And so there ain't nothing more to write about, and I am rotten glad of it, because if I'd a knowed what a trouble it was to make a book I wouldn't a tackled it and ain't agoing to no more.

—Mark Twain
Adventures of Huckleberry Finn

SUMMER

1

Maybe it was on accounta it was a full moon. I dont know. It's a whole lotta things I use to be dead certain about—like, day follow night and night follow day—things I wouldnt even bet on no more. It's been that way since me and Squirrel broke up and that's been yeahbout fifteen-some-odd years ago, *odd* years—July the Fourth.

If I was to wake up tomorrow and read in the headlines where it say it aint gon be no more full moons cause the atmosphere done got too polluted or somethin like that, it wouldnt hardly faze me none.

I'd just lay back and figger, well, maybe by men all the time goin up there foolin round with the moon and stuff, that maybe they done messed that up too the way they done the air and water so cant no full moon get over no more without undue difficulty.

I'd just shake my head, move on to the sports page or the comics and figger another good thing done come to a close.

But this full moon, this big old yella-lookin full moon was up there shinin its ass off, just big enough to fit in her bedroom window which was pretty big. She got one of them fancy places, you know, real big with nice rugs down on the floor feel like you steppin in deep velvet when you walk out barefoot to go to the bathroom.

I'd seen her before, lotsa times in Adamo's. She'd come in there lookin like royalty and order up seventy or eighty dollars wortha booze and snacks just like that! I mean, no pain whatsoever. I'd be up there at the counter next to her countin out my little quarters and dimes and pennies to pay for my fifth of Eyetalian Swiss Colony Port, hopin the man let me slide if I'm a coupla cent short, and she just whip out her fancy BankAmericard, sign, and the clerk flag a boy to tote her stuff out and load it in that white Mercedes she drive.

Then one night she come in there, got her dark shades on with a expensive rag tied round her head. Her long dress was draggin the floor. While she chargin up some vodka, some Wild Turkey and one of them teensie cans of caviar cost fifteen dollars, I checked her peepin over the topa her sunglasses at me but I didnt pay it much mind cause one of the integral aspects of my personal philosophy is to be cool. Even when jive get way outta hand I tries my best to maintain my cool. You ask anybody that know me well—Willie G., the Professor, Broadway, Miz Duchess, any of em—and theyll tell you how I strives to comport myself with coolness and discretion dont care what the situation.

She grin at me while I'm still buyin my wine and head on out the store with her purchase. She was walkin kinda shaky, weavin a little like she done already had a few. She slow down and turn my way and say, "Hi!"

"How you doin tonight?" I say, kinda wonderin what a old woman like her see in a old man like me. Probly just bein friendly, I tell myself.

Next thing I know, I'm walkin out the store with my bottle under my arm when I hear this voice, the same woman settin up in her fancy sedan got her head stuck out the window. "Do you have the time?"

"You talkin to me?"

"Yes, yes, what time do you have?"

I walks up to the car and say, "I dont wear no watch, lady, but the clock in the liquor store say nine-fifteen."

I was bout to walk on off—it's only ten minutes by foot to my room at the Blue Jay—when I hear her hollerin after me again.

"Mister, could you give me a hand? . . . Please? . . ."

Now, this here where the full moon come in. I look up in the sky and shonuff it's a giant-size for-real full moon hangin up there over the whole scene, and I know for a fact that when it's a full moon out people gon naturally start cuttin the fool and clownin and carryin on.

See, moon in Latin is *luna,* you know, same as in Spanish so that's where we get the word *lunatic* from. I dont think I need to go into it any deeper than that. I studies these things. The Professor gimme this big dictionary for a present a coupla years back. I be steady readin round in it to enhance my word power. I cut this article out the *National Enquirer* that maintain how you can succeed and develop yourself and transformate your whole personality by buildin up your vocabulary.

Anyway, I see it's gon be one of them old off-the-wall summertime nights. I ease back up to the car and ask her what's the matter.

She turnt her head to one side and cough some, then she commence to grinnin again. What with the moon so bright and the neon light flashin off the liquor store sign upside her face she didnt look all that old. She kinda red in the face and her skin a little rough-lookin from drinkin too much. Up close I can see she dark-complected somethin long the order of a Mexican or a Portuguese or one of them Creoles I use to know a whole lot of back south when I was livin on the Coast.

"I'll tell you the truth, honey," she say like we old friends or somethin. "I'm a little . . . I'm a little bit, well, too tipsy to drive home and I was wondering if you could—"

She let out a belch in the middle of what she was bout to tell me and I could smell garlic all mixed up with liquor and stuff but I didnt even bat an eye.

"You need somebody to drive you home. That what you tryna say?"

"In a word—yes!"

I just looked at the woman. Just so happen I had other plans.

"Please, pleeeease," she starts whinin in that halfway-

5

beggin—halfway-playin kinda way some women'll do when they after you to do somethin and they half tore-up. She slump down in the seat with the backa her neck against the leather headrest and shut her eyes real tight like she either fixin to break down and cry or else do somethin outrageous.

Now, me, I dont go for people goin into they crazy numbers up outta the blue, dont care who it is. You put me up round the Queen of England or the King of the Zulus or the Head Mucky-Muck of the Eskimos and I'm ready to get my hat the minute they start puttin me thru any kinda unforeseen, elaborate or unnecessary changes.

I looked at this drunk woman. I looked at her real hard and I looked at my wine all bagged up so nice and I'm thinkin to myself: Well now, Sidney J. Prettymon, here you stand once again on the threshold of destiny, temptation and fate.

Now, that's *bad!* Lemme run thru that one again so yall can savor it. . . .

Here you stand on the threshold of destiny, temptation and fate. Should you run the risk of drivin this drunk woman home to a neighborhood that probly aint too use to seein no niggers—and what you gon do once you get her there, walk back home?—or should you just mind your own business, go drink your wine, climb in bed and study the next chapter of your *90 Days to a More Powerful Vocabulary?*

My better mind told me to get my butt home. Yet and still I hated seein anybody in this kinda predicament, stranded *and* wasted. I asked her where she live at.

"Atherton . . . on Primrose Path. You mean you . . . youre gonna drive me?"

"Naw, that aint what I said. I just wanted to know—"

"Listen, I'll make it worth your while if you do get me to my place. I'll send you home in a taxi, OK?"

She opened the door and slid over.

It was a good old comfortable shift car like that raggedy Plymouth I'd been gettin round in until I parked it in one of them tow-away zones up in San Francisco a little while back. Went in to holler at this old frienda mine and when I come back out theyd done shonuff towed that damn pile of junk away. Cost too much to get it back so I just let it stay over there at the garage where theyd hauled it. I got enough problems anyway. Got fifty unpaid parkin tickets and I was tireda slippin round thru the streets scared any minute some cop gon jump up in my chest talkin bout, *I got a warrant for your arrest!*

"What's your name?" she say.

"Sitting Pretty," I say.

"No," she say, "I wanna know your name."

"Sitting Pretty *is* my name. What's yours?"

"Marguerite."

"Glad to meetcha, Marguerite. You gotta gimme some directions."

She start tellin me how to get to her place but keep on slurrin her words and gettin all mixed up. I keep tryna imagine what it look like to the public with me at the wheel and her up next to me in that shiny white Mercedes-Benz drivin down El Camino Real at nine o'clock at night.

Every time she get her directions mixed up, insteada reachin out and touchin my shoulder or my arm the way most people would, she reach over and lay her hand on my johnson. I mean, she dont just touch it, she rub it kinda.

I just looked at Marguerite and back at the road again.

I started laughin to myself at the way the moon was shinin down thru the windshield and thought about my white port right there in my coat pocket just itchin for me to twist the cap off and get at it.

2

First thing she done after we got to the house was to ask me to make myself comfortable on this giant couch, musta been ten feet long if it was one inch.

"You can stay a minute, cant you?" she say. "I'll fix you a drink. What do you like?"

I set back, taken out my bottle and plunked it on the coffee table. "Dont put yourself to no trouble, ma'am, I brung my own. Wine bout the only thing I fool with anymore."

"Well then, save yours, Ive got wine up the kazoo. What's your pleasure—burgundy, gamay, zinfandel, dry riesling?"

"Port, port will do, just a little glass with maybe some ice if you got any."

"Ive got just the thing—some delicious tawny port my husband had shipped over from Funchal last fall. It's so good I even serve it over ice cream sometimes for dessert."

Wine and ice cream? Funchal? Her husband? What kinda inordinate setup was I steppin into? I know rich people the weirdest of all—they can afford to be—but, I swear, I couldnt get a good fix on where this broad was comin from.

"Relax," she say, "I have to make a trip to the little girl's room and then I'll be back with the best port youve ever tasted on that sweet tongue of yours. You just relax."

So that's what I done. I laid back and closed my eyes and figgered what the hell, I'm in the shit now. I'd have me one expensive drink and then ask the woman for my cab fare home. I'm the kinda dude can relax anywhere. Gimme a minute and I can relax in it. Unlax is what I call it. Gimme five minutes and I'm dead asleep like somebody done hypmatized me.

A hour coulda oozed by or maybe just a minute or two. I got off into one of them things where you kinda dead but you still alive, I mean, you be dreamin funny little untogether things, things that sorta mean somethin the moment you dreamin em but they keep changin and meltin into somethin else. Yet at the same time all this be happenin it still look like you wide awake and keepin tracka what's goin on in the room you settin in only that's parta the dream too.

Next thing I know, I'm openin my eyes and it's this little white poodle dog got a red ribbon tied round his neck layin up in a easy chair cross the room lookin at me like I'm stone crazy. It was hate at first sight. I cant stand a damn poodle with they high-strung ways. It's people starvin and scufflin and here they is round here chompin on steaks and tranquilizers and got charge accounts at the beauty parlor and shit. I got hot but that damn dog, I must admit, was cool. He just set there, stylin out, starin at me. Some slick white boy on the record player was imitatin the blues, probly knockin down a coupla grand a week.

Marguerite come in the room with a trayfulla stuff—two big ice-tea-lookin glasses of drinks, a coupla bottles, a bowl of ice and some corn chips.

Good gracious alive! She got on one of them see-thru nightgowns and, even tho I didnt really wanna see what all she got to present, I couldnt help focusin in on her fine behind, that pudgy protudin puddin belly, them hips she got on her, them big sturdy legs and the way it all got to wobblin when she walked.

"Desirée!" she shout, reachin for the dog. "Desirée, I want you to meet a very nice man."

The dog leap on her lap and she pat him some with one

9

hand while she liftin her glass with the other'n. She taken a big swig and then she and the dog kiss one another on the mouth. They do that a coupla times before I just up and quit lookin at em and knock back a good stiff slug myself. That funnystyle wine she laid on me wasnt half bad. It taste more bitterish than what I was use to, a little more heavy and serious, guess you could say, so I reckon it was spose to be more sophisticated.

"Desirée, I want you to meet Mr. Standing Pat. He drove mummy home out of the kindness of his heart because mumsy-wumsy was a wee bit tipsy and . . . Do you like dogs, Standing Pat?"

My stomach was startin do flip-flops. I taken a really big swallow and looked the woman dead in the eye. "It aint Standing Pat, it's Sitting Pretty," I tell her.

"O do forgive me . . . I'm really embarrassed. I . . . I knew it had something to do with being OK or something like that but . . . O please dont . . . I hope you wont think I'm making fun or anything. Do you like Desirée?"

"Aw, I guess he all right."

"She."

"Hunh?"

"Desirée is a she. . . . My little bitch . . . My widdle bitchy-witchy thoroughbred . . ." Here she go huggin and kissin on the dog again, rubbin its forehead up against her forehead. "Poor little thing. She's been fixed so she cant really get into all the delicious trouble her mumsy-wumsy gets into. She doesnt even know what it's all about."

By now I'm ready to throw up for real. I take a cigarette out the wooden box of em on the coffee table and light up.

"Ah, what a wonderful idea. Would you light one for me too?" She snap her fingers and the dog jump down outta her lap and land on the floor lookin shame. "Time for babies to be in bed. Go back to your room and go to sleep!"

Desirée do like she told and disappear.

Marguerite go to smokin on the cigarette I lit for her and talkin all outta her head. She light another cigarette offa that one and talk till both our drinks is drained.

Talk, talk, talk about her problems, all the crazy things she done been thru, includin her husband—his third marriage, her fourth. He work for some big research outfit and spend pretty much all his time on the road but pull down a whole heapa bread, like enough to set me up for the next decade. She liked that, him bein off someplace mosta the time. That's how come she married him.

"What he be researchin?" I ask her.

"Damned if I know. He doesnt really like to talk about it. O he's a character, a regular goddam character, that Harry. Works for this division called Urban Systems. I think it has something to do with, you know, efficiency, getting city things to work more smoothly, that sort of thing, but that's just a guess. All I really know is the government's backing the Institute's research and I'm well informed enough to know that whatever the government's behind is apt to be sneaky and dangerous. I dont quiz him too closely. What do you do?"

The question hit me like a missile. I wasnt ready for it. Aint nobody asked me nothin like that since I moved into the Blue Jay.

"You dont have to tell me if you dont want to," she say. "Just being curious. I'm always curious about us."

"About . . . us?"

"Yeah, you know. . . . We have to sort of keep tabs on one another."

"I dont understand."

She ease over on the couch and throw both her arms round my neck.

"I'm a sister, silly! Cant you tell?"

"A sister? How you mean?"

She commence to whisperin somethin in my left ear all sloppy but I cant make out a word she sayin. She draw her head back and laugh and then start slidin her big old fat wet tongue round in my ear and up and down longside my jaw and chin. Then she tease the corners of my mouth, stabbin and lickin round the edges. Before I know it, she done slipped that thing dead in my mouth. Taste like whiskey and cigarette smoke only it's soft and real warm.

By this time my johnson is turning flip-flops.

Now, my johnson got its own ideas bout things. Its got its philosophy and I got mine. We been friends goin on

11

fifty-five years but a long time ago we drew a line whereupon it was agreed we was gon follow our own separate paths. I wasnt spose to get in mister johnson's way and vice versa. We still tryna make it work.

Imagination is a wonderful thing—and all I mean by imagination is the way stuff look when you pull back from it and give it some reflectin room—but when you come right smack back on down on the ground to the stone nit-nat, then you into that other world, this so-call reality, you wanna call it that. I never much cared for it myself. It just dont make much sense.

When I be up there in my room at the Blue Jay, readin or drinkin or just listenin in on some of the talk shows on my little transistor, mister johnson and me'll start havin fantasies and reminiscin bout all the good times we done been thru together—thrills and spills and intimate moments you might say. It be somethin like that old record Howlin Wolf use to have out bout how he done enjoyed things that kings and queens will never have and can never get and dont even know about. *"And women?"* he say. *"Great kooklymookly!!!"*

But out here in this whatchacall reality is this Marguerite, bout as drunk as the moon is full, massagin my thighs and belly and erogenous zones and even got her old juicylip mouth down round my crotch breathin hot air thru my britches, got poor mister johnson and me both twitchin and steamin.

I really hadnt been in the mood up until then. I really didnt like the broad all that much after I'd done seen for myself how bad she strung out behind alcohol—and I aint no one to talk! Watchin her kissin on that dog was what done it tho, plus the fact I'd done been thru a hard week, got in a argument with Aristotle, my son. He a lawyer. Got a pretty good practice goin up in Oakland with a coupla other sharp young dudes. It really hurt me some of the stuff he said—bout how I never encouraged him or his sister and how I walked off and left they mother and them stranded to make ends meet. He dont really understand how it really went down. If it's the last thing I do I gotta make him and Cornelia see how I am not the irresponsible villain they mama Squirrel like to make me out to be.

"Uh, excuse me please. Excuse me, lady, I mean, Marguerite, but, like . . ."

"Something the matter, honey?" She look up, all teeth or dentures—I couldnt tell which—and her head go to weavin round while she starin at me like she fixin to work some kinda spell or put me in a trance. She dont look all that repulsive when she grin. Fact, that grin probly knock maybe ten years off her age which I calculated to be—by conservative estimate—somethin like forty-seven, forty-nine, pushin the hell outta fifty at any rate. Considerin all the changes I done been thru behind women and this thing they got about never gettin outta they teens or twenties, I sure as hell wasnt gon ask her how old she was.

I taken another look at her head-on like I'm some kinda cold-blooded official the City done sent out to do a little appraisin. That good-quality wine was openin my eyes. I can see she got dark hair only it's sorta reddish when you look at it close with the light from the ultramodern lamp shinin in backa her.

Mister johnson gigglin.

"I could use another little teensie-weensie," she say. "How about you?"

"Suit yourself. I'm fine, thank you."

"But your glass is empty." She drop some more cubes in and head for the bathroom. "Excuse me again. Gotta tinkle, you know. Help yourself. I'll bring more ice."

It was already enough ice still stacked up to build some pint-size Eskimo a igloo but she snatch the bowl anyway and carry it off with her.

I set there gazin at that luxurious tushie of hers—Jewish word for what we use to call totches in my day—and relax like the world bout to come to a close, watchin it wobble off in the distance again.

It's a whole lotta things I could say about that night. All I kept thinkin was what that old Alabama guvnor use to say: "Let's put the hay down on the ground so the goats can get at it."

She didnt have shade or curtain or venetian blind the first

on her bedroom window. Didnt need none, I guess, on accounta all you could see when you looked out was plants and shrubbery. That full moon still shinin down like movie projector light. Fact, I felt like I was in some movie.

Willie G. and Broadway and them all the time tellin me how wild these little young girls spose to be, be boppin round here you can see they titties bouncin and some of em, from what I hear, dont even wear no draws. Wait till I tell em bout this monster I lucked up on. Naw, on second thought, I wasnt gon tell em nothin!

We got to tusslin and jammin so hard round there on that big round bed of hers until at one point I thought I was gon have a heart attack.

The Professor was right. I need to get more physical exercise, joggin maybe or swimmin at the Y. She even taught me some things I didnt even know people did.

The woman literally picked the seeds outta my watermelon and put a pillow up under my head.

One thing tho kept gettin on my nerves—that damn dog was up under the bed and every time Marguerite get to moanin and cryin and squealin and carryin on, the dog start yippin and howlin and runnin round the room.

"Cant we put, uh, Desirée out?"

"Why? She bugging you?"

"Somethin terrible."

"OK, tell you what. I'll put Desirée out if you'll take your socks off."

"Well . . . I really dont think you want me to do that."

"Well then, Desirée stays. Besides, this is her room as much as it is mine. That's just like a brother. Always trying to boss his women around."

"You must be stone crazy, you *got* to be!"

She just push me down and climb back on and laugh.

I had to laugh myself.

Poor mister johnson too tired to even crack a smile.

"It aint funny to me," Broadway was on the telephone tellin somebody. "It just aint funny worth a damn. And I'll tell you somethin . . ."

It's always like that. Every time I got a important call to make or some business to take care of, here he is or else the Duchess monopolizin the pay phone in the Blue Jay lobby. I got up feelin like this was the time to get somethin done for a change. My back was still achin from that workout Marguerite gimme a few nights ago. Was it a Wednesday or a Thursday? I lose tracka time and have to look at a newspaper to see what day it is. Today was Monday, I do know that much, so I'm figgerin it's as good a day as any to turn over a new leaf. *Carpe diem,* like they say in Latin. Save the day.

"What?" Broadway sayin. "He cant mean that! Who's he supposed to be anyway? Tell him I want my money. I done the job and I wanna get paid for it same as he pay them sillyass hippies. Dago must dont know who he messin with . . . Hunh? . . . Well, dago, frog, kraut, polack, spic, whatever the hell he is . . . O yeah? . . . They all just a buncha hunkies to me and I dont care—What you say? . . ."

I never really like listenin to Broadway talk on the phone. Life for him look like it's just one big interminable hassle. Nothin's ever right far as he concerned. I use to feel kinda sorry for him. Now I just wanted him to hurry up and get on off the phone so I could call Aristotle bout helpin me get my car back from the Law. When I went to see him bout it in Oakland, we got in a thing the minute I set foot in his office bout how come I went round lookin so shabby and need a haircut and my shoes need shinin and re-solin. He love to pick at me, look like, specially when I be in dire need of both spiritual and material consolation. It's bad enough when strangers try to put you down and make you feel bad much less your own kin, your own son, your own flesh and blood.

I started thinkin bout callin Cornelia instead. She always was a little more tenderhearted than Aristotle. I always could get over to her better'n I could to Squirrel or Aristotle. He resent me so much he even go round callin hisself A. Win-fred Prettymon. Why? Because I'm the one give him his first name and that's his way of gettin back at me. I wanted him to stand out and be distinguished and be the bearer of a name that smack of dignity.

Broadway up there leanin on the wall in his leather golf cap, his chartreuse jumpsuit and his five-inch platform heels with his purse slung over his skinny shoulder was drivin me outta my mind! I moved around to where he could see me, got right up in his face and flipped my dime and started breathin heavy and lookin mad.

"All right," he say. "Solid. Yeah, that's slick. . . . You tell him that . . . I refuse to work for him anymore unless he pay me what he pay them two white boys he use all the time . . . and if he dont, tell him I got a little bit of influence too, you know . . . I'll talk Dagmar, Jennifer, Lee Ann and that blonde bitch superstar ho of his—Irma Yolanda—I'll talk every one of them bitches into never shootin another flick with him. Dont none of us like him anyway with his freakish, tightass rootypoot rap. He must think we rumpkins. . . . OK, Eddie . . . check you later . . . yeah."

Broadway finally hang up and poke his finger in the coin-return slot to see if he got any money back like he always do. Everybody stay at the Blue Jay do that. Then he turn round real slow, look straight at me and break out grinnin.

"Sitting Pretty! Say, brother, I aint seen you in a week. What's goin on?"

Then he reach over and jeck my hand out my pocket and go to yankin and twistin on it like he practicin some kinda secret jujitsu hold, the object of which is to irritate somebody to death.

"You lookin good, Sit, you lookin bad, my man! I can sure relate to the way you stylin your wig out these days. Now, that's creative." He step back and flash for a full second on my hair. "That's truly creative, Sit. I'mo have to try that. I'm tireda these cornrows and Superfly do's. How you get that downhome continental, you dig, tribal effect?"

"Easy. I just let it grow out to where I shoulda got a haircut six months ago, then I sleep on it and dont comb it for two or three days."

"That's bad, brother, that's slick and together! Say, you get your ride back yet?"

"That's what I been waitin to use the phone to get taken care of."

Broadway grab hold to his purse strap with one hand and twist the corner of his thick long mustache with the other'n.

"Awwww, Sit, I hear you, brother! I didnt know you was waitin to consult with Mister Bell." He come extendin his old mosquito-lookin arm toward the phone with that hammy kinda flourish he like to affect. "Here, by all means, be my guest." He even go in his purse and hand me a quarter which I accept just like I done went for his play-actin.

Broadway one Negro can talk more bullshit than a fertilizer executive, shake your hand fifty different ways and still dont know nothin bout common courtesy and bein considerate.

Words like *jive* and *corny* just dont seem to get it when it come to verbally pinpointin somebody like that. I use to try to school him in how to be cool when he first turnt up at the Blue Jay last fall but he got so much soul he couldnt be bothered with my advice, that raunchy kinda soul that put you to sleep even tho you old enough to be his youthful grandfather.

I got Cornelia on the line and come right out with the problem.

"Listen, sweetheart, I know you dont know anything about

17

this, but my car got towed away. A fine's accrued. I havent paid it. I cant pay it. I went to talk to Aristotle. He never gave me a chance to explain. He got on me bout the usual stuff—how I never done anything for you or him or your mother—and I need you, I'm askin you, darlin, to run a little interference for me."

"Hi, Daddy, it's so good to hear your voice. When are you going to come visit us? The twins—theyre eighteen months old now, keep asking about granddaddy. You really should come around more often. Heard you had the flu."

"Yes, well, I was laid up with the flu but that was . . . that was last spring . . . April. How's Marcus?"

"O Marcus is fine, doing very well. He just got promoted."

"Again?"

"Yes, he's working for the Rand Corporation now. Youve heard of them, havent you?"

"Yeah, sure, who hasnt heard of the Rand Corporation?"

"He's still a thinker but with this exception—he doesnt even have to think about anything specific now. They dont assign him any particular problems now. Whatever crosses his mind, he simply writes down or diagrams and they collect it from him and file it away to make use of as they see fit. Isnt that wonderful?"

"Yes, that's a little bit of all right, Cornelia. Sometime I wish I had his kinda mind. Just lay back and think stuff and know it's gon fit in some way to the general scheme of things and help make the world a better place to live in."

"Never envy anyone, Daddy. You never know what . . . what weaknesses plague the very people you admire."

This the sorta conversation I'm always gettin into with my daughter. She married into a goddam fifth-generation California family and teach school herself, state university level. I know I aint got no business sayin this, but it's been times when I been sorry I ever contributed one red cent to my children's formal educations.

"I know, Cornelia, it's like that great poet and philosopher say: 'For everything you gain you lose somethin, and for everything you lose you gain somethin.' Now, can you tell me where that come from?"

18

"The Bible?"

"Nope. Well, actually, you probly could find in the Bible where it do say the same thing another way, but I already told you it was a poet and philosopher."

"I dont know, Dad—Thoreau maybe?"

"Naw, but you close. Take a guess."

"Honestly, Dad, I give up. It's too early in the morning. My brain doesnt begin functioning anymore until I get the kids to bed at night. It's awful. I'll bet my I.Q.'s dropped considerably since they were born."

"It was Ralph Waldo Emerson said that, remember? I taught you that when you was in junior high."

"Hmmm, I guess you did. Anyway, what do you want me to tell Risty?"

"Tell your brother I need my car back. It's hard gettin around down here on the Peninsula without one. It's different up there in San Francisco where yall live. You can take the bus pretty near anyplace you wanna go but this deal down here is set up for private transportation."

"I understand, Dad. I'll give him a ring. Should I call you back or what?"

"You just talk to him and sound him out and—"

A bleep and a click come on the line. Here the operator come cuttin in, talkin bout, "It is now three minutes please signal when finished. . . ."

"Dad, are you still there?"

"Yeah, honey, I'll check back with Aristotle at home tonight. My love to you and the family. Bye-bye."

"Bye. Do come see us, OK?"

I hung up fast, then taken the receiver back off the hook again so the operator couldnt ring me back for that extra ten cent. I aint got nothin but the vastest contempt for the Phone Company. Leeches and rascals! Need to be investigated.

I went down to the California Department of Human Resources and picked up my last two unemployment checks. Somethin sinister bout that place. I dont dig it at all. Take the name they call it by—human resources—like I'm some kinda walkin, breathin coal mine or oil field or electrical plant or somethin!

They got me classified there as a janitor, maintenance engineer, but they aint been able to help me find job the first in six months. Now my benefits done run out and I was feelin glad about it in a funny sorta way. Time to knuckle back down and get on a schedule again. A hundred forty dollars wasnt gon carry me that far into the future when here I was needin to buy some clothes, some shoes, get a haircut. After I paid my fifty-dollar room rent and set aside that dollar a day it take to keep me in port, that didnt leave too much for eatin much less anything else.

At Walgreen's on University Avenue they was outta *National Enquirers*, so I hung around the newsstand readin this article in *Psychology Today* about how psychiatrists done finally got around to studyin how people have to play different kindsa roles to keep theyself together. Masks they call em. A joker be one way when he round his wife and kids, another way when he be on the job, another way when

he with somebody from a different social or ethnic background—and like that. They tickle me these professors and
headshrinkers and things. They all the time comin up with
some new discovery I done pieced together and peeped forty
years ago. Yet and still I like to check em out and see where
they heads at from time to time. Every once in a while they
will hit on somethin worth worryin over or thinkin about.
People need they masks, heh! Aint a black person in the
world dont already know that. *Been* knowin it, had to know
it to keep functionin.

"What you doin lookin at that magazine all hard like that,
Sitting Pretty? You know you cant read."

It was Willie G. done tipped up behind me, bustin into
that loud laugh like he always do in public places.

"Hey, where you been, Willie? I been keepin a eye out for
you."

"Had to go down to L.A. to visit my sister. She got the
flu and I fooled around down there and ended up catchin it
myself."

"The flu in the summertime?"

"Where you been, Sit? You know these people out here in
California keep some kinda flu or disease goin around. Get
me mad. They always tryna blame it on somebody else,
some other race—the Asian flu, the Hong Kong flu—when it
aint nothin but that good old, aggravatin California plague."

I picked up a Palo Alto *Times* to check the want ads and
we went down the street to the Ocean Cafe to get a sammich
and some coffee. Willie G. wanted his beer, a big cold glassa
Slitz.

It's quite a few people in there I recognize from the Blue
Jay but I dont really know em to speak to. The Blue Jay the
kinda place where it's always people comin and goin. Me and
Willie, the Duchess and the Professor done bout been there
long as anybody, goin on two and a half years. The Duchess
been there a lot longer, ten years maybe. A lotta peripatetic
types come thru there, if you know what I mean.

Wing Lee come out from the kitchen and run the new
waitress off when he see me and Willie settin down at the
counter. He own the place.

"Well, well, so it's that time again!" Wing Lee say, noticin

I had the classified section of the paper out. "You look around for a job again."

"Yeah, Wing, you know bout anything?"

Wing in his early sixties but look younger'n me or Willie G. We bout the same height—five-ten—which is pretty tall for a Chinese dude. He keep trim and healthy, not like me. I probly weigh two hundred to his one seventy-five which is what the doctor say I oughtta slim down to.

"You wanna come to work for me again? My dishwasher and cook help is moving up to Portland."

I didnt know if I was ready to go thru them changes again. I'd worked in the Ocean Cafe kitchen durin a bad spell over a year ago. I got plenty to eat and all but couldnt make no money and got bored pretty quick.

"I'll have to think about it."

"OK, you think about it but, remember, I got to know by day after tomorrow. You want coffee and a grilled cheese on whole wheat, right? And what you like, Mistah Gee?"

While Wing was off gettin our orders I told Willie all about the Plymouth and the fight with my boy and how I had to get some kinda job right away. He sipped on his Slitz and listen real careful, shakin his head and frownin. That's how come I like Willie G. Now, he one outrageous Negro and do a lotta crazy stuff that'd get me killed shonuff but he quiet with his shit. He keep it cooled down, somethin Broadway aint gon never learn to do. Willie give you the shirt off his back and then turn around and go steal another one for hisself.

"Why cant you go back to work for Sam?"

"Mmmm, I dont know. Sam kinda funny and sometimey, you know. I dont mind workin for him when he in a good mood but—aw, we be cleanin up and washin these places down at night and, you know, I like to have me a little taste in the evenin. I mean, I can take care of stuff OK. You dont see me stumblin round sloppy drunk or wasted or anything like that but Sam, well, he just dont want you to be drinkin or smellin like you been drinkin or actin funny or lookin funny or nothin!"

"I understand. I met him, remember? Straight-line nigger. But I can understand where he comin from. He's a family man, a church man, finally struggled up and got that jani-

22

torial service goin, took his son into the business, got two trucks and contracts with a lotta these good solid businesses round the area here—banks and some of these bigger stores. I know he had to hustle his butt off to get to that point. Shoot, I wouldnt want anybody fuckin up a good thing either if I'd done worked as hard as he has to build it up."

"Yeah, I know."

"You gotta learn to compromise, Sit. I mean, you know me. I like to go out and cut the fool with the best of em but I know how to ease up and act right when it come to earnin bread."

"You still on vacation?"

"Unh-hunh. Got a week and a half to go. It's kinda slow right now over at the wreckin yard and bein round that jive all the time is startin to get to me—old nasty, rusted-out, smashed-up cars and parts and broken glass and grease and shit. Getcha down after while. I'd go back to cleanin and polishin cars on that Ford lot in Redwood City in a minute if I could get on again. At least be around some new-lookin merchandise for a change."

"Yeah, Willie, but I was talkin on the radio to my man Ed Jason the other day bout how people done stopped buyin up all these big-ass Detroit cars like they use to. Cant afford em no more. Gas costin too much and them smog devices aint exactly helpin what little mileage you do get. You better think about gettin on at one of these Datsun lots or Toyota lots cause them's the cars that's movin right now."

"It aint that bad yet but I have been thinkin ahead. My sister—the one in L.A.—done put this supermarket idea in my head and I been thinkin bout it seriously."

"Supermarket idea?"

"That's right, goin to supermarket school and learnin how to check out groceries. You gotta put out a little money to put yourself thru but it's worth it in the end. You get to be a checker and the pay aint bad."

"That would drive me nuts."

"But look at it this way. You know if I get backstage in one of them markets, I aint gon never starve. I'm gonna get me some groceries some kinda way."

We laugh over that and Wing Lee come back with our

sammiches. He push his chef's hat back on his baldin head—
the only clue that he got a little age on him—and reach
back under his apron and take his wallet out.

"Look at that," he say real proud, got his billfold open
to a color picture of two little Chinese babies, couldnt be
more'n a few weeks old, wrapped up in blankets, they eyes
all squinched shut.

"My first great-grandchildren. Twins. What you thinka
that?"

Willie and me smile and reach cross the counter, shakin
Wing's hand and pattin him on the back.

"That's wonderful," I say. "I got twins too but they just my
grandchildren."

"Ah but you dont know what this really mean," Wing say.
"We Chinese we dont have twins too often. Use to be considered a curse back in the old country, so I guess we just
stopped having them. Me, I never believe in all that superstition hogwash. I think it's sign of a great blessing, so I am
happy. You looking today at a very happy man. I never
thought I would live to see such a thing—and my own great-
grandchildren."

I felt happy for the man but started gettin depressed at
the same time.

"You two eat up. This one is on me, OK? But you got
to tell me if you still want the job."

Wing disappeared again and I told Willie I wish I was in
a position to do more for my own family.

"You cant win," he say.

"How you mean?"

"You all the time complainin about how you done failed
your wife and kids and grandkids, and I'm still wonderin if
it's too late for me to still have any."

"Too late? You just now turnt forty. You can still have kids."

"O I know that. I know I'm still a good stickman and all
that. I just wonder if I could stand that bein a father and a
husband-plus-a-provider scene. That's like doin time, man."

"Wrong. It's worse than doin time, but it's still somethin
a man oughtta should go thru."

"Why?"

"I dont know. Maybe just so he can know what real freedom is all about."

"You feel free?"

"Dont I look free to you?"

"I'm gonna do you a favor, Sit, and not answer that. But I do think you should check Sam out again. He pays pretty good, dont he?"

"Best job I ever had since I moved down here."

Willie G. swallowed the last drop of beer and hold his empty bottle up for the girl to bring him another'n.

"What would you like to be if it wasnt anything holdin you back, Sitting Pretty?"

"You mean . . . anything?"

"Anything."

"A radio announcer or a disc jockey or somethin long that line."

"That how come you always listenin to these talk shows and phonin in and stuff?"

"Hadnt thought much about it but your analysis is probly correct. I even got a few fans already just from callin into Ed Jason's show on KRZY. Some people wrote in letters and postcards sayin how much they like that old dude Sitting Pretty, say I be *tellin* it! One old joker down in San Jose say he dont go for me tho, but I can tell he just one of them redneck reactionaries, dont like to hear a nigger that can articulate and express hisself persuasively."

Willie lookin at me all incredulous, smirkin kinda.

"I got the letters and things up in my room you dont believe me. The station forwards em on to me. I'll show em to you."

"I believe you, I believe you!" Willie start shoutin, bobbin his head up and down a little too much, bout to go into his boisterous public thing again.

People was beginnin to look over at us.

Elsie, a poor old colored woman you always see walkin round downtown all day long, settin down at the other enda the counter. It's ninety degrees outside and she got a heavy black sweater on. She turn on her stool and holler cross the room, "Attaboy, Willie G., you tell em, sweetnin!"

"Aw, keep it down, Willie," I tell him, "else people'll be thinkin we crazy."

He straighten his tie, brush a little brew off the collar of his shortsleeve shirt and say, "And we cant have em thinkin *that* now can we, Sitting Pretty?"

5

You never know where another person comin from. I mean that literally. You never know where another man or woman really stay at and where they comin from when you think they steppin out they door. Aint no way of tellin what ground they standin on, what planet they own that's theys alone. It was like that with my father.

My daddy had a lotta the Henry Ford in him. I mean, he was *mean!*

One time, I remember, it was cotton-pickin time and hotter'n a burnt skillet in the fields so I went back to the house and set up awhile in the cool of the porch cause I was feelin sickly. He seen I was missin and come lookin for me, real big man—musta weighed two hundred fifty and six foot two. He found me settin up there with my twelve-year-old self, haul off and spit a big gob of whatever he was chewin ten feet cross the porch out into the yard and say, "Anybody can go set up in the shade when it's this much work to be done need to have they butt grow into they seat and stay stuck that way forever!"

I aint never forgot that.

My old man, Nebuchadnezzar Josiah Prettymon—I still carry his middle name—was a hard-drivin farmin man outta

Quitman, Missippi. It still scare the daylights outta me just thinkin bout him. He had one of them low voices that make the ground go to rumblin when he speak. And when he get mad his voice get real high pitch and everybody in the family—Mama, the six girls and all five of us boys—we just all stiffen up like wet laundry hung out to dry in January.

When I finally left home it was to go in the army and all thru the war my daddy stayed on my mind. I decided I wasnt gon raise my kids the way he tried to raise us—to be scareda him and to have contempt for everything that wasnt hard work. I dont know if I failed or succeeded. All I do know is aint none of my family too intimidated by me, never have been, but I sure wish sometime they would show a little more respect.

Then too I wish I coulda really got to know Papa better before he died. He wouldnt hardly let nobody get close to him, not even Mama, not even his own woman. Once in a while I'd see him standin on the back porch early in the mornin, say, or bout when the sun go down, and he be dippin hisself up some water out the bucket we kept back there to wash with or drink. He might go to lookin way off in the distance and I could tell he was gazin past the corn-field on past the pasture on out past the low ground way out yonder beyond the horizon even. *Wonder what Papa be thinkin bout?* I be askin myself.

One mornin I got the nerve up to come right out and ask him.

"What's on your mind, Papa? Look like somethin troublin you."

He turn and look at me real harsh, then his face muscles loosen up a little and he walk over to me and pat me on the head and gimme a little hug kinda round the shoulder. All the time he shakin his head real slow and aint said nary word. That's the only time I ever seen him do anything like that, least round his sons.

Last night he come to me in a bad dream I was havin bout all my problems and hug me like that again and didnt say nothin. But I could tell what he was thinkin, you know, somethin like telepathy. He was sendin me good thoughts from wherever he was. That happen to me and my sister Catherine a lot but it's usually Mama that come to us.

I dont have to be sleep to get in that state of mind. That's how come psychology and stuff like that innerest me. It's moments when I can actually read what's on people's minds and it's other times when I can tell you bout somethin that's gon happen to me or to people I know or to the Bay Area or the whole country or the world. I aint never been wrong yet. But I cant always do it. I mean, I never know when I'mo slip into this thing and start gettin these long flashes. It's like everything inside me get real quiet and I get goose bumps all over my body but at the same time I feel warm and then . . .

But where was my old man comin from? What did he dream about? If I was to ever meet up with him again, what would we say to one nother?

I got up feelin all relaxed and unbeatable, like wasnt nothin I couldnt do. I figger somebody somewhere done said a prayer or maybe burnt a candle for me.

I knew I had to swallow my pride and go see Sam bout a job again.

The whole history of my life is the history of bullshit and mistakes mixed in with forgiveness. God must like me, least some of the time. Every time I bounce back from a bad period, I tell myself I aint gon never fall down no more and then I go off and mess up again. Goin down slow. But when you get to be my age you can get pretty tireda the world, just plain tireda livin on the earth. Hardest thing for me is to keep fightin doin that give-up.

You take this earth we all live on. OK, when you come down here, the way I see it, you steppin into the oldest trap known to man. You come here figurin the world owe you somethin just cause you here and then you commence to gettin bitter and uppity and evil and sick if things dont go exactly like the way you think they oughtta go.

Now, say you do get hold to a few things—some property, say, beautiful womens, fine cars, clothes, a good education (somethin I always wish I'd got), prestige, a taste of power, like you get to be the president of China or someplace—then you get to thinkin, well, I'mo hold on to this and squeeze everything I can outta it.

So what happen? So what always happen? You get old, that's what happen. You get old and, same as everything else, you crumble on away and turn to dust. Dont care how perspicacious or slick you think you is, aint no way you gon get outta this world alive.

Now, I been knowin all this since I was five years old, no lie. Yet and still here I am wallowin right down in the dirt with the best of em—kings and queens, rebels with and without a cause, bigtime stars, generals, professors and scholars, diplomats, rich gangsters, evangelists, union leaders, civil rights leaders, society people, bigshot Communists—all of us goin down slow.

But I keep tryna move on. I left a good job and a good family, lookin for that somethin else. It was gettin to the point where I felt like I couldnt breathe, and yet I still feel horrible for doin what I figgered was best for all concerned. Even tho I depend on bein able to look back and say to myself, *Well, Sitting Pretty, you blew it that time, maybe next time you can do a little better!* I still keep takin long looks at different parts of myself. Dont nobody feel the same way bout everything every day, so I keep on hopin it's still some hope for me.

So what do all this mean?

It mean that sometime it do some good to tell what you know real slow to yourself so you can get it fixed in your own mind good.

Sam was in his office with a new hat on, smokin his pipe in his coveralls.

"I'm gonna level with you, Sit," he tell me after I'd done got thru statin my case and aint neither of us said nothin for ten minutes feel like. "You know I like you as a person. I'm a fairly easygoing fella. Business is going along pretty well right now and I could use another hand to help out three nights a week. As you already know, I believe in paying my men well. OK."

30

Sam pause and trail off a lot when he talk. He a reddish complected man got a thick scar cut into one of his cheeks so he all the time rubbin at that side of his face. He rub on the scar and smoke on his pipe and look at me like he bout to come to some big decision.

"All right. I *will* do this. Ive got a man who's about to take a leave of absence for a year to go backeast and be with his mother who's having health problems. He's a good man and I hate to see him take off but he wont be leaving for another month. I'll put you on for the three nights a week and, if that works out, then perhaps you can take his place full-time during the time he's away."

"Aw, Sam, I'd really appreciate that. I'm much obliged for your kindness."

"But wait a minute! Look here! I dont like anyone running games on me. There will definitely be no fooling around on the job—and I think you know what I mean. The first time you show up on the job with liquor on your breath, the first time I or any of the other workers catch you sneaking a drink during working hours, it's hat-getting time, Sitting Pretty! Now, need I make it any clearer?"

"I think we understand one another."

"What you do off the job is your business but what you do on the job is *mine*."

"I understand, Sam."

We shake hands on it and Sam say, "I'm not a man to hold grudges but I never give anybody more than a second chance. You start work a week from tomorrow and youll be working with me and my sister Wanda."

I nod and hold my breath and let it ease back out a little bit at a time.

Night comin on and it was coolin down fast. These aggravatin summers down here on the Peninsula can really put you thru some odious changes.

We go thru week after weeka this hot dry heat and then up outta nowhere itll break all of a sudden and drop from a hundred degrees back down to sixty. Itll do this between the time you finish eatin your dinner and go out for a walk and maybe, for the hell of it, stay round in the low sixties or drop into the fifties for a coupla days then, just when everybody gettin into a fall or spring frame of mind, itll skeet back up right quick and start bakin people's brains out again.

But I'll tell you somethin. It can be swelterin down here and you ride up to San Francisco and folks walkin round in overcoats.

California? Love it or leave it, I say. Or else, if the scene is gettin you down, just wait a few minutes and see what happen.

I keep thinkin I done seen it all happen—and I have—but the *way* in which it happen keep changin.

Take right now. University Avenue gettin dark. I'm settin up on one of the benches in Lytton Plaza with the hippies and the old folks. The kids done got permission from the

City to throw another concert, this time providin they dont let shit get outta hand like they kept doin in the past when theyd be up there screamin and yowlin with they amplifiers blastin. A riot would break out, windows'd start gettin broke and the City would cut off the electricity and arrest everybody.

That's how these so-call concerts use to go, but now it's done cool down some. The kids is cooler, they hair is shorter and you dont read too much about Vietnam in the papers no more. O it's still wars goin on all over the globe only now everybody just tryna figger out what the next big thing to be doin is. Beside, they got other things to worry bout.

I sure wouldnt wanna be in these young folkses shoes nowdays. It's too much phenomena and data to decipher and evaluate and no time to lay back and just enjoy bein childish and uninformed.

Miz Duchess come waddlin over toward me while the band tunin up, got her shades on, that sea cap'n cap, her long trenchcoat and sportin her little made-in-Hong-Kong cane.

You might think she blind the way she come tap-tap-tappin her way to my bench. Aint too many people assembled yet but they all get outta her way. She kinda like for people to think that, that she cant see too good when, you wanna know the truth, she probly could spot the date on a dime in the dark layin on the sidewalk halfa block away.

She plop down longside me and reach for my hand.

"Sitting Pretty."

"Yes, Duchess."

"Feel my hand!"

"I'm feelin it."

"How does it feel?"

"Like your hand."

"Well, I'm ice cold. Cant you tell?"

"I'd say you was more like lukewarm, Duchess."

"Ah, youre like all the resta them. You wanna put me on and talk a lotta fool flattery. Well, you know what I say? I say *horsefeathers!* I'm ice cold. Ive been ice cold all day long. You know what the doctor said? Told me to go home and go to bed for a coupla days but to walk and get lots of exercise. Now, what do you think of that?"

Under the plaza lights which'd just then come on, I can

33

see how black her hair still is. It's short and curl at the nape of her neck. She tan from walkin all over town all day which is all that keep her goin. Cut out them walks and Miz Duchess is dead. She admit to bein seventy-five, for three years she been seventy-five, so I figger she gotta be eighty at least. She a good-size woman, bout my height, but dumpy kinda and grouchy tho she always walk tall.

"Sitting Pretty," she say, "I got two things to tell you. The first is that I want you to drive me up to San Francisco."

"When?"

"Tonight."

"I cant, my car's been impounded. Now, what's the second thing?"

"Wait a minute, wait a minute! Let me show you this letter I got. CBS wants me to join their staff. They sent me an invitation to audition as an announcer. Ive got it right here."

She hand me a crumpled-up letter from outta her shoulderbag sent to our Blue Jay address. It's from the Columbia School of Broadcasting and right up at the top they got a disclaimer that explain how they aint connected up in no way or fashion with the real CBS, the Columbia Broadcasting System.

All it is is a pitch. They send these promos—I know a little somethin bout advertizin—out to everybody that somehow got on they mailin list. What they do is train you to be a radio announcer. You the one do the payin. Any breaks you get after that is gravy, but Miz Duchess had it all wrong.

"Youre a spoilsport, Sitting Pretty," she tell me after I explain and run down all them intricacies to her. "I thought theyd somehow narrowed their search for a real reporter who wouldnt pull any punches down to me. I do know everything about everybody, you know. I can tell you stuff'd make your nappy head spin!"

Then she mumbled a few phrases I couldnt understand. I asked her what was goin on. She giggle and snatch the letter back.

"I was calling them all kinds of bastards and sonsofbitches in my own tongue," she say, "the Cherokee language. I'm a fullblooded Cherokee, you know, but there's a little of their blood and a little of, ha ha, your blood mixed up in it

34

too, you know. What does that make me, Sitting Pretty?"

"We a little bit of one nother," I tell her.

"I was afraid you were going to say something like that. I dont know. Are we really? Nah, I guess maybe we are. My granddaddy was a fullblooded Cherokee way back when Oklahoma was just territory. Used to say we were all a part of the Great Spirit. The Great Spirit. But you gotta remember that was back before the white man had really gotten his foot in our door and we were still free. I dont think he meant to include the white man when he said we were all a part of this Great Spirit, do you?"

"Hard to say, Duchess. Course, I didnt know your grand-dad and—"

"Ah what the hell. Skip it. Whatre we doing sitting out here anyway?"

"I'm just takin the air and lettin my thoughts cool out."

The band started up. Some little blonde gal with overalls on—couldna been more'n sixteen—was up there shakin her boodie round with a redhead boy play guitar. Both of em tryna sing Lowell Fulsom's tune "Tramp" the same way Otis Redding and Carla Thomas recorded it. People eatin it up. I'm diggin on how these young white kids be workin so hard to get the authentic Negro music down and thinkin back to the time when "Tramp" first come out by the man that wrote it, when me and Squirrel was doin all right, not raisin much sand but doin OK. I use to bring her home flowers and candy and ice cream when I got off work Fridays. That's how beautiful it was in them days.

Miz Duchess customarily be tightlipped and cautious but she break down and smile watchin the kids do they number. I check her goin thru this change and say, "You blowin your cool, Duchess, you blowin your cover."

"How's that? You know how I hate the current slang. If youre gonna talk American then say what you mean!"

"But that just aint the American way," I tell her, kiddin her like I always like to do. "The free-enterprise system and democracy say you can do anything you wanna do just so long as it turn a profit. And that include how you talk."

"Well, I find that unacceptable."

She got up to go and some hairy, short, thick-neck-lookin

joker with a ring in one ear come over and rattle a money can in her face.

"Would you care to make a contribution?" he say.

"Nope!" say the Duchess, drawin her cane back over her shoulder.

Kids dancin all round her while Miz Duchess tryna make her way thru the crowd and back to the Blue Jay.

I get up and jog after her.

"What was the second thing you wanted to tell me?" I ask while she usin her cane to knock folks out the way.

"Second thing? O yes! You got a call on the lobby phone and I answered it and took the message. What was it he said? Ah! Now I remember. It was your boy, gotta funny name, he said for you to call him first thing in the morning, said there'd be complications, that's all."

I did understand.

"That number was cute," she say, "but I cant stand the noise, it makes my stomach hurt. I'm still trying to get over Nat King Cole. Wasnt that awful, him up and dying on us like that?"

I'm wonderin if Miz Duchess got anybody in the world to look after her. She too old to be draggin round these streets, holin up at a hotel.

She turn and tap-tap her way off thru the crowd. "Outta my way, sonny!" she growl, wavin her cane. "Youre loitering on public property, you know."

Some big colored dude with his hair braided come over with this pretty little Japanese girl hangin on his arm.

"Want a hit off this, brother?"

I take me a giant swig that go straight to my knees and hand him back the bottle, paper bag and all.

"Not bad," I say, "but what is it?"

"What it is, what it is," his girlfriend say, gigglin.

What with all that racket and commotion and the drink I'd just taken, I was startin to feel randy—a term the Professor use, British word for horny—randy for my own private bottle of sweet wine. Got a job lined up and just *know* Aristotle gon spring my Plymouth loose.

Celebration time!

Time to do that quiet furlough down to Adamo's again.

7

Dont ask me how come but it felt like one of them nights —people racin round crazy in they cars all up and down El Camino like nights and cars was goin outta style. You can feel things out better, least I can, when you do a lotta walkin round a scene that's motorized.

I'm probly more sensitized to these things than most people anyhow. It's a parta me that, when I'm in my right mind, operate like radar. I can pick up on good clean righteous thoughts from someplace deep down inside myself that belong to a whole different person. But if I get juiced out or stoned, my own body dont even belong to me.

It's spirits, you know, dead people's souls that be floatin round in the environment. They can slip into your body and take it over after you done drowned yourself out cause they aint got no bodies of they own, so while you all fuzzyminded and outta control they do they own thing thru you. I know that might sound ignorant but I know bout these things and it's what God love, the truth.

The night just wasnt feelin right, that's all.

I get to Adamo's and it's a goofy-lookin buncha kids crammed inside a VW bus out in the parkin lot, lookin at me all peculiar like they been waitin all this time for me to finally make my appearance.

The shaggyhead boy in the driverseat wave me over and say, "Sir? Excuse me, sir, but can I talk to you a second?"

"What yall want?"

I knew what they wanted but, like I say, I plays my cards up so close to my chest until sometime I have to scoot back my ownself to peep what I'm holdin.

"Sir, we were wondering if you could, you know, buy us some beer."

I'm feelin pretty mellow and figger what the hell, you aint settin no example, get the durn kids a coupla sixpacks and let em enjoy theyself. Better than them bein on that doggone dope. Beside, they just might gimme a tip.

"What's in it for me?"

"Here you go, mister." He hand me a ten-dollar bill. "We want three sixpacks."

"What brand yall drink?"

A coupla the kids in the back start snigglin.

"We dont really care, any kind. You can mix them up if you like. You can keep the change too."

Mmmm, I'd be comin out a good two dollars ahead for bout three minutes' work, not bad, but I didn't want no trouble. I told em, say, "Listen, I can get in a lotta trouble doin this."

The back window slid open and a hand shot out with another dollar bill in it. I snatched it, crumpled it up in my coat pocket and say, "Yall wait for me up the street here at the Shell station, OK? I'll walk by with it."

"O *really*, Mark," the gal settin next to him say, "this dude might just turn out to be another burn artist!"

I handed the boy back his ten dollars and was feelin for the other balled-up bill when he say, "No, no! We'll be there at the service station parked near the phone booth, is that cool?"

They start up they engine while I look around good before goin inside.

"Well, well, a little beer to go with your wine tonight," the little yella-headed clerk say to me at the cash register.

"Yeah, decided to stock up on some suds for the weekend to celebrate."

"I can go for that, getting a few days' jump on the weekend, eh? Whatcha celebrating?"

"The weather coolin down," I tell him outta my head. In other words wasnt none of his business.

"Have a long happy weekend, man!" the little clerk say, tackin that word *man* on at the end the way white folks'll do sometime when they talkin to a Negro and dont know how to act. They figger that *man* business spose to put *me* at ease when all they really doin is allowin me to ascertain they own discomfiture.

I walked cross the street to the gas station to give the kids they beer, got my coupla dollars made! Yet and still I'm checkin everything out like somebody got some sense. That walk I do take me from Palo Alto cross the border into Menlo Park where the police dont always wear uniforms and aint necessarily doin they gettin around in marked cars.

Just like we agreed, they parked right there on the station lot, one of em slick enough to be in the phone booth makin out like he havin a conversation while the rest of em waitin on him.

"Hey, great!" the boy was doin the drivin say when I hand him the bag. "Thanks, buddy, we really appreciate it. Trying to get this party together, you know, and without a little beer there's no party, right? Say, can we give you a lift anywhere?"

"How far yall goin?"

"To the end of the world," some little girl in back call out.

It was innerestin back up in there. They got the backa the VW fixed up like a regular room—got pillows, mats, a rug, a little kerosene stove, tape recorder, some books. On the wall they got a picture of Jesus taped up longside one of Hitler, plus pictures somebody just set down and drew—foolish-lookin stuff with a lotta nekkid people even tho you gotta sit real still and look at em hard to make out what they actually spose to represent.

It's maybe nine of us scroonched up in there but dont nobody say too mucha nothin.

Everybody nod at me and a coupla kids ask how I'm doin or what's goin on.

It's four girls. One of em set there lookin down at the cigarette she fixin to light, a Virginia Slim. Just set up there cross from me, rollin her eyes at the cigarette, hair all down her back and got them overalls on like the rich white kids like to wear nowdays. Back when I was comin up if you went around in overalls it didnt mean but one thing, that you was too poor to afford anything else and you was expected to do the best you could to scrape together some kinda presentable-lookin clothes to socialize in.

But it's a brand-new day. It's always a brand-new day and my philosophy is to sorta roll with the times.

Virginia Slim look over at another brown-hair girl and say, "O wow, I cant believe it's really happening!"

All of em laugh at that.

"Just wait a few more minutes, give it some time," a little Negro say. We the only two back there. Like the joker in the plaza gimme a pull off his wine, this boy got his head all plaited up too, stickin all up on the topa his head make him favor a pickaninny, one of them original Gold Dust Twins use to be on the fronta the soapbox.

He tickle me.

I cant forget how me and a whole lotta other people use to picket and boycott shit like that, how the N Double A CP stayed on companies' ass to get them kinda images up offa us—the Gold Dust Twins, Amos and Andy, Stepin Fetchit, Little Black Sambo, all that jive—and now here this young Afro-American squat, eyes all glazed, got his legs drawn up and his hands wrapped around em. All he need is a bone thru his nose. I just ignored the fool.

Roll with the times but that dont mean I gotta get behind every simple-minded style that come down the pike. Anyway if the kids get together and decide they wanna go sloppin round in overalls or with they hair standin up on end, it aint for me to say that's wrong. It's done got so now I can spot this jive comin a coupla years away—like I knew as soon as that picture *Superfly* come out that Negroes was gon start back to straightnin they hair—and it always take longer for these things to play out than it do to get em goin.

My true feelins on the matter, long as we on the subject, is that we slidin back into prehistoric times. White people done slid back to caveman style and Negroes done gone back to cannibalism, not that the two is mutually exclusive, you understand. Them's just my feelins.

It do say in the Bible where each generation was gon get wiser and weaker. It'd been me writin up the Bible, I think I'da slipped somethin in there bout how they was gon get dumber and more uppity too but, to give credit where credit is due, it's a few of these younguns—damn few but a few—that's bout half smart, that's got a little sense. Sense and wisdom two different things.

The bus windows all curtained off so aint nothin to do but hunch up like everybody else and keep quiet till they let me off on Hamilton Street. I get to studyin them pictures of Jesus and Hitler and think to myself, Now, that's two controversial figgers the world aint gon never forget because, say what you will, they was *hell raisers,* both of em!

While I'm lookin round at these washed-out kids—all of em young enough to be my grandchildren—it's a parta me wonderin what Willie G. see in these overall and longdress-wearin gals and another part wonderin what Marguerite doin right now.

That's when the siren come whoopin up behind us and the bus slow down and pull over.

Didnt nobody move but me.

8

Everything probly woulda been OK if it hadnt been nothin but a van fulla white kids.

Well, lemme put it another way.

Everything probly woulda been all right if the police hadna peeped inside and seen me and Gold Dust back there with all them young girls.

"That was a red light you ran back there," I hear one of em sayin.

"But it was a blinking red light," the boy explain.

"What's that supposed to mean?" the other cop say. "A red light's a red light and youre obliged to stop. Where'd you get your driver's training anyway?"

"Pali High."

"Palo Alto High, eh? Well, dont they teach you over there that youre to come to a full stop every time you see either a red light or a stop sign? May I see your driver's license?"

I couldnt actually see what was happenin up front so I just reckon the boy was gettin his license out to present.

Everybody piled in back is scared, includin me. I wanted to disappear, turn invisible, and swoop on back to my room undetected. At the very least I'm hopin aint none of em done

42

already cracked open one of them beers. My palms itchin and my head startin to hurt.

Gold Dust unzip his boot and cram a little packet of somethin down inside it.

One of the girls—a fat one in a long purple dress, got curly black hair—she snatch up somethin was layin on topa the tape recorder and jam it down her big bosom.

The side door swing open and there we set. The youngish cop with his babyface and light-brown hair look like Mister America. He shine his flashlight on every one of us and all cross the floor and walls. When he come to the pictures was taped up, I can see him do a little subtle double take. His Adam's apple commence to bobbin.

He focus right in on me.

"I'm just a hitchhiker," I tell him, "just tryna get back to the Blue Jay for a good night's sleep."

"Everybody out! I want to see some identification!"

Nazi Germany is runnin thru my mind while I'm climbin out on the sidewalk like everybody else, climbin out that goddam Volkswagen bus.

Already I can picture myself sayin to the judge, *Your Honor, I served in the European Theater and was decorated for bravery beyond the call of duty overseas in Itly back in 1944.*

It was really a silly bust.

They end up citin the boy for runnin the red light, for not havin a side-view mirror and for faulty windshield wipers. I knew his folks was gon get on his case when he got home and told em about it. Theyd cuss him out, pay the violation and that would be that.

Me they radio a warrant check on—"Just routine, Mister Prettymon," the babyface cop say—and find out bout all them tickets I been duckin and aint paid yet.

"You guys can go now," the other Chicano-lookin cop tell the kids, "but drive carefully and watch the lights. I'd take care of that citation first thing tomorrow if I were you, young man. I'm afraid we're gonna have to detain your passenger a bit longer."

The kids done they best to look shameface and stay cool but I seen a couple of em lookin relieved as they all pile back inside the VW.

A redface boy with a ponytail stickin out from under his derby hat ask the Anglo cop, "Whatre you gonna do with him?"

"O nothing brutal or discriminatory if that's what's worrying you. It simply appears that the gentleman has a number of outstanding traffic tickets that I'm sure he might wish to discuss with us."

Cop been lookin at television.

Wasnt nothin much to say. They college-trained cops from what I could tell, courteous and hip. The Chicano one even offer me a cigarette from his pack. I tell him I dont smoke.

On the way down to the station another cop car pull up longside em and a Negro in uniform stick his head out and say, "Everything OK?"

They laugh and joke with one nother. The Negro cop say how he cant wait to see how the Giants come out in that doubleheader Friday.

"You and your Giants," the Anglo say. "Took my kids out to Marine World with that last ten bucks I won off you. Ready to kick down some more bread, baby?"

"Let's talk about it over coffee."

"See you in half an hour at Jack-in-the-Box."

"Nah, I'm sick of that place, how about the Pancake House?"

"The Pancake House," the Chicano say, "that place aint got no soul."

"There's no place open this late that serves chili peppers with coffee," the Negro say. "Pancake House, OK? I'm buying."

"Youre on, half an hour!"

Half an hour later they done granted me my phone call which I placed to Aristotle after Marguerite didnt answer. Izetta answered, his wife, and told me he was out but she was gon tell him the bad news soon as he got in. She say she was shocked but not to worry bout a thing.

By the time the officers was goin off-duty to keep they little coffee rendezvous, they done booked and fingerprinted me, said they gon hold me for twenty-four hours or at least until somebody went my bail, taken all the stuff out my pockets and my belt. I was locked up with a buncha knuckleheads aint nary one got no wine or anything worth readin.

I cried without sheddin a tear.

9

Jail is dull, dont care what anybody say. It's all calculated to be that way. It's all worked out to make you feel crummy, to make you realize how good it really is to be able to move around on your own schedule insteada somebody else's and to be able to carry out little ordinary plans like settin up in the privacy of your own familiar john for as long as you feel like.

The joker on the bunk next to mine—a little scraggly Okie bout forty years old, got big bug eyes and bad breath—he kept dozin off and wakin up and sayin stuff like, "Betcha one thing . . . betcha when they let me outta this rathole, betcha I go right back to Sunnyvale and do a number on that bitch! Betcha that! I'll break the bitch's legs. Yeah."

He kept this up all night until I couldnt stand it no more and finally just told him to knock it off, goddammit! He shut up after that but keep on droppin off and wakin up lookin stupid.

The other fool they got me locked up in the same cell with, he a big neat-lookin, expensive-clothes-wearin clown. His shoes look like they set him back, say, seventy-five dollars and his shirt and cuff links look custom-made. I kept wonderin what he was doin in there with us. He dont say much. Every

46

once in a while he come out with somethin like, "I never felt so alienated from a culture or a society, not even when I was AWOL in Vietnam."

He do a lotta pacin up and down which can get on your nerves when you pretty pissed off in the first place but still tryna get in a few winks before daybreak. Remind me of sweaty old William Bendix bout to stage a prison break in one of them old-timey convict pictures they run on "All Nite Movies" come over TV. I use to look at them things at the picture show when I was a kid and believe every scene and every word was said.

But this cornball! Not only do he be pacin, he be scratchin at his johnson a lot. He even jam his hand down inside his britches and play with hisself like dudes'll do while they lookin at *Deep Throat* or flicksa that type that play in them theaters in the city. Stag movies they called em back in my day.

That's where that imagination thing I was talkin bout come back in again.

It's like you be settin up there in the dark tryna be cool, checkin out some old raunchy porn flick. Some simple-minded pervert settin up next to you in real life whip out his thing and start gettin all rigid and breathin heavy and you actually ready to go get the management or some kinda cop to come and arrest him for indecent exposure.

Aint nothin romantic bout bein behind bars.

Now, I have known people that get they jollies behind the idea of bein locked up, but they was either middle-class white or colored kids that's into some kinda shaky revolutionary hype or else they the kinda incorrigible jailbird that find they true peace of mind in the joint. Like Broadway.

It was even a time not too long ago out here in California when all you had to do was get put away, type up a few letters or essays or poems, get one of these liberals to sneak em out and print em up and the next thing you know you had it *made,* jack!

Free Sidney J. Prettymon! Victim of racist imperialist oppression! Free all political prisoners!

I thought about it, Lord knows I did, but the real scene was I'd done gone and fucked up, gone and fucked up bad.

The real scene was every one of my thoughts involved Aristotle who I was prayin would turn up the next mornin to get me out.

Please, son, with your silver tongue, please dont fail me now!

The people that listen to KRZY was definitely gon hear about all this.

"A conservative is quite apt to be merely a liberal who's been mugged," the fancypants joker that scratch hisself was sayin to the Okie over oatmeal.

"Horseshit," the Okie say, "youre just sayin that because you think it sounds good. Ive been mugged, Ive been jumped in alleys and outside bars from here to Seoul, Korea, and I still think Amurica's the greatest. You dont see me runnin around low-ratin this country."

"I'm not low-ratin the country, as you choose to put it, I'm merely expressing my personal opinion which holds that in a democratic society such as ours—"

"There you go," the Okie cut in, "*democratic,* that's the basic point. We live in a democracy, not a dictatorship. Why, over there in Russia and China and Cuba and some of these goddam commonist countries, I hear you cant even blow your nose the wrong way without some stool-pigeon secret-service asshole turnin you in. Here I can snap on my television or radio any minute of the day and get people runnin down the government. That's all I'm talkin about. We're free to say whatever we wanna say but I think we overdo it. I think we need to dwell more on the positive side. Sure, we got problems, what country doesnt? I got a lotta beefs too but I pay my taxes and keep my nose clean. I'm a good joe and I believe in the integrity of our free-enterprise system even if I am sittin up here now in the goddam Palo Alto jail!"

You didnt have to be all that observant to pick up on the fact that Fancypants was pissed. He fumble with his coffee and tell the Okie, "In a democracy you have a majority rule. All I'm trying to get across is that this has ceased to be the case. Now, I'm a businessman. I run a telephone-answering and secretarial service. I pay my taxes too. I served in the

48

armed forces the same as you. I would simply like to see—
and I say this as an American and a native-born Californian—
a little more respect for individual liberty demonstrated by the
way in which the authorities deal with individual problems."

I was tryna get down some of my oatmeal but them lumps
was holdin me back. Yet and still I figgered it might be innerestin to find out what each of these monkeys did to end up in
jail, so I just come out and asked em.

"I beat my old lady up," the Okie told me, "but she had it
comin. I feel sorry about it, not like last night, but she still
had it comin, hair-assin me about some stranda blonde hair
she found on my coat, I mean, just like in the funny papers
or offa television. I work hard, I pay the bills, I think I deserve bein able to whoop it up a little every now and then. The
blonde hair she got hot about, it probly came off Sally's head.
She's one of the gals over at Dynamite Massage in Mountain
View. I drop in there sometime to relax. Theyre cool, I mean,
they dont do that outrageous stuff like serve you some head
right there on the premises. You can arrange to see the girls
afterward. But they do give a sensitive massage and—hell,
why'm I tellin you guys all this?"

Fancypants done got all dreamy-eyed listenin at the Okie
but then he snap outta it and tell me, "You black people think
you have all the problems. Well, it just isnt so. We white people have some too. One of my secretaries, a male, said I tried
to rape him. Now, what do you think of that?"

The Okie just went "Ho-hooo!" and cluck his tongue and
get so quiet I can hear the ashes burnin in the cigarette he
smokin.

I nodded real polite and even swallowed a coupla oatmeal
lumps I wouldna done otherwise.

What I look like anyway gettin in the middle of two white
dudes' argument? Push come to shove they gon both come out
aheada me.

I was just bidin my time till my son, another native-born
American like me, appeared on the scene and got these people
told!

10

Aristotle come thru like a little champion. He posted bail, got my court date arranged and had me back on the street in no time.

Outside we set in his Jaguar sedan and size one nother up while he shake his head and yawn.

"So . . . otherwise how's it going, Dad?"

"Otherwise things seem to be lookin up, son." I felt so shame I could hardly look at him. "Got a job lined up anyway, pretty good one too. If things work out I'm thinkin bout movin out the Blue Jay."

"And where would you go?"

"O I dont know, maybe get an apartment."

It's only ten in the mornin but the heat already comin down heavy and both of us sweatin. Aristotle undo his top shirt button and loosen his tie a little. I can tell he pretty disgusted with me, or else he done give me up as a hopeless case—one. Couldnt much blame him.

"Dad, you have breakfast yet?"

"Tried to get down that mess they serve back there."

He nod and start the engine up.

"Let's go grab a bite someplace. There're a couple of things I'd like to discuss with you."

The lunch crowd was startin to trickle in and we still nursin our third coffee apiece and digestin our eggs, toast and sausages. It felt good bein in a nice big air-conditioned restaurant in Town & Country Village, lookin out at people roastin and the traffic long El Camino Real.

"She really wants to see you," Aristotle was sayin. "I think it's pretty serious that tumor of hers, more serious than either she or the doctors care to admit. Please go see Mama, Dad."

"I'll do that . . . even tho . . . well, you know how me and Frazier dont get along too good."

"Frazier's a good man. He's been a pretty decent companion to Mama. I know you have your differences but all that seems so petty under the circumstances."

"Youre right, I know that. I feel pretty guilty bout not comin up to see Cornelia and the twins too. How do yall put up with me?"

Aristotle go in his billfold and pull out a Diners Club card. "We dont put up with you, Dad, we love you. But you ought to come around more often. Izetta wanted me to ask you for dinner last week but I was still pretty hot under the collar about that last big scene we had up at my office. Which reminds me . . . I checked on your car and it's already been auctioned off."

"Auctioned off?"

"Yes, once a vehicle's been impounded they only hold it for so long before it goes up for sale. Sorry. There was nothing I could do at that point."

Now, that really got my dander up. "Auctioned off!" I couldnt believe it. "Wonder how much they got for it? I cant believe they actually went and done that, Aristotle. Why wasnt I notified?"

"You probably were. Did you ever bother getting the registration changed on it when you bought it like you were supposed to?"

"I think I did. Yeah, me and Willie G. went down to the Motor Vehicle Department together and—"

Aristotle gettin up to go but he stop and look at me when I break off in the middle of what I was sayin. "What's wrong, Dad?"

"O nothin. I just now remembered that I did get some kinda letter from them traffic people but I was in a hurry and just stuck it in my pocket without even openin it. It probly got lost cause I never did see it again after that."

My son shake his head and we both head toward the cashier to pay the tab. I cant help noticin how handsome he really is, favor his mother more'n he do me—well-groomed, clean-shaved, wear his hair a little longish but it's neat and clean. Make any father proud to have a son and a daughter like mine. A big lump come up in my throat and I look off hopin he dont see me goin soft.

Back out in the Jaguar on the way to my hotel, he hand me a check for fifty dollars.

"What's this for?"

"It *isnt* for getting drunk on. I'd like you to spruce yourself up a bit and go see Mama as soon as you can. Bring her a present of some kind. You know how much she likes that. Why dont you plan to spend the weekend with us?"

"I'll go visit Squirrel but I dont know bout acceptin your invitation. Look like it might bring you and Izetta down havin me around to cope with."

"Goddammit, Dad, will you quit feeling sorry for yourself! That's your problem you know, one of them at least, you drag around taking pity on yourself when you ought to be try-ing to change your life. If you dont like the way you are then change! Doesnt that make sense?"

"I'm, I'm, I'm tryna get things back together, son. Gimme a little time. Gimme a few weeks."

"Youve got all the time in the world. In fact, if you fool around and miss your court date—"

"I'll be there, dont worry."

"Youll be there all right because I'm going to drive back down here and see to it that you be there. Do you know how much youve run up in unpaid tickets?"

"Round two hundred fifty dollars, aint it?"

"Do you have any idea where youre going to get the money?"

I just rub at my chin.

"No, you dont, do you? Well, youd better start thinking about it because it's a serious sum of money and I'm not going to pay it. I bailed you out and I'll act as your legal counsel.

52

I'll even consider *lending* you the money. But I'll be damned if I'm going to pay hard-earned money out of my own pocket to settle your irresponsible debts!"

At the Blue Jay I thanked him for all he done and we shook hands while the motor still runnin.

"I'm sorry," he say, "I didnt mean to raise my voice or swear at you. Ive never done that before but . . . but sometimes you make me furious."

"No hard feelins. I had it comin. Thanks for the check. I'll pay you back, promise."

"Take care of yourself and dont forget Mama. See you around, Dad, I'm going to try and keep a one o'clock appointment in Oakland."

"So long, Aristotle. I'll be in touch."

I got out and slam the door.

He beep the horn at me just as I'm turnin to go back up to my old sorry room. Funny what time do. I use to drop him off at his roomin house sometime back when he was at college. Now it's me the one livin in a room. I walk back to the car and stick my head in the window.

"Just wanted to say I caught you on the radio the other day. You were very articulate and stated your argument well. Both Izetta and I were impressed. You must spend up a fortune making toll calls to that station."

"It cost all right but it do me a lotta good soundin off like that. I figger it save on psychiatry bills."

He wave and drive off.

I'm standin on the sidewalk, sweatin like a mule, thinkin how lucky I am, forgettin all my headaches.

The sky looked bluer.

Even the heat felt good.

"We love you," he told me. That's what he said all right. "But, Dad, we love you." Aint nobody said that to me in so long it's like magic done come back in style.

I could coast a long ways behind a few words like that.

11

O I tell you I slept like a baby in my own bed, slept like a baby caterpillar wrapped up in a cocoon for bout nine billion years. It was that good deep dreamless sleep where cant nothin get thru to you but peace and rest. Now, if that's what dyin is like, as some people maintain it is, then what's all the fuss about?

I didnt never wanna come back but got up recharged when the knockin at the door got too loud.

Got up feelin like I was just learnin to walk for the first time. The sheet was wet and all tangled up around me. My little discount electric fan hadnt done me much good. I stomped to the door, buck nekkid, trailin sheet.

"Uh, who is it?"

"The Professor, are you OK?"

"Well, I guess so."

"Should I come back later?"

"I dont know. What time is it?"

"I dont know."

"What you mean you dont know? Aint you got a watch or a clock or anything?"

"I cut all that out. It's getting dark outside if that helps you any but there's still a bit of sun in the west."

"West?"

54

"Way over back up behind Stanford University."

"O yeah, that's right. Well, listen. I just now woke up and I'm slightly whatcha might call indisposed."

"Well, get disposed and drop by my room. Ive got a package for you someone left."

"Who?"

"Darned if I know. I weighs a ton and it's beautifully wrapped."

"Then how'd you get it if you dont know who left it?"

"This isnt making sense, Sit. Just come to my room, OK?"

"Gotcha. You want me to stop by, right?"

"Brilliant. Where were you last night anyway?"

"Due to circumstances beyond my control, I was briefly detained from returnin home."

"Tell me about it later if you feel like it."

"I will if I can remember."

"Dream on."

Funny he should say that—*dream on*—cause that's what I was tryna do standin at the door, tryna remember if what happen last night'd really taken place or if I'd kinda just dreamed it. I still wasnt woke up good.

Usually I look forward to seein the Professor. You walk into that room of his and you steppin inside a world. That's what I like about the cat. He one of the very few you know from in front where he be comin from. The Professor known for puttin out good vibes wherever he go and that's more'n rare, that's ridiculous.

This night tho I walked in with an attitude. See, it's another side to all this actin crazy and fuckin up, just like you take a man that's considered a success. All his life he done the right things, made all the right moves at all the right times, survived and prospered, made his name, copped the bread and all the good things that come with it. Now, people look at this joker and go, "Wow, yon go one of our most prominent citizens, an asset to the community! I sure wish I had it made like him." Me, I dont look at it like that cause I know deep down someplace that person probly hurtin and doubtin the validity of all his so-call accomplishments. If it aint that, then it's somethin else. It's always another side to everything and everybody. Well, it's the same with the way my life done went. People see me actin jolly even tho they know I'm mosta the time down and out and shit, so probly they figger somethin like, "Now, there's one old friendly spade that bear his burden joyfully." And that's bullshit too.

I stepped in the Professor's world that night—wide awake finally, showered down, clean clothes, fresh and depressed— with every bad break I'd ever been thru on my mind, all fifty-five years' worth. The burdens I was totin musta weigh a hundred tons, like somebody tryna carry the national debt round on they back in nickels, dimes and quarters!

The Professor the most observant person I met since my sister Lottie died. She could tell you stuff like what Mama serve for dinner the Fourth Sunday in August—which was a big day for the colored Baptists downsouth—back in 1933 when she couldna been more'n ten years old at the most. And Mama made a big thing outta never repeatin her special-day meals. Forty years later Lottie could tell you this, or what I was wearin the day I left home to join the service. She was kinda whatcha might call the historian in the family. I regret to this minute I didnt make her funeral here a while back. Bout the best I could do at that time was send her husband a telegram and wire some flowers.

The Professor say, "You look troubled, Sit."

"Feelin kinda down."

"What's the matter this time, you let yourself get run down again? You'd better watch that at your age."

"Naw, Professor, it's another kinda down."

"I understand, just up against it, eh?"

I plop down on one of his oversize pillows. The Professor just dont believe in regular chairs like most folks. And like with everything else he got a whole theory bout how people really sposed to sit on the floor or on the ground—somethin bout how it's beneficial for the back and the spine.

"Sometime," I tell him, "I wonder if anything is worth the trouble. Like, what's the use of keep fightin when you aint gon end up no place but in the grave. Like, I could die right now, right here on this pillow, and wouldnt nobody be all that fazed, not even my own kin."

Professor go, "Ho hum!" and take a deep breath and

scratch at the collar of his blue cotton work shirt, the kind hardhats and workinstiff people you see around quit wearin back about the time when Ike was in the White House and I was drivin a bus for the Muni up in San Francisco. Hard to believe I was just still in my thirties back then when I was draggin round feelin miserable and old as black pepper. Anyway, it's only kids and funnystyle people you see sportin them work shirts anymore. Beside, cotton done got to be too damn expensive. Japan done bought up all the cotton and wool and silk and natural fabrics. I clipped an article out the backa the *Chronicle* about it.

So I sat there still sleepy—even tho I just now got up—and listen at the Professor tellin me, "That's very dramatic what you say, Sit, but it's like Langston Hughes wrote. You ever hear of him?"

"Who aint heard tella Langston Hughes? Wrote *Simple Speaks His Mind* and all like that? My daughter Cornelia got every book he ever put out and he put out a whole slewful. What you fixin to quote from what he wrote?"

"You know that poem of his, 'Life Aint Been No Crystal Staircase'? Well, all I'm saying is life's never really been easy for anyone. We darker-skinned peoples dont have a monopoly on misery."

"Hmmph, well you sure coulda fooled me!"

Actually, I didnt feel too much like listenin at the Professor go into one of his pedagojical raps bout first one thing and another. No, not tonight! Like, OK, I know it's lotsa things, lotsa problems and hurts I could avoid and prevent by bein sensible and moderate and judicious and cool. It's even been times when the Professor—a pretty together young man, twenty-some years my junior—done me a lotta good by just gettin on my case and everybody else's, tryna force me to see how it's higher things to aspire to in this life other than just gettin by and makin ends meet.

I understand all that.

I understand all his good intentions and respect him for all that book-learnin and soul-searchin he done gone thru just so he could arrive at his own ideas bout how things go and follow his own mind, his own intuition.

The Professor know I dig him and done learnt a lot from

him but tonight I just wanted to get down inside my own head good. Sometime you feel like bein sad and fucked-up all by yourself.

"You want to be alone, dont you? That isnt hard to see. Frankly I just wanted to get this package out of my hands and into yours."

Now, for some reason, dont ask me why, I wasnt a bit more studyin bout that box or what might be in it than I was a man or a woman in the moon. I remembered him mentionin it when we talked thru the door but my mind was on other things, namely wakin up.

He fling open his clothes closet door. Closet got more books and papers and record albums jammed up inside it than it do clothes. The Professor kind of a slight-built dude with a big head, broad features, curly hair, brown skin, eyes slant a little. He got a little of that Oriental blood in him, Filipino on his mama's side. His old man a spook, Afro-American, which is to say aint no tellin what he was since most American Negroes got Indian and maybe even a little paddy in em from someplace back there. You see the Professor for the first time and you do a double take tryna figger out what nationality he belong to. What he is is Spookapino, only he got great big hands and feet.

He grab that big box wrapped up all pretty like a Christmas present and stand there holdin it in his big hands, talkin bout, "Would you like to open it here or in your room? I can carry it over for you."

"Is it really all that heavy?"

"Here."

It just about brought me to my knees.

He helped me get it to my room where we dumped it on the bed. I was still breathin heavy.

"Ive already told you about getting more exercise," he say. "You arent doing yourself any favors at your age leading the kind of sedentary life you do. Have you recovered from last night, you said you were *detained?*"

"I got picked up for unpaid parkin tickets and spent the night in jail."

"Were you drunk?"

"Unfortunately, no. It was a jive deal. I hitched a ride with

58

some kids, they got stopped, I got checked, they got a traffic ticket, I got the shaft. My boy got me out on bail this mornin and I gotta be in court in a few days."

"That mustve left you feeling rather exhausted and anxious, no?"

"Anxious isnt the word for it, Professor, I feel downright eager—eager to go someplace and hide, sleep, till all this shit blow over!"

Professor dont say nothin. He set down on the edge of the bed and start pattin the package.

A picture flashin thru my head—Aristotle and Cornelia and Squirrel, how many years ago? They all settin round me at the dinner table lookin sad while I'm up there explainin how I cashed the Christmas check, tucked the money in my billfold, dropped into Lucky Chuck's for a beer and had my pocket picked. Aw, that hurt, I cant tell you how much that hurt! We wouldna had no Christmas shonuff that year if it hadna been for Mr. Critchlow bein kind enough to advance me two weeks' pay outta his own pocket.

I squeeze my eyes shut and shake my head and make the picture go away.

"You really do need more rest," the Professor say, "but are you going to open this box or what? The suspense is killing me!"

I tear at the paper, sorta lookin for a tag or a note of some kind.

"Who you say left this?"

"I didnt say. Johnny at the desk downstairs gave it to me to bring up. He said some messenger delivered it by taxi. Mysterious stuff, Sit. You must have some real devoted fan out there in Radio Land, heh heh!"

I ripped the resta the paper off and tore open the topa the box. Staples went flyin every whichway.

"Well, I'll be doggone!"

"Looks like a case of some type of expensive beverage, Sit."

I take one of the bottles out and hand it to the Professor. He hold it up and read the label.

"My, my, my," he say. " '*Vinho Tinto do Porto Santo* . . . A Product of Portugal.' Say, this is good port wine, Sit. Comes from Madeira, the island off the coast of the Portuguese mainland. Now, who'd be laying something like this on you? I was over there once in the Azores, pretty place."

"Funchal by any chance?"

"Funchal, yes. Hey, you know about that? You never told me you'd traveled in that part of the world."

"I havent," I say. "I just happen to know somebody that know somebody that's been there."

"Well, they sure must think a lot of you to send you this for a gift. Do you know how much this wine costs in the stores? It's probably gone up since I was back in my lightweight wine-collecting period, but I used to pay around seven dollars a bottle. Seven times twelve is . . . Wow, Sit, that's eighty-four bucks right there. Whatre you going to do with all this?"

"Give one of em to you to start with. The rest? I dont know. Maybe I'll throw a party and have everybody over."

"Right here in the room?"

"Why not? This joint could use a little livenin up, dont you think so?"

The Professor like a little kid all of a sudden, settin there readin the wine label and tiltin the bottle up to the light.

"Thanks, man. I'll savor this port."

"Savor it *nothin!* Just drink it," I tell him. "It's plenty more where this come from."

I was thinkin bout the way Squirrel use to grab hold to me in her sleep like she dreamin bout something good. I'd reach back, run my hand up under her nightgown and rub down long her soft warm belly down to where she fuzzy and tender. Maybe tonight she'll reach around and grab mister johnson! But she never hardly did, least not much after the kids was born. She push me away and turn over real sudden and say, 'Not tonight, Sidney, I got a headache, I'm tired, try me in the mornin when I'm rested.' Mornin always came on time but she was never rested.

I was thinkin way back in my mind what it's really like to grow old slow with nothin to show for it when the Professor stand up with his bottle of wine and a smile on his lips. He pat me on the cheek and split.

Everything's complete. I'm all alone now, lonely as the devil, just like I thought I wanted to be.

12

Takin the train up to the city? Aint nothin I like better unless it's hangin out with people you like and exchangin good talk on one of them days when aint nobody got appointments to make or any dismal thoughts cloudin up they mind.

Far as I'm concerned, the train the last civilized forma transportation that's left. Look at it this way. I drive in on 101 or 280 and gotta all the time be worried bout keepin my eye on the road and lookin out for other drivers messin up. I cant read, I cant relax, I cant really think. Cant do nothin but set up there behind that wheel like some robot, hopin I aint gon run into no traffic jam or accident. I always think a protective ring of white light around my machine before I take it out on the freeway. You can laugh if you want to but I believe in stuff like that. It's done seen me thru some close scrapes too. The time gon come when people'll look back on all this racin round in carriages of metal and glass and see how it truly wasnt nothin but folly, one of them barbaric phases man had to evolve up from.

Now, on the train—the ten thirty-two outta Palo Alto, put me in San Francisco by eleven-thirty—I can stretch out and rest up, think my thoughts, read, walk around, talk with folks or just lay back and nap or check out the passin scenery. That's what I call civilized!

The rush hour over so the train relatively uncrowded— housewives with they kids goin shoppin, some old folks, a few of them tensed-up, suit-wearin dudes with they attaché cases and *Chronicle*s and *Wall Street Journal*s, lookin at they watches every five or ten minutes.

I'm dressed up myself this mornin, got my fat tie on with that good old Windsor knot and a nice brown corduroy suit I bought at the Thrift Shop on California Avenue and had cleaned and pressed. Bought that there and a paira good shoes which I aim to get shined in the city someplace. I was lookin pretty good if I must say so myself.

The towns go zippin by—Menlo Park, Atherton, Redwood City, San Carlos, Belmont, Hillsdale, Hayward Park, San Mateo, Burlingame . . .

Some school kids get on at Burlingame, junior high age. Must be a private school they goin to cause they all got on the same little brown britches and green button-up sweaters.

One freckleface boy tell another one, say, "You really oughtta should come out for the team, Tim. Next month we're playing San Jose. I can hardly wait. You ever been there?"

"San Jose? Wow, that's a huge place. My dad works there."

"You think San Jose is huge," another boy join in. "My cousin lives in San Francisco and that place is like an airport!"

I always eavesdrops on kids to pick up on where they at. That airport part tickle me a little. So that's the kinda place the little kids think of as big nowdays? I still aint forgot the time Mama carried me and Lottie and my brother Nehemiah over to Meridian with her on the Greyhound bus. We set there scrooched up at the backa the bus when it roll into Meridian. We aint *never* seen no place that big! All we ever knew was Quitman and them little places round in there, most of em got a general store, a post office, the jail, and a place to tie your mule or hitch your wagon. I musta been ten years old. Meridian to us was like the real Big Time and wasnt no place to go after that except Memphis or New Orleans.

. . . Broadway, Millbrae, San Bruno, South San Francisco.

I'm lookin at all the shabby little streets and houses and back-yards with wash hung out that run down long beside the rail-road tracks.

At one stop it's a ganga little teeny kids—white, colored, Mexican, Oriental—bunched together with they tricycles and wagons, wavin at the train, all of em poor as church mice but in that new modern installment-plan way.

I lean toward the window and wave back at em while the train go whoooo-whoooo and chug and whip along thru the hot sunshine.

It's like every telephone post, factory and junkyard flash past represent a century outta my long sorry life.

"Yeah, we livin in the days of Sodom and Gomorrah," the shoeshine dude say while he brushin polish on. "These people round here they love that pornography."

"Do you know where that word come from?" I ask him, feelin devilish.

"What you mean, it come from out the newspapers, dont it?"

"It come from the doggone Greeks. You can break it down into two parts—*porno* or *pornē* which mean prostitute or slut, and *graphos* which is like graphic in English, you know, writin. So all pornography mean is writin that's about ho's and nasty bitches."

The shoeshine dude, looked to be round my age, wipe some of the sweat off his face with the backa his hand and cut his big old wrinkly eyes at me funny.

"Well, I'll be!" he say. "Live and learn. All I know is these San Franciscans really go for that mess. It was even a joker I use to shine his shoes opened him up a topless shoeshine joint right over here in North Beach right off Broadway except I heard the men'd come in there and some of em'd get too worked up over the deal and go to grabbin at the gals' titties and things. That musta been somethin! He was cleanin up tho for a while there before it got too much outta hand. I kept kickin myself for not thinkin of it first. Man, this white man somethin else, aint he? Excuse me, mister, but do you want the deluxe or the regular Wax Shine?"

63

"What's the difference?"

"Twenty-five cent."

"I'll take the regular."

He got em to lookin bout as good as it was possible. I was settin up there feelin like some kinda potentate, figgerin out what the first thing I say to Squirrel was gon be. Been years since I last laid eyes on the woman. I was genuinely developin what the Professor call a complex about it.

All along I been checkin out subliminally, you understand, this theater cross the street called Peep-O-Rama. The markee advertizin what's playin say: BOX LUNCH & OTHER MEALS STARRING IRMA YOLANDA RATED XXX.

"How much I owe you?"

"Seventy-five cent."

I hand him a dollar and step down.

"Uckfay ouyay irsay!" he shout out at me.

"Beg pardon?"

"That's Latin," he say, "pig Latin. You can figger it out since you so high and mighty and know everything."

I couldnt much blame him for showin his ass. Shinin shoes a hard, hard gig. I done a little bit of that too. Last thing you want is somebody jumpin up in your face talkin a whole lotta off-the-wall shit even if it is informative. People resent that. Beside, if I'da been a white man, his attitude woulda been different.

When I trotted cross the street to drop two dollars on the man and check out *Box Lunch,* it was a sign taped to the door say: HAVE A FREE PEEP ON US.

They got a little window in the lobby there where you can actually peek in and see the picture in progress.

All I actually get to see is this big blonde Amazon-lookin broad settin up reared back on a red sofa. She got a white blouse on and a white miniskirt with her legs spread. On each side of her is a dude, still dressed, one of em white with long brown hippy hair. The other one got a cap on and he real emaciated-lookin and black. All three of em grinnin while the dudes workin they hands all up long her thighs up under the skirt bout to peel her panty hose down.

She give the white dude a big old nasty sloppy kiss, then she turn and slobber all over the colored dude's mouth.

The camera move in for a close-up and I see just what I had a hunch I'd see. There Broadway is with his snaggly-tooth self, lookin like the last joker in the world I'd want my daughter to be associatin with.

Next shot is the broad take they hands away and pull down her hose—she aint wearin no draws—and then it's just a big wide floppy quiverin nekkid vagina starin you in the face. This aint just no innocent beaver shot like they features in *Playboy* nowdays. This the real thing—meat—moist raw human pussy in technicolor, like, what it must look like under a microscope! How these people pull these numbers in fronta a camera and then go out walkin round like aint nothin the matter with em? I figger they got to get stoned to do it. I know Broadway stay lit up behind that cocaine.

"Your free time is up," the fat man say. "You wanna buy a ticket or what?"

I just shrug my shoulders and shake my head.

What happen was I come outta there grinnin like a chesscat because it felt so *good* to be gettin back out in the fresh air and sunshine that dont even cost me one red cent!

On the bus all the way up to Portreo Hill I catch myself thankin God for seein to it my kids got raised up decent and proper.

It's somethin bout Squirrel that every time I see her for the first few minutes I do a mental trip that take me all the way back to San Francisco 1946.

That's when we first met up and clicked.

Tell you what it is, it's them eyes. She got big sad prettylookin eyes that's brown as the earth is round. Look like it aint nothin ever happened or been thought about in the world that you cant see reflected in em. Her eyes tell a story use to speed my blood up. They still do.

She was waitin tables at a little place called Zola Mae's Cafe over in the Fillmore and I use to come in there two-three times a week to eat—and I mean it was some *choice* greaze in them days—greens, cornbread, chitlins, black-eyed peas, butterbeans, ribs, fried okra, sweet-potato pie—oooweeee! This was back before bein black got to be big business, way before everything was Soul this and Soul that! You could eat this

65

kinda food in peace and enjoy it for what it was—just the kinda good somethin-to-eat downhome colored folks liked and was use to.

The world done changed so much since then, it scare me to even think about it. In them days, for example, you didnt go round tellin nobody they was funky—least not to they face—unless you was shonuff lookin to get your block knocked off. Funky didnt mean but one thing then and that pertained to individual body odor. B.O. they use to call it in the Lifebuoy Soap advertizements. Now somebody say you funky and that's spose to be a compliment. Everybody tryna be so hip. Wasnt nobody hip in 1946 except beboppers, Father Divine, Daddy Grace and a whole lotta rich white folks—and the beboppers was scufflin to stay alive.

Me, I shudder to think how square I was, just out the army and punchin a clock to sweep floors at the Shipyard. Check this! Just because I'd been discharged in San Francisco, that's where I ended up stayin.

Squirrel was vacuumin the flat when I got there. She come to the door in a flowery shift dress and gimme a big strong hug with tears in her eyes.

Well, right off this was a new one on me. She hadnt hugged me nowhere near anything like that in a good ten years. I didnt know how to take it.

"Understand you havent been doin so good, Squirrel."

"You heard right but it's worse than that even."

"What's the matter?"

"Cancer."

"Cancer?"

"Cancer, Sidney."

I wanted to change the subject to anything else. It's like you just walked in on somebody and they buck nekkid only you want em to pretend like they aint so you can go long with the joke and dont get embarrassed.

"How long you been knowin about it?"

"Six weeks now."

"How bad is it?"

"They say they dont know yet but I got my own ideas about that. For one thing, it's in the region of what they call the lower abdominal track and I happen to know that's plenty serious. Theyre gonna have to operate."

"When?"

"Doctor's supposed to let me know next week. I'm still going thru tests."

I'm standin there lookin down at the rug, tryin my best not to let our eyes meet.

"O Sidney!" Squirrel break down and say, big raindrop tears slippin down her cheeks, her voice soft and wavery-like. "What in the world am I going to do?"

She come lungin at me with her arms held out. I get one glimpse of them big sorrowful eyes and start flashin like clockwork on that dark Sunday mornin we got up and drove out down the avenues in my old beat-up DeSoto and parked by the ocean in the pourin-down rain. We set there lookin out thru the windshield at the water splashin and churnin, everything so stormy and watery it was hard to tell where the Pacific leave off and the sky begin. She was sharin a flat with another gal name Lee Julia. Lee Julia had to go back to St. Charles, Louisiana, on accounta her daddy'd died. I got to spend that Saturday night with Squirrel, our first time really alone. We even slept in her bed together but all we done was hug and kiss on one nother. She'da shot me if I'd tried to take it any further'n that. That's how decent people was back then even tho I'd done already been with a coupla women before— Martha Lu Montgomery in the eighth grade in Quitman and Francesca Corradini in Naples, Itly, a beautiful olive-complected woman that wanted me to marry her. Even her daddy and brothers treated me like I was one of the family. That's another story. Squirrel I proposed to settin there in that storm. She was beautiful too. She accepted. That was November the twenty-third, 1946.

All this streak cross my mind in the split second it take for her to reach out and come crashin in my arms, cryin all over my pressed suit. Sometime you aint got time to stop and figger what the correct thing to do is. You follow your blood. My blood led me to huggin on Squirrel with all my might and sayin stuff like, "It's gon be all right, dont worry, baby, it's gon all work out OK."

67

She start doin that little thing I'll always remember her for. Squirrel dont just caress you when she got her arms around you. She got a habit of squeezin up little portions of your flesh with her hands. She'll do a slow soft squeeze and then ease up and then bunch up another hunka your back or shoulder or whatever with her good-feelin fingers. That's just one of her own personal traits, you understand.

We stand up there with her carryin on like that and cryin for a hour look like.

Pretty soon she let go of me and step back and wipe at her eyes with the fresh handkerchief I offer her.

"How's Frazier?" I ask her.

"O he's all right. He had to run up to Sacramento on business but he'll be back in the mornin. How you been doing? It's been a long time, hasnt it, Sidney?"

I didnt wanna talk about it.

"I hear you over the radio sometime. Youre getting to be real popular, you know."

We drink a lotta coffee and yak about the old days. I know the only liquor Squirrel'll drink is brandy which she keep on hand for what she call medicinal purposes but I finally get around to suggestin a toast—"To the success of your operation that's comin up, OK?"—and that little libation loosen her up to where we actually communicatin together like old true friends.

"You still drinking as much as you use to, Sidney?"

"No," I lied, "I cut way down. In fact, I'm almost a saint these days. We've all got our problems of course."

"Aristotle tells me you got arrested and have to appear in court in a few days. What happened?"

I told her, careful to set the record straight.

"I wish you hadna left me, Sidney," she finally say. "At least not when you did. We coulda done all right together. We woulda made things go, you know, Jesus be my witness."

Aw, man, this was somethin new. Squirrel wasnt one to come on with all that Jesus talk. She'd finished high school and done a lotta readin and thinkin. All thru our hard marriage she'd been the angel and me the devil, the only difference bein she never did cotton to that Sunday school stuff whereas I was always callin on God to sanction jive I knew was hopeless.

"I went back to school, did you hear?" she say. "Got my B.A. from San Francisco State."

"What in?"

"Social work, sociology. I'll never use it."

"I heard you was takin courses but that's bout all I heard. What ever possessed you?"

"God," she say. "God and our children. Frazier, by him being in real estate, was pretty encouraging too. Aw, Sidney, I wish it coulda been different. You know I aint never really loved anyone like I loved you!"

She squeeze my fingers in that special way and I look down at the lasta the sunlight oozin cross the table we settin at in the kitchen at the backa her flat.

I coulda laid a rap on her thatd exonerate me from years of blame, suspiciousness and irresponsibility, but we had to be at Cornelia's for dinner and it was time to get ready. Aristotle and Izetta would be there too.

We drove over in her and Frazier's Chrysler. Squirrel set up thigh next to mine while I maneuvered the car to Ashbury Heights. It was just the way we use to ride around together years ago.

I kept wonderin what in the hell was the matter with people. What was the matter with *me?*

13

Blam! Sometime it hit you—the importance of bein together, belongin to a family—and you set there in a big old comfortable easy chair next to a Tiffny lamp with your glassa good wine, brimmin with good cheer, wonderin where your head was at all the resta that time.

Marriage aint for everybody. It wasnt for me. Maybe I was too young, too childish. I dont know. I'll never know now. I resented the hassle, every bit of it—gettin up to hurry off to a job I hated just to put food on the table and pay the bills and save up for a down payment on a house. I resented the way everybody both on the job and off just taken me for granted. Squirrel was workin too, I got to admit, but even so look like she got more respect on her job sellin neckties and socks at Sears Roebuck than I did drivin a Muni bus. She got more respect from the kids at home too. They was crazy bout they mama. Nothin I done seemed to please any of em.

We went to shows together, had picnics, took trips. Me and Aristotle played baseball and football together and went salmon fishin up on the Sacramento River. I never did go in much for church—and neither did Squirrel—but we did try to set a good example by teachin em bout the Bible and doin right unto others. Cornelia even joined the local Methodist

70

church on her own just so she could sing in the choir with a girlfrienda hers. Me and Squirrel started goin there every once in a while so as to make her feel and look good—which is sayin a lot for two parents that was both raised Southern Baptist. Squirrel from outta Texas. Her folks moved up to California when she was in her early teens.

Both Cornelia and Aristotle was always good about gettin they lesson in school. They got good grades. They loved to read and discuss things and participate in the various activities the school offered such as sports, the science club, the debatin team and all like that.

Aristotle always was a good fast talker. I shoulda known he was gon turn out a lawyer. When he got a track scholarship to San Jose State—he'd made all-city runnin the mile in high school—I knew he was on his way. He later transferred up to U.C. Berkeley. "Daddy," he use to tell me, "I'm gonna show the world that we colored can accomplish anything we set our minds to!"

Cornelia started out wantin to be a professional singer like Ella Fitzgerald or somebody, but after giggin around on weekends round town with a little group made up mostly of people she went to San Francisco State with, she changed her mind and, always bein a charitable kinda person, figgered she could better help colored people improve they condition by devotin herself to teachin school.

They was good kids. Didnt neither of em ever get in no trouble with the law like a lotta the kids they grew up with. I loved my children. I thought I loved Squirrel. So what went wrong? Where was it I jumped off the track and how come? Why? I still think it was on accounta I hadnt come into my full senses yet. See, a man he develop at a different rate than a woman do. Squirrel probly knew exactly what she wanted outta life before she left Corpus Christi and all she was doin when I run into her was scufflin round out there tryna get at it. Me, it's only been in the last few years I know kinda what it is I want and that's peace of mind—and where you gon find that in this evil fool world?

I can say all this now because it's easy to see. Age'll do that for you if you let it, clear stuff up so you can see it better.

Back when the shit was comin at me hard and steady, all I could see was things like I couldnt get into the bathroom when I wanted to to read the paper, or we finally move into a nice apartment on a quiet street with lotsa room and reasonable rent when what Squirrel really want is to *buy* a place, or I wanna spend my vacation just sleepin and restin up and watchin the ball game but Squirrel and the kids they wanna *go* someplace, or I wanna have some of the boys over for poker and a few drinks and Squirrel wanna have us do our socializin out in the garage, or some of my relatives come to pay me a visit and Squirrel get all uptight but it's OK for her parasitic relations to move in on us right there in the house and free-load long as they like.

I could go on like that forever but one of the main things it finally came down to was she didnt seem to need me around as a man after we'd done got the family thing goin along OK. I reckon now that's how it musta been with pretty near everybody in that situation but back then I taken it personally and figgered it was just me.

One time I remember we had a little block party over on Buchanan Street, the same Christmas I'd lost my check, and all the men was out in the kitchen swappin lies and downhome what we use to call tall tales.

Booker Critchlow was there, the same dude that was my boss on the Muni who advanced me a coupla weeks' pay that time, and he was listenin to me tell about how after I been out alone for a big night on the town and come slippin home, easin the car motor off as I pull into the driveway, tip up to the door, snuggle the key in the lock, take off my clothes in the livinroom and step real quiet into the bedroom. "Every time," I told em, "my old lady click on the light just as I'm slippin into bed and holler loud enough for the neighbors to hear, 'And just where in the fuck have you been, Sidney Prettymon!' "

Critchlow who bout as hip as they came in them days, he just laugh and say, "Well, you got the wrong approach, Sitting Pretty. What I do is pull up to the house and sit out front revvin the engine for a few minutes, come stompin up the front steps, make as much noise as I can gettin the door open, sing a few bars off the jukebox tune at the bar I just left, open and slam the icebox door loud as I can, run the water in the bathroom full force, crash into the bedroom and leap on the bed, pat Mirna on the ass and shout, 'Baby, you *gots* to gimme some trim! I need a piece of tail so bad I can taste it!' Know what she does? She turns over on her pillow and rubs her head and says, 'O not tonight, sweetheart, I have this terrible headache!' "

Style and simplicity, that's where it's at. Keeps takin me all my life to find that out.

What I mean to say is there I am up in Cornelia and Marcus' big bay-windowed dream house on Stanyan Street. It's even got more style than Marguerite's because my daughter and son-in-law love art and pretty things and got a lotta taste. Class, baby! They flat out cultured. Got paintins and sculptures and enough books to start they own lightweight Library of Congress.

Marcus settin there smokin on his pipe. He on the couch cross from me with Izetta and Aristotle. Cornelia out in the kitchen addin last-minute touches to dinner.

"Why dont you move up to the city," Marcus is sayin, "so that we could see more of you, Sidney?"

"Practically everybody I know tryna get outta the city, but I must confess it's always good visitin yall up here. Are the twins in bed already?"

"Yes, Cornelia deliberately didnt put them down for a nap this afternoon just so she could tuck them in early tonight. Cute as you might think they are, theyre really no fun when we're trying to entertain and enjoy a special supper."

Izetta with her fine longhaired self say, "Didnt I tell you Sidney'd ask about the kids first thing, Aristotle? You love your grandchildren, dont you?"

"I love the whole family."

Aristotle say, "I guess we'll have to hurry up and provide you with another set of grandchildren to love, eh, Dad?"

"Naw, yall take your time. Me and your mama taken ours, didnt we now, Squirrel?"

Squirrel just set there smilin kinda, lookin elegant as all

get-out in her long bright dress and with her hair put up all salt-and-peppery, the same color's mine. She favor some angel I use to be on intimate terms with, only now I can appreciate her better due to experiential distance—if yall can get to that! Her whole dark face is radiatin light so much that it was hard to believe she bout to be operated on for tumors. Sequoia Jo Rawlins, my dream girl from the forties who never would take no for a answer. Wonder who it was first nicknamed her Squirrel?

She come with me down the long hallway to the twins' room, Marcus leadin the way with his fancy pipe. "Just be quiet when you peek in at them," he say. "Sean you'd have to really shake hard to wake up but Amanda's an extremely light sleeper."

"Dont worry," I whisper, "we wont make a sound."

He crack the door and we peep in. They got em in twin cribs next to one nother. Sean got his space-age bottle clamped in his hand and all the covers is twisted up around his little pajama'd neck. One of his legs is pokin thru the railin long the side of the crib. Now, little Mandy she layin there on her stomach, covered up all prim and proper, got her eyes half-shut like she either fixin to go to sleep for real or halfway ready to wake up. She huggin on the stuffed panda bear from the supermarket I gave her. Boy, that make me feel special!

Marcus tip on off back to the livinroom and leave me and Squirrel standin up there in the doorway all by ourself.

"I see em just about every day and I still cant believe theyre almost two."

I wanna grab Squirrel and hold her like time done stood still, but all I do is kiss her on the forehead. We look at one nother funny but with that cozy old feelin between us.

"God is wonderful," she whisper, straightenin my tie, "isnt He?"

I didnt know what to say to that so I didnt say a word. I escorted her back to the front room just in time to hear Cornelia call out: "Dinner, such as it is, is served!"

Aw, I wanna tell you if the people at the Blue Jay could see me now theyd start treatin me with a little more respect. Roast

Cornish game hen, wild rice, asparagus tips, the real home-made yeast bread with lotsa whipped butter to spread on it and a ganga chilled white wine to wash it all down! Talk about the seven cardinal sins, one of which is gluttony—I was scared the Devil hisself was waitin outside the front door with his pitchfork to jab me in the butt.

"Where you learn to cook like this?" I ask Cornelia, got my napkin up to my lips to muffle a burp. "I mean, I know your mama could righteously burn but—"

The burp missed the napkin and came out loud only everyone pretend like they didnt even hear it.

"I'm glad you like it, Dad. If you only knew what it took to hassle with Sean and Mandy and get this meal together as well. I must admit, Marcus helped me out. He baked the bread and prepared the special dessert that's coming up."

Marcus tryna look humble but I can see how secretly proud he is. He and Cornelia exchange little looks, lettin me know how tight and together they really must be. I'm hopin my jealousy aint showin itself too much. It's a funny feelin to be envious of your own kids and they husbands and wives.

Aristotle like his mother. She never did talk much while she eatin. That night, in fact, Squirrel wasnt doin much talkin *or* eatin. She set there lookin pleasant enough but I can sense her mind is way off someplace, probly hangin in the air over the operatin table, poor thing! I'd rather I die than her anyday. But wasnt any reason yet for either of us to even be thinkin bout that.

"What's the big project youre directing all your thought toward these days?" Izetta ask Marcus.

"Nothing in particular," he say real casual, "but I will be working on something specific soon—strange sort of area."

"Can you talk about it?" ask Aristotle who, so I notice, never hardly talk about his professional stuff in public.

Cornelia get up and light out for the kitchen, I reckon to round up coffee and that surprise dessert. I'm ready for anything she come back with.

"Urban systems," Marcus went on, reachin in his jacket pocket for his pipe. He kinda favor me, Marcus do, the way I use to look back in what once woulda been called my salad

75

days—broad-faced, brown skin, mustache, handsome features, Clark Gable-ish, except he thinner'n I was and gotta lot more sense naturally. "It's a relatively unexplored field. I'll be working with a man named Harry Burns, have you heard of him? He's with that big research institute down on the Peninsula, very creative individual. Just got back from Portugal."

"Do you think what youll be doing will be in the best interest of black people?" Aristotle ask him.

"My conscience is clear," Marcus say. "I make it a point never to accept an assignment that offends my ethical sensibilities."

"Well," Izetta say, "just what is it theyre asking you to focus on with this urban systems project?"

Marcus light his trusty pipe and let his eyes follow the cloudsa thick smoke he puff on up toward the ceilin. He say, "To put it succinctly, studies have indicated the need for effective and efficient alternatives to the deteriorative trend which our major cities are presently reflecting in their rapid decline."

"Well, do tell!" Squirrel say all of a sudden. "That's generalized enough to qualify you as some kinda candidate for political office. Whatre they paying you think-tank people all that good money to do anyway—help put us all in concentration camps?"

"Yeah," Aristotle say, "every time they start talking about the decline of the cities I get nervous too because everybody knows that the majority of the inner big cities are black, non-white anyway. It's like that old phrase they used to trot out—"

"Slum clearance!" Squirrel shout out.

"Only now they call it urban renewal," Izetta say.

Aristotle clear his throat and say, "Whatever you want to label it, it's usually just another way of further disadvantaging blacks and poor people."

Marcus lookin disturbed.

"Ah, you guys are all just paranoid as usual. You read too much of that radical chic propaganda and put too much stock in that rhetoric."

The Professor use that term *radical chic* sometime when he get on one of his political kicks. Me, when I hear it, I always

76

get a picture of one of them zillionaire A-rabs got two dozen wives and holdin back on all that oil he own until the U.S., Europe, Japan, and them finally come around to seein things him and all his buddies' way. Now, that's a shonuff radical sheik! But here my family is bout to get in a argument I wasnt exactly in the mood to see happen, so I decide to ease my little two cent in and try to make peace before the discussion get to be too heated.

"Now, wait a minute," I say. "Yall ask Marcus what kinda project he currently workin on and bein a gentleman he told us. I dont think we need to start advisin him bout how he spose to conduct his own business. Cornelia, where that dog-gone dessert you went out there to get?"

"It's coming right up, Dad."

Squirrel say, "Sidney, no one's really upset with Marcus. We talk this way all the time. I, for one, simply dont trust too many of these big egghead studies and projects. I still havent forgot how they rounded up all the Japanese back here in World War Two and taken they money, land and property from em."

"And then turned around and dropped the atom bomb on Japan when they *knew*—as history now reveals—that theyd already been defeated anyway." Izetta talkin.

"I fail to see your point," Marcus say. "What's all that got to do with what I was talking about?"

Unh-hunh! It's startin to sound like one of them emotional exchanges that Ed Jason get into now and then on his KRZY call-in program. Boy, them communicasters must get ulcers behind havin to cope with that jive on a full-time basis.

Marcus say, "I think the point Izetta's making is pertinent and lucid. A great deal of the research and planning that went into the making of the atomic bomb was conducted in those lush, peaceful, bucolic hills right up behind Stanford University."

"By supercivilized professors and brilliantly educated white people. Notice they didnt drop no bomb on the Germans," Squirrel say, shakin her finger around in the air. "They didnt drop it on the Nazis and they didnt drop it on the Italians. They dropped it on colored folks, and dont you believe for one minute that the Japanese done forgot that! I havent forgot it."

Cornelia come back in the dininroom with two huge sweetpotato pies and a half-gallona vanilla ice cream. "They just came out of the oven," she tell us. "We can all help ourselves. Ive been overhearing the discussion and frankly I think youre all talking about completely different things."

"And I concur," I say, gettin up to help Cornelia clear the table some so everybody can get at dessert.

"Stay put, Dad, I can handle the dishes all right."

"In the first place," I say. "I was back there participatin in that Second World War as you all know. We bombed and killed up a whole lotta Germans and Eyetalians. Hell, you wanna get technical, the Germans wasted millions of them Russians they ownself. And dont forget how the Japanese run up into China and was givin the Chinese hell. My point bein, it was plenty white folks killin white folks and plenty colored folks killin colored folks."

Squirrel say, "OK, Sidney, we understand all that but tell me this—how many colored folks was it killing white folks?"

"Yeah, Dad," say Aristotle, sidin with his mama.

"Yeah-Dad nothin! I was over there, I was in it! Yall wasnt! It wasnt makin no sense to me then and it still dont make sense for us to set up here arguin like loonies over stuff that dont matter. Killin is evil, dont care who doin it and who it's bein done to. I still have nightmares over some of the things I had to do over there and then get back here and find out how didnt none of the colored soldiers outta Missippi get what was comin to em and rightfully theys under the G.I. Bill. That's the only reason yall was brought up in California insteada in the south."

I didnt know if I was makin sense either but I didnt care. I cut myself some pie and dipped up a big spoona ice cream.

"Calm down, Sidney," Squirrel say, relaxin. "We dont have to go into the family history again. What's a good discussion anyway without a few fireworks."

Marcus, who was puttin his pipe out again, motion with his arm held up that he would like a little attention.

"In the interest of clarification and for whatever good itll do, I'd just like to remind you for the thousandth time that most of the problem-solving with which I'm involved is of a technical nature. Ive never taken on anything political. On this urban systems project, for example, my concern is strictly with ways of improving mass transit systems, the reduction of auto traffic, energy preservation, ways of reducing on-the-street crime—"

"There you go again," Izetta say. "Crime. Crime is political. When the white man speaks of crime in the streets, what he's really speaking of is black people. What are we going to do about the niggers this time?"

"Aw, that's unfair," Marcus groan, "because youre over-simplifying a very complex human problem."

"Well, let's face it," I say, "black people are still killin and cuttin on and stickin one another up. Two little jokers pulled a gun on me coupla years back here right down there in Redwood City in a parkinlot and in broad daylight. All I had was seven dollars and a little change. I give em everything I had. You would too."

Cornelia say, "It's happened to me right over in the Sunset. You talk about black crime and immediately everyone starts putting you down and calling you an Uncle Tom but it's a hard fact of life. I dont know. I can only speak for myself, not for the race, but I think we better-thinking black people should stop allowing ourselves to be intimidated by all these trashy hoodlum elements. We've been listening to the cut-and-shoot-and-burn fanatics for a long time now and where has it gotten us?"

"I'll tell you where it's gotten us," Aristotle say. "We now have more black people in good-paying positions and jobs. Our media image has improved considerably. We've got black mayors, thriving black businesses getting a few of those juicy government contracts for a change. And youve got black children coming up now who arent saddled down with severe psychological complexes such as hating themselves because they arent white."

"Do you really believe all that, Risty?" Cornelia ask him.

"Just check out the statistics," my son's pretty wife say.

"I dont have to anymore, Izetta, Ive taught college and high school. Ive sat in on school board meetings until my behind got

79

sore and my throat ached from talking. The situation's worse than ever if you ask me."

Izetta just shrug.

Squirrel go to spoonin herself up some ice cream and growin quiet again.

"Please can we change the subject," I tell em. "This isnt leadin anywhere constructive. The shape the world is in today, everybody catchin hell. I know I am. I dont see how come every time Negroes get together all we know to talk about is the race problem. It it wasnt a whole lotta other problems to worry about, Marcus here wouldnt have a job. Izetta, you gettin your master's degree in psychology to help folks deal with their psychological problems, right? Cornelia, you dealin with problems on the educational level and I know what a mess that is because we done talked about it many a time. And Aristotle, you my son and you know how much I love and respect you, but, just think now . . . if it wasnt for all this crime and stuff we talkin bout, you and your law partners would have to shut down and get into some other racket, am I wrong?"

"OK, Sidney, you win," Squirrel say, laughin.

"Win what? I dont see yall that much and I wanna know all about how the twins gettin along and how we gon get behind Squirrel here and help us battle this cancer thing. Mmmm, this pie is good! Marcus, you and Cornelia both oughtta should get a prize of some kind behind all this good cookin. If yall only knew how good this pie was, yall'd quit squabblin and carryin on like niggers and dig in, *mmm-mmm-mmm!*"

"Daddy, you sure can run your mouth," Cornelia say, takin holda my arm.

"Always could," Squirrel say, pointin at Aristotle. "I keep on tellin this boy here that's where he gets his gift of gab from—from his daddy—but I still dont think he believes me."

"Well, I believe it," Izetta say.

Marcus just beamin.

That's the way the whole weekend go—with me visitin at both the kids' homes, stayin overnight at Cornelia's so I could play a little bit with the twins before headin cross the Bay Bridge to Oakland and hang out with Aristotle and his wife.

Much as I love the twins and bein round all that fine furniture and pleasant surroundins my daughter and Marcus live in (Marcus got framed pictures hung up of members of his family datin all the way back to the Gold Rush practically), it was still nice to get to the East Bay into a nice simple luxury apartment with a pool I could take a dip in to cool down, plus wasnt no worrisome babies to fool with. Poor Cornelia, at least she had Squirrel to help her do around a little.

I wanted to spend more time with Squirrel but Frazier got back in town that next day and I wasnt up to testin out whether or not I was ready to try to get along with him again. Maybe next visit.

It wasnt easy goin back to Palo Alto to worry bout how things was gon go for me in court and startin back to janitorin for Sam, and tryna keep my wine-drinkin under control.

The Blue Jay Hotel looked pretty cold and unappetizin behind all that gracious hospitality but home's still home and that's the only one I knew.

First thing I done when I got to my room that Sunday night was drag that case of wine Marguerite'd laid on me from out the closet.

I taken one of the bottles out, held it up to the light, uncorked it and placed it up under my nostrils. Man, it smell beautiful! Got a marvelous bouquet as Marcus might say.

I'd done had a coupla brandies with Aristotle and Izetta in the city before they drove me on to the SP Station and put me on the train. I was still feelin mellow and sleepy so I plug the cork back in and decide not to fool with no wine that night, not just then anyway.

Well, I musta dozed off listenin to Chad Whitmore's talk show over KRZY. They sign off midnight Sundays and play the "Star Spangle Banner." I wake up in the middle of the night and dont hear nothin but the toilet drippin and static comin outta my transistor layin there topa the other pillow I dont use.

After I get up to pee and try to fix the toilet, I remember it's still a coupla swallows left in a bottle of Swiss Colony Port I'd left twisted up in a paper sack in the pocketa my old coat slung over a chair back. I do that up, thinkin bout what

Marcus'd said about that dude he gon be workin with—urban systems. I hadnt let on then but that really struck me as kinda peculiar.

Back in bed, feelin warm and drowsy again, I snap off the radio and make two mental notes to myself. Usually I can get stuff to stick in my subconscious if I concentrate on it real hard just before fallin asleep. That's how I wake myself up in the mornin if I dont get too tore up the night before. Yet and still I knew I'd have to get a new alarm clock if I was gon try to hack this janitor job.

One: Telephone Squirrel and find out what hospital she gon be checked in at.

Two: Be sure and find out what Marguerite's last name is if we ever do see one nother again, or else look up in the Atherton directory and see if it's a Harry Burns that live on Primrose Path.

Even in my sleep it felt like the whole world was hurryin to come to a close. I kept seein train tracks and little kids and Squirrel climbin up outta swimmin pools cryin and all them old-timey pictures off Cornelia and Marcus' walls keep fadin in and out full life-size—and it's like I'm lookin at myself lookin at all this from behind bars that keep on zippin by while I'm tryna grab hold to em like scenery in the distance you be passin thru.

FALL

14

It's pretty much like goin on stage. I mean, I aint never actually been on stage or up in fronta no microphone or camera or anything like that but this is what I imagine it'd probly be like.

In the background I can hear Ed Jason gettin in his last comments on the woman that just now called in and cussed him out—they had to bleep out a lotta what she said—talkin bout how much she didnt care for his program and how he oughtta should balance his own views with somethin sensible once in a while, and on and on.

Ed say, "Funny isnt it how she hates the show but keeps on listening all the same. Would you say, would you even be willing to place a bet—O a dollar, say—that she must really get some sort of sadistic kick out of hating me as much as she claims she does? Would you be willing to put your money on that possibility? I would. I'd wager a buck. I'd wager . . . well . . . let's keep it down to a dollar. Not much you can buy with a dollar these days, true, but my wife may be listening to the show today and she's *awfully* touchy about foolhardy speculation, especially when it involves the family budget. Here's Vikki Carr with a message about milk and then I'll be back to take the next call."

A sexy woman's voice come on the line and tell me I'm next to go on the air. It's his producer, Passionate Patricia he call her, and by now she know my voice and call me by name.

"Be sure your radio's turned down, Sitting Pretty. Youre an old-timer around here. I know I dont have to tell *you* that anymore. Try and keep it brief because we'll be running into news time in just a few minutes, OK? Stand by, Ed'll be talking with you on line two in just a few moments."

Sure, I'm a little nervous but that's par for the course. Betcha anything O. J. Simpson still get butterflies before he go out on the field, or Flip Wilson or even my boy Stevie Wonder before they go out on stage.

Over the radio which I got turned down real low, the woman still ramblin on bout how milk got somethin for every body, but over the phone I can hear Ed Jason gettin in his wisecracks over the air. That's because of that seven-second tape delay thing they got goin so if anybody come on the phone sayin shit or dick or fuck and like that, they got plenty of time to bleep they ass *out!*

"Hello, line two, youre on the air. And what do *you* think about lowering the drinking age to eighteen?"

"Hi, Ed, this is Sitting Pretty."

"My, my, my goodness! Where've you been? I havent heard from you in quite a spell. What you been doing? How'd you come out on that traffic ticket rap?"

"It was quite an experience, man. I really been thru some changes since I talked to you last."

"Well, if you can tell me about it in about three minutes, I'd certainly be interested in catching up as I'm sure many of our regular listeners would."

"Well, I done a little time in the pokey as they use to say."

"*You,* Sitting Pretty? *You* mean to tell me *you* actually put in a few minutes in the slammer?"

"I'm afraid it was more'n just a few minutes. I got busted —you know, arrested, excuse the vernacular—owed a lotta money in back parkin tickets. I coulda hit on my son— he a lawyer—for money to settle up with the court on the fine, but I chose to go to jail instead."

86

"Why? Now, *this* is interesting."

"Why? That's hard to say. I reckon you could say I was fascinated by what I might learn from the experience."

"O???—"

"Yeah, you know how you get all these people callin in about prisoners' rights and—"

"Excuse me, Sitting Pretty, but as a long-timer tuner-in to the program, you know my feelings about that. You relinquish any rights you might think youve got the minute you walk into that liquor store and pull that gun on the attendant or rob that home or kidnap that girl or kill a cop or embezzle the government out of a million dollars or . . . whatever."

"I know your feelins, Ed. In fact, I admire a lot of em and I was thinkin bout you while I was doin time in the Palo Alto jail on weekends."

"On weekends? OK, now, you went in on one of those deals where you do your time piecemeal, on weekends, until youve served out the full sentence, right? Ive heard about people doing that but youre the first one Ive ever actually talked with who's done it. How did it feel? I mean, were you holding down a regular job and then on the weekend instead of working around the house or getting out in the yard or . . . well . . . instead of taking the wife and kids to the beach, you said, 'Well, honey, see you Monday, I gotta go change into the old striped suit and kick the ball and chain around. You and the kids'll have to check out the "Game of the Week" without me?' Just how did that go? How'd it work out?"

"Worked out fine, Ed. It wasnt quite like you imagine it on accounta I do have a regular job but, well, you see, I'm divorced and my kids're both grown."

"That's right, you did say you have a son who's a lawyer. Go on."

"Every Friday after I got off work, I'd go have me a good dinner someplace and then go check into the joint by six o'clock. Forty-eight hours later, which is to say by six that Sunday I'd be released and free to go on bout my business till the followin Friday."

"How much time were you sentenced to, Sitting Pretty?"

"Originally it was thirty days but the judge was lenient seein as how I'd been a pretty good joe and was claimin hardship. Also the fact that I was decorated for bravery in the war probly didnt hurt me none either."

"So . . . let me get my trusty pencil out here. Fifteen days at forty-eight hours per week would break that down to . . . O darn! I never was much at long division and multiplication, ahhh—"

"Came to eight days a month, Ed. Fact, they chopped off a day—"

"For good behavior, I hope."

"Nope, just because the jails're too full as it is and it really does cost the taxpayer more money than you'd think to feed and look after inmates. Took me somethin like two months to pay my debt to society."

"Two months of hard weekends. Wow, now that's something! I'll bet some of those dudes at San Quentin or Soledad would be appreciative if they could get it arranged to do their ten or twenty or lifetime terms that way, eh?"

"Well, that's a different matter, as you know, Ed."

"How'd you like it there in jail?"

"O it wasnt all that bad. The food's nothin to recommend. Your boy there, Max Felton—the one that broadcast the restaurant reviews—I dont think he'd give the jail menu too high a ratin. But other'n that I made out OK. Got more readin and thinkin done on them weekends durin September and October than I ordinarily woulda."

"Now, hold on, Sitting Pretty. You mean, they didnt have you busting up rocks or making license plates or anything like that? You just sort of sat around and read and contemplated the cosmos or whatever?"

"I made good use of my time. Most jailees dont. Most of em just set around lookin at television all day or playin cards, unproductive stuff like that. O I caught the big football games all right."

"Myyyy goodness! Now I know what to do if I want to get away from the old weekend grind at home and get in a bit of relaxation and meditation—let my parking tickets pile up and do time in jail on the installment plan. Sure beats washing and waxing the Pinto or laying new brick in the patio.

Whoops! Am I getting too close to home? Listen, Sitting Pretty, youve got a growing collection of fans out there in KRZY Land. How'd you like to come in one of these afternoons and be on the show?"

"Me? Are you kiddin me, Ed?"

"How could I kid an old authentic, crusty, dyed-in-the-wool cracker barreler like you? I'd sure love to have you if you can see your way clear to put in an appearance as we say in the business."

"Now, it's a whole lotta people out there heard you say that. I accept the invitation. What day?"

"O I think we can work that out. Stick around, dont hang up. Passionate Patricia'll come on the line and you can discuss it with her, work out all the particulars. News time's coming up. Did you have anything to add about lowering the drinking age?"

"Naw, not really. The kids gon get hold to the liquor dont care how you limit the age. When I was a kid back down in Missippi—and you grew up in the south, Ed—"

"Virginia, that's right."

"—So I *know* you must know Missippi for the longest was one of the driest states *officially*. We use to mash up blackberries, peaches, figs, anything. I musta been round ten when I first got in on it. We'd put a little sugar in, pour in a little water and let the stuff fer*ment* and drink it till we felt a buzz of some kind comin on. Now, you take somebody eighteen that's old enough to fight for they country and die for they country, you *know* they old enough to get drunk."

"That's an argument Ive heard delivered many a time, Sitting Pretty, and one I used to use myself but, really, I cant go along with it anymore. It's like saying I'm old enough to go out on patrol with a rifle and shoot somebody, so why cant I get drunk out of my mind and get in a car and run somebody down? You know what I mean?"

"Look at it this way then. The twenty-one-year-olds, they gon purchase liquor for they eighteen-year-old friends and the eighteen-year-olds, they naturally gon pass the thing on down and get they sixteen- and fifteen-year-old buddies whiskey and wine. So why not leave the deal the way it already is? Kids gon drink and smoke because they see they parents doin it and they parents aint gon be all that quick to condemn it because they think it's better'n shootin heroin."

"I go along with you on that, Sitting Pretty, and all I would add is: For crying out loud, why make something legal just because it's a problem we cant handle? Do you follow me? Legalize marijuana and it ceases to be a problem. It clears our courts, unclutters the jails, saves the taxpayers money—but is that really a valid way of coping head-on with the intricacies of the problem?"

"Well, good talkin to you again, Ed."

"Same here, Sitting Pretty. It's always a pleasure and, as pleasant as it sounded, considering the circumstances, I hope youll be able to steer clear of the law from now on. Stick around. Patricia's waiting to talk to you. It's news time now on KRZY and—"

I cut off the radio and, just like Ed say, there Passionate Patricia is on the phone, takin down my name and address and explainin to me how Ed wanna see me bout a very special deal, somethin that could lead to a little money if I was innerested, some kinda commercial promotion or—I didnt really understand but I agreed to be on the show and talk about it with him in private.

Patricia is in my ear, yes indeed, givin me a number where I can reach Ed off-hours. He wanna talk to me bout some kinda deal he cookin up and it could mean a little money if I'm innerested. I didnt really understand any of it but I got sense enough to be cool and discreet and scribble down what she say on the backa the envelope with my paycheck from Sam in it.

15

"What is it I do that turns you on most?"

"That's a tough one. I dont know as I can really say."

"Then ask *me,* why dont you?"

"All right, I'm game. What is it *you* like?"

"Promise you wont laugh?"

"Why would I laugh, is it all that funny?"

"To you it might be—with your ambivalent attitude toward sex."

"Ambivalent attitude? Now where you get that? All I said was it crack me up. The amount of time people spend thinkin bout it's unjustified when you consider the time it take to carry out the actual act, and you got to admit the positions is comical."

"*Preposterous,* I think, is how you put it a few weeks ago."

"All right, preposterous, but how's that make me ambivalent as you call it?"

"O I dont know. It appears to be rather impersonal with you. I mean, I enjoy making out with you but—"

"But what? You a married woman, Marguerite, and you gotta remember I'm always figgerin the worst can happen, like, your old man come bustin in on us any minute. Then we end up in a situation that's embarrassin for everybody concerned."

"I know, I know. That's probably one of the reasons this affair is so exciting, like all affairs perhaps."

"You gettin that far-off look in your eyes again."

"Am I? I certainly dont mean to. Turn over so I can massage your left side."

"Uhnngh! That feels so goooood! Where you learn to do that jive?"

"From my second husband, Leonard, he was an airline pilot. In fact, he was one of the first colored pilots to get a contract with a bigtime outfit. Strange man. I never really understood him. We lasted three years. Washington, D.C. He was very taken with Martin Luther King and the kinds of things he was trying to accomplish. Very race conscious. Every year we mustve written out checks for several hundred dollars to the Southern Christian Leadership Conference. I wanted a child—this was before I found out I couldnt have any—and Leonard didnt. My womb is funny. Gynecologists tell me it's immature. Anyway—I didnt mean to go into all that—he was forever raving about the massages those girls gave him when he was stationed over in Okinawa. I found a woman from Japan who taught me a little something about it."

"And you learnt how to do it better'n she could, betcha."

"O, Sidney, hold me, just hold me tight and kiss me, would you?"

Desirée out in the livinroom. She use to that now since I been comin around.

"Leonard said he didnt want to bring any kid into the world who'd have to endure the same racial situation he had to endure. For him it was a racially screwed-up world and he didnt have the temperament or patience to see any child of his thru it."

It's one in the mornin and I'm too tired from sweepin and dustin and scrubbin and waxin and polishin with Sam and his sister Wanda to wanna go too deep into *anything*. Marguerite'd picked me up, like she done every Tuesday and Thursday, right in fronta Uncle John's on El Camino. I'd have Sam drop me off there for coffee and wait for her.

"Sound to me like youve had a pretty innerestin life," I tell her.

92

"Most people would think so. I don't know. All in all, I suppose it's been pretty comfortable and, well, sheltered. I come from a long line of schoolteachers. My great-grandparents were free Negroes in Louisiana back before the Civil War. They did all right, spoke French, taught school, even managed to get a successful seafood market established which they later sold to a white family. My grandparents on my mother's side—my grandfather, I should say—had absolutely no head for business so he took up teaching and kept that tradition going. He was a history professor. His eldest son, my dad, took after him. He joined the faculty of Dillard College in New Orleans, teaching history. My brother went to West Point and went on to become a major in the army. He was a beautiful man. Tough, brilliant, rational but very warm and affectionate. I really loved him. He died in combat in Korea. Maybe that's why I married Leonard. I still think of my brother Alain a lot. My dad sent me upnorth to school, Bryn Mawr. He wanted me to be some kind of lady professor. I transferred to Oberlin in my junior year and took a degree in anthropology. That's about as far as I got. I met Stan, my first husband, while we were both undergraduates there. Nice guy, Pennsylvania German descent, sharp, ambitious. He wanted to break into politics. We moved up to New York where he'd been accepted for Law School at Columbia. Both our parents sent us money occasionally but we were really hard-up. I got a job doing library research for one of the anthro profs there at Columbia. One day he sent me over to Washington, D.C., to spend a week looking up some materials at the Smithsonian. That's where I met Leonard. You can figure out the rest of it yourself. I really dont care to talk about it any further except maybe to add that being married to Stan really didnt count. We were kids. We didnt know the first thing about life or each other. He buried himself in his law studies and I worked my ass off, going around frustrated, dammit!"

It was sorta inordinate for Marguerite to be gettin all this personal. I had a million things I wanted to ask her but feelin, as I did, a little shaky bout the relationship, I figgered the best thing to do was to hold off and just let her tell me what she wanted me to know whensoever she was in the mood to divulge it, right?

I wanted to ask her how it felt to be movin in and outta the race, how it felt to be passin. Far as I'm concerned, the woman was white but, like she herself was always sayin, society and upbringin do strange things to people's minds.

All I can get up the nerve to ask is, "Who was number three while you at it?"

She laugh and say, "That's funny, that's really funny. You ready for a drink? I'm on a ration and I try to abstain until late at night."

"Well, you know what I like. That was a good massage. Taken all the knots and kinks outta my tired muscles. What's so funny bout your third marriage?"

"Ha ha, ahhh . . . as you yourself might say—the dude was a *dud!* Lasted four months before I got an annulment. It was fun while it lasted tho, sort of. He was a musician, a piano player—or *pianist* as he called himself. I met him in Los Angeles where I'd gone to forget about Leonard. You know, to have a little fun in the California sun and all that sort of bullshit. He worked in this little cocktail joint but he really thought he was Art Tatum or Errol Garner or some giant like that. Little guy, shorter than me and very darkskinned and handsome. I was in my wild semibeatnik period, going on thirty-three and casting my fates to the winds, you know. Dad had died and left me some money and Leonard was still sending me alimony. I was running around in outlandish dress and trying for once to be a real soul sister. I was sick of being marginal. My idea was to commit myself to the prospect of undergoing complete negrification—or niggerization as Lonnie, that was his name, called it—and it cost me half a fortune. He had a lot of sycophantic friends that—"

"Sick-o-fan-tick?"

"Yeah, leeches, baby, in plain English."

"Hmmm, I'll have to remember that."

"Believe me there's nothing to remember. We had a good time I guess you could say—cut up a lot, stayed up all night every night, handed out money right and left to his friends, laughed, drank, smoked weed, jived around. We even got it in our heads one drunken night to fly over to Paris and *did it!* And guess who footed the bill for all this? Good old, desperate, guilt-ridden, super high yellow Marguerite, that's who! That con artist really had me believing he was going to make his mark as an influential jazzman. Hated the word *jazz* too. He liked to describe himself as a creative Afro-American composer, even back then, even in the fifties. O but he could talk that talk, as they say, and make me feel like heaven in bed. But his cocaine habit was getting to be a financial burden on me. After I left him, he got into hard stuff and never survived it. All I ever really got out of the deal was an LP he cut with a tune on it named after me called 'Sweet Marguerite.' I'll play it for you sometime."

"Play it now, I'd sure like to hear it."

"Cant, Sit, it's packed away. Harry cant stand it. He's rather uptight about all the men in my life who preceded him. That's understandable, isnt it? Lonnie's record to him is like an old love letter or something."

"You up and joined Alcohol Anonymous or somethin? You only had two double bourbons. That's how it's been for a coupla weeks now, what's up?"

"I'm trying to lose weight, honey. Harry'll be coming back from Europe soon. I'd like to look nice for him. I'm on that Dr. Stillman high-protein diet and, strictly speaking, I'm not supposed to fool around with too many carbohydrates at all and booze is sabotage calorie-wise."

"I oughtta should lose some weight myself. I been meanin to start joggin, even tried it a coupla times but look like I just cant get into it."

"I detest jogging. It's so boring. I swim and exercise at this club I belong to. Tennis, I play that too. It helps. At least you have your job to go to. Doesnt all that janitoring help you work off a few pounds?"

"Yeah, a little, but that wine . . ."

"Youve hardly touched yours, you talk about *me*."

"Aw, it's things on my mind."

"Squirrel?"

"I reckon. She aint doin all that well."

"You been to see her?"

"Yeah, a few times. She losin weight and gettin a funny look in her eyes, but she seem to have a pretty good disposition bout it, considerin. It's gettin harder and harder for me to be with her for any length of time tho. I get to feelin so . . . you know . . . down. While I was doin time in jail them weekends, that's what bothered me most. I was havin it easy, relatively, while she sufferin. She deserve better'n that. She the one kept the family together while I was off just—"

"While you were off just—just what? Whatve you been doing with yourself all these years away from them?"

"Ouch, there you go again. You really do know how to get at me where it hurt."

My glassa port right there beside the bed. I take a good-size swallow and go *hahhh*.

Marguerite, settin up next to me nekkid with her legs crossed, them big dannies she got floppin and quiverin every time she move—I take in the whole scene like I'm some kinda livin Kodak Instamatic and wig behind how pretty she look, chubby as she is, with her sweaty dark hair tied back in a ponytail with a red, red ribbon. It's shit you know you gon remember exactly the way it was at the time and this was one of them times. She done lit some candles and got the Sony radio over in the corner tuned in to soft mood music.

"Mmm, you smell so good tonight," I say, pullin her down on topa me.

"I had a long hot tub bath and plenty of time to sweeten myself just for you. Youre the only outside man Ive been with, you know, since Harry and I got married six years ago."

"Now, I bet you tell that to all the boys."

"All the boys maybe so," she say with that mischievous grin, "but I distinctly said man and I meant it."

I chuckle and scoot down to where her dimple of a navel up over me so I can lick it a little taste.

"O that—that tickles," she laugh, on her hands and knees now but at the same time inchin on up to the place where all I can discern is fur and that soft, slick, slippery saltiness. She ease down gentle and go to whisperin with all the breath she got, "Whew, dont stop now. O *please* dont stop!"

That loud whisperin and breathin must be what mister johnson like because just soon as that float out cross the air on down to where he been takin his rest, his ears prick up and he stand at attention.

By the time we pull up in fronta the Blue Jay, I'm so shot I could crumple up and melt. It's already goin on three-thirty tomorrow and I'm spose to be up and ready no later'n ten to get a ride with Willie G. up to San Francisco to talk with Ed Jason at KRZY.

Then too I wasnt feelin exactly what I call unlaxed because all the way from her house to El Camino we was trailed by one of them nosey Atherton cop cars. You know how the law in them classy neighborhoods make it they business to check everything that look even halfway suspicious. It wasnt the first time we'd been tailed. That's how come I talked Marguerite into takin the little Volvo insteada the Mercedes.

"Well," she say, "like Ive been trying to tell you all the way here, I'll miss you."

"I know. I'll kinda miss you too."

"Just *kinda?* I mean, do you ever think about me when we arent together?"

"Oh yeah, sure, I was thinkin bout you all yesterday."

"Really? What kinds of things?"

"O . . . about how crazy you were."

She make out like she poutin and say, "Is that how you see me—as some crazy lady you met in a liquor store who drinks too much and likes to—"

"Now, wait a minute, hold on! I aint said all that. Lemme put the words in my own mouth, OK? I mean crazy in a real good sense, like, in the old sense of where you see or do or experience somethin that's nice and you can relate to it so you up and say *crazy,* that's all. I go for you—period! Need I say more?"

"Why not? O I'm just insecure. I understand. Lonnie used to talk that way. Everything was crazy, wild, weird, bad. I simply dont know when I'll be able to see you again. Maybe it wont be necessary with Harry back. He's square as a cement block, only not as dense. I used to go to these encounter groups and sensitivity groups and all that sort of thing. Harry'd just laugh at me and ask me to bring back a report. Said he didnt need that kind of stimulation, that the whole world was a turn-on for him. Sometimes I wonder if he isnt a secret cockhound or something. I'll bet he really sampled some of that European pussy."

"Now, now, Marguerite, that last extra drink you treated yourself to is startin to show."

"Listen," she say, turnin the ignition on, "call me sometime, would you? Do it during the day, early. Harry's usually home by four."

"I will do that."

"Did you understand tonight?"

"Did I understand tonight?"

"I wanted to make you feel better, cheer you up. Youve been so morose lately. It's really been something of a bringdown. That's all Ive ever wanted to do—make you feel good and lift my own spirits in the bargain."

I already knew all that but it's good hearin her say it.

"Next time you see me I'll be at least ten pounds thinner, honey."

"Well, dont get too thin, you might cave in."

"Come again?"

"Aw, nothin. That's just somethin I used to tell Squirrel when she got off on one of her losin weight kicks. Listen, baby, I'll be in touch but in the meantime you can listen for me on the radio on Ed Jason's show."

"What time is he on and what station?"

"KRZY, the middle of the dial, the middle of the day."

"I havent the faintest what you mean by that but I'll try and listen in. I'm signed up for a pottery class out at Foothill College that's scheduled to meet three afternoons a week."

"Well, do what you can."

"Hope Squirrel gets better. I feel as if I actually know the woman after all youve told me. Is she still at Kaiser Hospital?"

"She goes home in a few days. Listen, I'm dyin."

"Then good night, good night! I think youre pretty crazy yourself and sooner or later I'll pin you down on what youve been up to for the past couple of decades. You are one evasive bastard, you know that?"

She poke out her lips and lean toward me. We get soppy and all sloppy. And I use to cringe lookin at her do that same number with that doggone poodle Desirée.

16

Willie G. might know all about cars, how to rip em apart and put em back together, but he one of the scariest drivers I ever had the displeasure of ridin with.

He slouch all down in his seat, use his left hand to steer while he be steady twistin the radio knob and smokin with his right. He dont signal when he change lanes and he *keep* changin lanes. It aint nothin for him to just all of a sudden shoot from the slow lane straight over to the fast—no turn signal, no hand out the window, nothin—just zip right over there in fronta some big monster truck and then speed up till he right on topa the car in fronta him and tailgate the hell outta it and honk his horn, really mash on it, so that either the lead car gotta get out his way or else he gon zoom back into the lane to the right and try and overtake the sucker just so he can feel like he the leader of the pack or some fool nonsense.

All the time this mess is goin on, he got the radio blastin or either he reachin and feelin round the topa the dashboard or up under or back round behind the seat tryna find some particular eight-track cassette to shove in this new tape do-hickey he done just had installed. It's tape cartridges scattered all over the front and back seats along with girlie magazines, old racin forms, newspaper, rags, rusty car parts, tools, Coke bottles, Dr Pepper and Slitz cans, cigarette and candy wrappers, potato chip bags, old Colonel Sanders take-out boxes with dried-up chicken bones stickin up outta em, mitchmatch socks and shoes, spare neckties, shirts and britches all crumpled up, cans of Maine sardines unopened, half-eaten ice cream cones, orange peels, coils and coils of used dental floss, LP albums with no jackets all warped outta shape by the sun, Vicks inhalers, Christmas tree branches, a paira psychedelic women's underpants and aint really no tellin what-all since buried down underneath all that is stuff I cant even make heads or tails outta.

What it is is a miniature version of the city dump, a travelin nuthouse on radial tires. This rebuilt Chrysler jacked up so high off the ground with the shocks he put in until if you wasnt careful to check yourself right close when you opened the door to step out you was subject to fall to your death. I mean, sail right to the pavement and dash your silly brains out!

The racket from the radio and tapes so damn loud you gotta holler and shout and even scream just to be heard.

"JUST A MINUTE NOW," Willie G. shriek while I'm tryna tell him bout Marguerite and Squirrel and how much it mean to me to be ridin up to talk over this deal, whatever it was, with my man Ed Jason. "HOLD ON, SIT, I GOT SOMETHIN YOU JUST *GOTS* TO LISTEN TO! IF I CAN JUST LOCATE THE DURN TAPE—"

Now, here he go feelin and fumblin round the floor again, aint lookin at the road or nothin, swervin all in and outta the lane.

My throat sore from shoutin and my nerves—every single one of em done shriveled up and collapsed. I just flat out give up.

For some reason, dont ask me why, I'd got up that mornin feelin like, well, Marguerite she goodlookin and educated and even sensitive when she lighten up on that bourbon, plus she consider herself some kinda soul sister and *love* to whip on me all that well-aged exquisite what the late Mr. Ian Fleming refer to as Pussy Galore. You ever see that picture, *Gold-*

finger? Yet and still, behind all that, I still found it hard to fill her in on what's been happenin with me all this time I been away from my family. How come? I dont rightly know but it worried me all in my sleep, so I figgered I'd lay the whole thing on Willie G. drivin in that mornin.

Facta business, wasnt nothin much to tell. After you hit thirty, twenty years dont really seem like no time. Look like it flash past faster'n you can swat at a gnat. That great Persian poet, old Omar Khayyam, he did write them lines that go: 'The bird of time hath but a little ways to fly, and lo the bird is on the wing,' now, didnt he?

I was gon tell all this to Willie G. I tried, I swear, only he never heard a word I said. All that stuff about carryin luggage out at the airport, drivin a Yellow Cab in Oakland, breathin them chemicals in a drycleanin plant, parkin cars for fancy San Francisco restaurants, cleanin up nightclubs after hours with this insane joker call hisself Black Buddha, jack-leg bartendin with a pistol closeby at a joint call Booker's T Club up there round Marin City, bein the janitor for a TV station in San Jose—which, combined with bein round clubs and bars, I learned a little somethin bout showbiz— not to mention short-term gigs such as substitute mail carryin, short-order cookin and dishwashin at places like Wing Lee's Ocean Cafe, plus workin for people like Sam. Damn!

That's what make time go by so quick. Just to tell about that'd take more'n a book and that dont include all the women I got messed up with, the hassles with people, the drinkin too much, the times I spent throwin the shoppin news and puttin junk advertizements up on people's porches just to keep up my room rent and wine habit which, as you might guess, got outta control from time to time even tho it's really pretty regulated now. All them times I was ready to give up but didnt, them evil dawns and afternoons—how you gon tell somebody was raised by professors the shit you been thru? How you gon explain it? On what basis? Aint no way they can comprehend it, dont care how many library books they done laid up in and pondered and empathized with.

Willie G. grinnin and I can see his mouth movin as he jam another cartridge in the tape mechanism but I cant make out what he sayin to save my life. What I really need now is for Miz Duchess to be there with us. She claim she can read lips when she feel like it.

Luckily it's a slow tune he put on, a ballad, got soft violins and stuff in the background in place of all that car-shakin bammity-blam-boom give a deaf-mute a headache. He still play it loud but I can kinda hear myself think for a change.

"What's this?"

"Roberta Flack. Man, she sure can sing, cant she?"

"Say, Willie, I know it aint none of my business but dont you ever throw nothin away?"

"Be with you in a second, Sit."

He cut over two lanes to the right and almost got smashed by a Greyhound bus. I'm bout to lose every bit of my breakfast.

"What was that all about?"

"Sorry, man, but I had to get outta that lane or else we'da ended up way over on Van Ness Avenue."

"But that's where I wanna go. The station's not too far from there."

"Is that right? I thought you told me it was downtown."

"Well . . . Actually you can get there from downtown pretty quick. At least you done got me to San Francisco."

"Just relax, Sit, a few minutes aint gon make that much difference. Now, what were you sayin to me back there?"

"Aw, nothin, it wasnt important. But—would you tell me this? Well, it's two things I wanna know really. First off, what's the significance of all them neckties you keep in the back seat?"

"No big thing. I just like to change ties whenever the mood hits me. I know it's strange but that's just me. I'll be drivin someplace and suddenly I'll pull over and put a fresh tie on, spruce up my image. Ties is it. I see a broad I wanna impress and *shhhoomp!* I whip my dark tie off and throw on my bright multicolored can-you-dig-it tie. You know, it was one time a tie saved my life. Way back in the sixties when the Watts riot broke out, I was toolin round down there in L.A. lookin for a job, had my sharkskin suit on, beautiful shirt and this respectable tie, lookin like I'm really together, you see. I didnt know the riot was goin on but, like, the closer I get toward Watts I start noticin how hostile the niggers on the streets is lookin at me at them stoplights. So finally I pull into a Texaco station, black-owned, you know, and while I'm gettin a fill-up I ask the dude how come people actin up so funny when they see me. He say, 'O that's easy. You must aint heard bout the riots yet. These kids probly think you with the Establishment because you are dressed rather clean and bourgie, if you dont mind my sayin so.' That's all I needed to hear, Sit. Shoot, I took my jacket off, my shoes, unbuttoned my shirt and let it hang open to my navel, found some old plastic thongs in the backa the short, put *them* on, combed my hair all every whichway until it looked all nappy and fucked-up, took the purplest tie I could find and wound it round my forehead. Shit, after that I drove clean thru Watts past flamin buildins, fire trucks, niggers bustin windows to get em a leather coat—and not one of them clowns ever even looked at me except to flash me the victory sign or somethin, heh heh!"

I couldnt really see the main point of Willie G.'s story but that didnt matter neither. I went on anyway and popped number two on him. "Uhhh, what's them damn technicolor draws doin back there?"

We rollin off the freeway now and Willie really crackin up. He laugh and snort and bang on the dashboard until it's tears seepin out the corners of his eyes. I'm still wishin he would look at where he goin some.

Roberta Flack singin bout how she taste just like a woman, and a light rain startin to come down. I sorta laugh a little myself just to keep Willie company but I'm still waitin on his ass to straighten up and answer my question.

"Whoa me," he say, simmerin down, "you sure a nosey dude, aint you? What's so funny is I aint sure myself whose draws they is but I think they belong to this little broad I picked up works at the A&W over in Cupertino. I took her to the drive-in to see this vampire flick and it hadnt been on fifteen minutes before she come snugglin up next to me. You know what she say?"

"Naw, what she say, Willie?"

"She say . . . *hee hee hee,* crack me up! She say, 'Ooooo, man, this is too freaky and scary for me. I havent been this grossed out since *The Exorcist.*' Then she lean back, reach down and slide her draws off. I thought at the time that she stuffed em in her purse but—well, whosoever they belong to, I left em back there where people could get a look at em. They really are a conversation piece, arent they?"

He go to havin another laughin fit and keep it up till we pull up in fronta the KRZY studios. I keep on forgettin how crazy Willie G. really is.

"Here you go, Sit. Hope you get back OK. I'm runnin over here to check on this security-guard job but I wont be headin back for a good day or two. There's this chick stay over here in Twin Peaks I use to fix cars for her mother. Watch your step comin out now!"

I kick some calcified french fries and well-gnawed bobby-cue sparerib bones out the way, open the door and take a deep breath before I make the big leap.

"HEY," Willie G. come shoutin after me as he pullin off, "TELL THEM PEOPLE YOU GOT A GOOD FRIEND THAT WOULDNT MIND BEIN ON THE RADIO TOO, HEAR?"

Two old ladies hobblin down the sidewalk, leanin up against one another, stop and turn around to look at him like he *got* to be tripped out.

I'm cool and pretend like I dont even know the fool. If it hadna been for me concentratin on circlin that damn car with white light before gettin in it, I might not be here today to tell yall all this.

17

Ed Jason look pretty much the way I'd pictured him—a medium-size man with grayish brown hair and a dark mustache. His eyes real dark and big and gaze right at you when he sayin somethin. Comin from the south like he do, he got that old-time way that's been handed down of seein if a Negro can look him straight in the eye. The way I do them people is to look em directly between they eyebrows so that they think we makin eyeball contact. With Jason it's different. Intuition let me know right off he a warm person thru and thru, so it aint no strain to look right at him.

The office part of KRZY is a big modern room with these long rows of desks. He settin at one of em eatin yogurt with a little plastic spoon right out the paper container. In the background it's secretaries typin and a few teletype machines clickety-clackin out news just like the ones down at that TV station in San Jose I use to dust off and study kinda, only these dont make as much racket.

I take one look at Ed Jason's desk piled up with papers and letters and packages and books and say, "Good gracious alive, Mr. Jason! How in the world do you find time to keep tracka all this stuff and be on the radio too?"

"Ed," he say.

"Beg your pardon."

"Youve been calling me Ed on the air for a couple of years now. Why this Mr. Jason business all of a sudden?"

"You right. That's funny. It's easy to call a celebrity—which you are—by they first name when you havent ever met em face to face. Excuse me—Ed."

"I suppose youre right but I certainly dont feel like any celebrity as you call it. Now youve just been let in on one of the secrets of this business. For every hour I spend on the air, I probably put in two to three hours preparing for it—and that's not counting the time my wife has to put up with when I'm tossing and turning in bed over things that went wrong or remarks I made during broadcast time that I later regret or feel nervous about. It really gets to be hellish sometimes."

"I can believe it."

"Listen, Sitting Pretty. A sort of unusual situation's come up. Perhaps I should call it an opportunity. The station management's decided to kick off a new campaign to ballyhoo our talk shows to prospective listeners, that's to say, people who, for one reason or another, arent familiar with what we do yet. We've held a few brainstorming sessions and I come up with the idea of getting a few of the station's more popular callers into the act. Rather than lay the entire promotion bit in the laps of slick professionals, I suggested it might be a novel tactic to try the homespun approach. Do you follow me so far?"

"I'm right there with you every step of the way, Ed."

"Attaboy, Sit, now dig, and I'll try and get right to the point. We've already signed Mrs. Mucci, you know, the lady with a hard-on for the governor, the one who also sees the global political situation as a reflection of the rivalry between Pepsi and Coca-Cola."

"The Soft Drink Conspiracy Lady—I know exactly who you talkin bout."

"Well, the management really went for my idea. Theyve also contacted Louie Matlock."

"O yeah, that old guy with the frog in his throat, always be carryin on bout this earthquake stuff and how he keep his own charts on it and how the lost continent of Atlantis gon rise up out the ocean again by nineteen eighty-four and all like that."

"That's right. We're picking three of our most popular callers to the station to feature in a number of radio and TV promos that'll be aired starting around January."

I feel my stomach lightenin up and go to tiltin-like, the way it do when you on a elevator sometime. I'm listenin at Ed Jason run all this down to me yet it's difficult to believe I'm hearin what he actually leadin up to.

"You mean—"

"I mean, I'm asking if you'd be interested in being number three. There's a couple thousand bucks in it for you and, for whatever it's worth, you can sit around and catch yourself coming out of the radio or playing on the idiot box every few hours for the rest of the winter. We'll be starting work on the tapes two weeks from today and would sure love to have you aboard if it sounds like the sort of project that might interest you. Whaddaya say?"

The words come tumblin outta my mouth before I even knew what I was gon say.

"Well, yes, yes. I could—I could really go for that, Ed, but, like, well, you know, I'm committed to workin a swing-shift kinda job now and—"

"Are you free mornings and weekends?"

"Sure."

"Youve paid your debt to society," he say, pushin his yogurt aside and smilin, "and dont have to spend the Sabbath behind bars?"

"O no, that's all over and done with."

"Great! That's just fine, Sitting Pretty. If you'd be willing to put in a few mornings and maybe a Saturday afternoon working with us, I'm certain we could wrap this thing up and get it on the road in no time. I'd like for you to stick around—if youve got the time, of course—and talk over details with Colin Crews. He's head of public relations around here and a big fan of yours. He's the one who'll be handling all this—drawing up contracts, taking care of scheduling. You wanna save all your big questions for him to answer. You look a little nervous."

"Well, no, not really. Just tryna figger out what I'mo be sayin and doin."

"That's only natural, Sit, and Colin's the man to put you

at ease. His idea—which he got from me—is to set up a more or less hang-loose series of spots. Theyll run anywhere from ten to thirty seconds."

"Aw, is that all? That sound like a breeze."

"I know, but it's work. Remember what I told you about how much preparation goes into my program. Well, doing good canned commercials can be even tougher. Youll earn your pay but that doesnt mean you wont also have a little fun while youre at it. Personally, I think youll do quite well for that very reason. You enjoy being on the air."

"Yes, I do."

"All right then, can you stick around for a few minutes?"

"I think that can be arranged."

"That's all I wanted to hear. Come and I'll introduce you to C.C. as we call him around here. C. C. Rider's what I nicknamed him."

Ed Jason got up and we shook hands again. Followin him over to C.C.'s office in another parta the buildin, thoughts and feelins is clickin inside me faster and quicker'n what's comin in over the teletype machines. I cant really grasp none of em, but, like Ed ask me to, I stuck around. I stuck around a few minutes and then some.

Why not?

I didnt have no place special I had to go. Far as I was concerned, wasnt no place left now to go but up.

It was kinda like what my daddy said the mornin I was packed and ready to go serve in the army. "You aint got nothin to lose," he told me. "Nothin to lose but your life. And you old enough to know by now that a black man's life aint worth a plug nickel in this white-run world. I'm sho hopin it dont happen, but at least if you die your soul will be free of this hell down here and you can sail on into heaven, safe and clean."

He said this in private, nudgin me on the chin with his big old knotty knuckles, with a little tremble in his voice. The very words of Nebuchadnezzar Josiah Prettymon—who passed on suddenly right after my discharge from the service —as recollected by his unkillable son.

18

It's rainin like God fixin to get ready to go out and recruit Hisself another Noah, and it's been doin it for days.

I been readin in the *Chronicle,* the Pali *Times* and the San Jose *Mercury* all about how lettuce and onion crops gettin ruined down in the Valley and how people's houses that's built on topa hills done got to slidin off they foundations like they all the time doin when it's a heavy rainy season.

These folks out here clever and resourceful but they aint never had good sense. They keep puttin up buildins and houses that's gon go just like *that* the minute a hard rain or a good flood come up or a strong enough earthquake. That's how come I always pay attention to that nut Louie Matlock when he call up KRZY. He say the whole state gon be shattered by a earthquake and sink down under the sea. I'll probly go down with it if I live long enough. California aint never been my style exactly, but it's done got to the point now where it's the only beautiful country I know. Aint no place else I can imagine myself livin now.

It's a hour to go before I have to be at work. I'm in the Ocean Cafe and it's just my luck to be settin up drinkin coffee with Broadway and Miz Duchess who was already there when I bounced in to unlax and do a little vocabulary study in peace.

"Hey, what's that you got there?" Broadway ask right off, lookin cross the table at the little Woolworth notebook I write my word lists down in.

"None of your business," Miz Duchess say. "Man's gotta right to carry a tablet around, doesnt he? Dont be so durn nosey!"

Now, you have to remember Broadway got one of the heaviest attitudes of anybody alive. Fact, that's all he is is this one big attitude struttin around held together by breath and britches and a awful lotta nerve. He cut his eyes real slow at Miz Duchess and then turn to me, breakin into one of them tight-jawed, ridiculous, un-for-real grins—one of them masks like they was talkin bout in *Psychology Today*. He done got his hair processed and it's hangin down over the collar of his ruffled shirt and Edwardian jacket, I reckon you call it. He tilt his Last Tango in Paris hat forward on his head—you know, the kind that French broad wore in that flick—and pick up his coffee cup and say, "Well, tell me what's goin on, Sit, aint seen you around much lately. Nasty weather we're havin, eh? How's that, Duchess?"

Miz Duchess just turn her head and look off toward the counter where Wing Lee drinkin a cupa his own coffee and talkin with a lady in Chinese.

"Been pretty busy and tied up," I tell Broadway, "what with having to keep runnin back and forth between here and San Francisco."

Miz Duchess say, 'O yes, you told me about that. That's awfully sad, Sitting Pretty. How's your wife doing? Is she any better?"

Broadway drop his grin and say, "Wife? You mean to tell me you been married all this time, brother? She been sick or somethin?"

"Sick, indeed! The man's poor wife has cancer."

"Aw, shit. That right, Sit? Damn, man, I'm sorry to hear that, real sorry. That cancer, wow, that's one terrible joint! My sister live back in Milwaukee she just got thru havin this operation on her toochie-wootchie behind that stuff but she

110

say that's pretty common for a woman nowdays. Golll*lee!*
I cant even stand to think about it!"

"On her *what?*" Miz Duchess say, snappin up the cap part
that go with her yellow rain slicker. "I swear, Ive been sitting
here talking with this young man for over half an hour and
I can only make out about a tenth of what he says. I barely
know what he's talking about—ever! Of course, I dont let
that worry me any. I quit paying most people any attention a
long time ago. Keeps my head peaceful, you know what I
mean?"

"Aw, Duchess," Broadway say, "you just testin me out,
aint you? She always testin me out, Sit. Miz Duchess here
so fulla jive I betcha anything she could probly talk a blind
man into buyin a truckloada mirrors. You oughtta been a
salesman of some kind, baby."

She shake her finger in Broadway's face and go, *"Baby???*
Baby, my posterior! Fanny to you, buster! I'm practically old
enough to be your great-grandmother. Dont you come handing me that *baby* malarkey! And be careful how you speak
about the blind because I almost qualify as one of them
myself. Why, any morning now I expect to wake up and find
my eyesight's gone, just—"

"Now, ease up, Duchess," I bust in and say. "You done
climbed up on your horse and dont wanna get down. Broadway just playin with you."

"No, I'm not either, Sit. I may joke but I dont play. Miz
Dutch here, she—"

"Dont mean to cut you off, Broadway, but it seem like to
me both of yall just tryna stage some type of who-can-get-on-
whose-nerves-the-most contest for my benefit. Yall was gettin
along all right until I set down with you."

"That's only because I was letting him do all the yakking,"
she say. "And another thing, Mr. Broadway, before I forget
it. A salesman, the way I learnt it in school, is a man who
sells something. Do I look like a man?"

"You really want me to answer that?" Broadway ask her,
snigglin and winkin at me.

I pretend like I dont see him winkin and just shake my
head with a sigh, rear back in my chair and start drummin

on the table with my fingers. My head hurtin and I got enough on my mind without foolin with these two past-grown people. It's one thing I done found out stumblin round thru the world. Stay the fuck outta other folkses arguments, fits, caniptions and politics. It simply dont pay, specially with these jiggedy, outta-touch types that check in and out the Blue Jay. These people got problems nobody's even studied about yet. They lonely, they frustrated, they alienated, they disenchanted, they livin at what's now called poverty level and below—and they are definitely on the edge. I mean, they be's *out* there! I know.

"Caught any good movies lately?" I ask that to be devilish, lookin at least to cool Broadway out.

Miz Duchess say, "Movies? You have got to be joking. I doze off looking at a lot of them on television in the hotel lobby, but the last picture I actually paid good money to go in and see was . . . O what the heck was it? . . . O yes, now I remember—*Pinocchio.*"

"Now, here she go again with that jive," Broadway say, got his face all screwed up while he smoothin down a sideburn. "*Pinocchio.* I dont believe it. They played that joint for us way back in third grade. I can even remember hunchin up in the school auditorium rootin for that little untogether, wooden-headed chump, scared to death he was gon get iced. Shoot, I know they musta shot that joint before I was born because it was old by the time I got around to peepin it. *Pinocchio* by Walt Disney? Where in the world you been, Miz Dutch?"

"All that was unnecessary, Broadway, as usual. I saw it right up here at the Stanford Theater four or five years ago. It was playing with *Fantasia* which always makes me dizzy to look at. I really loved *Pinocchio* even tho I had to threaten to call the management on a few dozen kids to get em to pipe down so I could hear what was going on up there on the screen."

"What you do, Duchess," I ask, "go durin the Saturday matinee?"

"You better believe it. What's wrong with that? It would surprise you how much money you save. My Social Security

112

and pension money'll only stretch so far." She shake her head slowly from side to side. "That was one heck of a good story. I cried all the way thru it. There was so much to learn from it. I'm Pinocchio. Youre Pinocchio. Even Broadway here with his funnylooking flamenco hat could be Pinocchio."

"Speak for your ownself," Broadway growl. "Quiet as it's kept, I'm that sly, slick, ruthless fox."

"Well, you can go on and be the fox. The nasty old world's gonna get you anyway—in the end. Isnt that how it is, Sitting Pretty?"

"I dont know about *gettin* you but I sure can testify that it does have a way of gettin *to* you. It got to me all right and I'm still tryna figger out ways to get back."

Broadway got his head down on the table, tryna act like the conversation puttin him to sleep, but I can see his little skinny belly quiverin under his spose-to-be-fancy coat which let me know that deep down he crackin up and too damn stubborn to show it.

I'm in just enough of a signifyin mood to come out and tell him, "Say, Broadway. I was walkin round the Tenderloin up in the city the other day and come across this movie house call Peep-A-Rama. Guess what they was playin when I walked in there?"

He hunch up his shoulders, raise his eyebrows and flatten his hands palms down on the formica table. "Search me, Sit. What was they playin—*Jesus Christ Superstar?*"

"Not hardly. They was featurin a little number the title of which is *Box Lunch*—you know, *Box Lunch* starring, heh heh, Irma Yolanda?"

"Was it good?"

"Hard to say, I only caught a few minutes of it."

"Well, I read the reviews and the critics think it's pretty good, excellent in fact."

"What critics you read?"

"Obviously, the ones you dont—haw haw haw!"

He let it all come rushin out now, all the stuff he wanted to laugh at but was holdin in. He go to slappin his thigh, bout big as my wrist, take his hat off and run his fingers thru his process, bang on the table till his eyes start waterin and just laugh and laugh, got me and Miz Duchess lookin and smilin at one nother.

I got to hand it to the little unscrupulous Negro. He cooler'n I am. He dont never let down and admit to nothin. Miz Duchess and me start gigglin a little too, only we each got our own private reasons. I can tell. That's what so nice about anything that's funny. Everybody got they own angle on what it is about it that's really comical or ridiculous. Now, me myself, I'm all the time flashin on the whole idea of it bein a world out there, outside my head, crowded with fools and rascals like me who be bumblin they way thru life from crib to casket, aint got the slightest idea what it's all spose to be about. Who know what the Duchess is seein in her real mind when she laugh? And Broadway—the bullshit that's gurglin round in his head probly best be represented by comic books.

"*Box Lunch,* my stars!" the Duchess say. "The titles theyre giving to movies these days!"

"What's it like being in a picture like that?" I up and ask Broadway point-blank, cold.

He wipe one smile off his face and replace it with a new one. That's what that little brass monkey did, plus got the nerve to come tellin me, "I aint never seen the flick but I'll let you know after I do, Mr. Sit. Sure hope that sickly wife of yours can get that cancer under control."

"That goes for me too," Miz Duchess say.

I wanna leap cross the table and hug her, whereas Broadway I'd be delighted to serve a big, fat juicy knuckle sammich to—and for dessert just choke him a little.

19

Wanda the one I gotta be careful around. Like, take to-night for instance. I'm comin off my break at the Bank of America where we cleanin up. It's our last stop. All night long we been workin like dogs on accounta Sam either up-set or uptight about somethin and when he get in one of them kinda moods it aint too much laughin and jokin go on. Sam'll come in, set up and hit that cleanup *hard*. He dont say much and if you perceptive you better not say too much neither. You better get busy hustlin and workin up a sweat that's at least as heavy as his is.

Wanda she got this irritatin habit, with her fat self, of followin in behind me, checkin out what I'm up to, peepin over my shoulder at what I'm readin, eavesdroppin the phone calls I make which mostly be to Marguerite. You bet-ter know I aint crazy enough to be usin some client's tele-phone to make toll calls to Squirrel.

Now, it's two ways I got of lookin at Wanda. One is I know she dont mean me any harm because she kid me a lot and like to brush up against me every chance she get. She really not all that badlookin either, say if she was to take off fifteen-twenty maybe twenty-five pounds, get her teeth fixed and quit straightenin her hair and packin it down with all that grease. She could boost her image up a hundred-ten percent, at least in my eyes anyway.

The other way I look at Wanda is to never forget she Sam's only sister and she definitely not the swiftest person I ever worked with. She work hard and try hard for somebody thirty-three years old, but it's somethin tell me Sam done put her up to spyin on me which is understandable. I mean, I know he hired me on again out the kindness of his heart and, bein the astute and concerned kinda businessman he is, it's important for him to know whether I'mo actually work out or not. It's a drag bein looked at, studied and watched but that's somethin I got use to a long time ago.

I know I been actin a little bit too happy lately, plus a little too goofy to boot. It's them KRZY commercials comin up got me carryin on like that. If you was to take a picture of what be's on my mind, you might find that halfa me in high spirits while the rest still broodin on Squirrel, the kids and mess that shoulda been resolved or at least ameliorated way back before I had all that time on my hands to just lay back and scheme, the way Marcus my son-in-law pull down a livin.

"Who that white woman pull up in that fancy car to pick you up?" Wanda ask me in the backa the janitorial truck where we busy storin all the cleanin equipment. Sam still stationed in the bank at somebody's desk, figgerin somethin out with a pencil and paper. He use to didnt be that way but lately he let us do mosta the loadin up while he hang back and fool around with paperwork.

"Hey," I tell Wanda while I'm rasslin with this big-ass floor polisher. "Gimme a hand with this, hunh?"

Wanda bout strong as Muhammad Ali anyway. She help me get the doggone contraption into place and then say, "Sit, you hear me?"

"Hear what?"

"I asked you a question. Who that Caucasian woman that be—"

"Now, Wanda," I say in the softest voice I can manage, "I was hopin you could take a hint and wouldnt come at me two times in a row with a off-the-wall inquiry like that."

116

"Dont go takin it the wrong way, Sit. I'm not tryna get in your business or anything like that. I was just—"

"You just nosey, right? Well, for your information and since you so curious and direct, I want you to know that the woman aint white. She a good frienda mine and—"

"You dont have to tell me nothin else. Shoot, I can take a hint. Forget I ever said *anything*."

She standin there with her mouth open, chompin on a peppermint Life Saver. It's dark in the truck so I cant really see her all that good but I can sure smell that peppermint and hear it bein crunched on.

I say, "It's all forgotten, Wanda," but she just keep on smackin and lookin with her big light-brown eyes. She and Sam both got them light-brown eyes.

Suddenly, without warnin the first, I lunge toward her at the same moment she done got it in her mind to come lungin toward me. It was one of them old crazy things that happen before you even know it's takin place.

Now that we actually pressed up against one nother—and aint neither of us really ready for it—all I know to do is pull her closer and go to kissin on that Life Saver-tastin mouth. Bits and pieces of chewed-up candy get all over my tongue while I'm busy squeezin on her broad back and chubby butt the way Squirrel do my arms and shoulder and neck, a handful at a time. She sorta mash her sweaty face into mine and ease her mammoth tongue up against my tonsils and then go to flickin it round inside my mouth and nibblin on my tongue real soft like her teeth made outta marshmellow. She got a heavy raincoat on and I'm wearin one too, but when she jut right in up next to mister johnson—*awwww,* I tell you, we all get to quiverin shonuff and you can feel the sun startin to shine out from underneath them coats!

Next thing I know, we done tussled each other down to the floor with me on topa her, layin up there between the vacuum cleaners and the rug shampooers and buckets and mops and the push-brooms, howlin.

"I'm sorry, Sitting Pretty," Wanda say, "but have you ever tried to get over to somebody and look like the only way you can connect is to physically just reach out and grab em?"

Before I can catch my breath to answer that, Sam come stickin his old rain-sprinkled head up inside the truck. "What you all doing?"

Wanda dont even so much as bat one eye. "We was tusslin with that damn floor polisher and tripped."

"Yeah," he say, standin there, rubbin at his jaw, "I can see *both* of you must have tripped all right. Now, get on up from there and let's get this show off the ground."

That's so much like Sam, me and Wanda both gotta peep at one nother and smile. That's him right down to a T.

Later on that night back up at the Blue Jay, I run into the Professor in the hallway. He all dressed up with a tie and jacket on underneath his army surplus rain poncho. I can tell he even done taken time out to polish his scuffed-up cowboy boots.

"What's up, Professor? I cant recall seein you this clean and spiffy since J. Krishna however-you-say-his-last-name hit town and spoke over here at Stanford."

"I'll have none of that," he say, "but you are just the man Ive been waiting to see."

"You mean to tell me you got all decked out for my sake?"

"Not on your life, Sitting Pretty, but I did want to hit you up for a bottle of that Portuguese wine if it's OK with you."

"You want it, you got it. You know that. What you celebratin?"

"Nothing, I'm going to a party."

"In the middle of the week at this time of night?"

"Now, since when have you or I ever been fenced in by temporal convention, Sit? Ive got a date with a young lady—no, it's a little sticky to say that currently, isnt it? I have a late rendezvous to keep with a youthful female person who's about as beautiful as they come."

"O yeahhh? Where'd you meet her?"

"She's a student. We met last week at the coffeehouse on campus where she works nights. Youre gonna have to meet her. I mean, this woman's got a mind that's so soulful and active, I come away from being with her with my whole body charged up. It's really refreshing to know someone like that."

"Sound to me like she stone got your nose open."

"Nose open?"

"Unh-hunh, got it open so wide I betcha I could drive a Mack truck up thru there and you probly wouldnt even feel a thing."

The Professor must aint never heard that old standby before. He shake his head, grinnin, and follow me to my room where I dig him up a coupla them Porto Santos.

"You need a bag or somethin to carry em round in? I should have one round here someplace."

"No, thanks, Sit. I can take care of that. We're just going over to hang out with a few friends of hers for a bit. Theyre all into this consciousness-raising thing."

"Is that right? I read about that stuff but I kinda thought it went out."

"No, it's still very much around. Personally I think Ive gone beyond that stage but Karen's fascinated with it and it doesnt do any harm."

"Well, me, that's the last thing in the world I need is to have my consciousness raised."

"Really? Why do you say that?"

"I say it on accounta I'm already *too* conscious of what's goin on around me. What I need is to get my head cooled down some, get my consciousness lowered to the place where I can cope more better with shit."

The Professor look hurt. I reckon he musta been thinkin bout all them deep discussions we done got into down thru the months where we be busy takin everything apart, examinin society and humankind and delvin around with the cosmos and the universe and whatnot.

"I think I understand what youre saying, Sit, but I'm not so certain you mean that."

"We can talk about it. In the meantime, have a good time and make sure you enjoy some of that good wine."

"We will. Thanks again. You ever find out who your benefactor was—who sent over that case of port?"

"Yeah, I found out."

"Anyone you know?'"

"Nah, just a casual acquaintance."

"Well, thank him or her for me too whenever you see them next. Hey, I meant to tell you—I got a new job."

"A new job? You never had an old one, what doin?"

"The old trust fund's been wearing rather thin lately, so I went out and applied for reviewing gig with the Pali *Times*. The pay isnt all that great but it should cover the rent here if I dont get carried away and spend it all up taking Karen out."

"What you gon be reviewin?"

"O, you know, movies, plays, concerts, things like that. I'll be up in the city a lot and maybe she can go along with me to cover some of them."

"I gotta meet this Karen. She done really got up next to you it seem like to me. You still keepin up with your readin and studyin?"

"All the time."

"Then more power to you. I'm fixin to do a little branchin out myself."

"In what area?"

"It's gon surprise you, Professor. I'm not talkin till it come to pass but you gon hear bout it, I guarantee you that."

He back up to the door, open it, and tell me, "I'll be watching and listening. Well . . . good night . . . I'd better be going."

"Yeah, get your old happy butt on outta here. I'm mad at you anyhow."

"Mad?" he say, lookin panicked and shocked. "Mad about what?"

"Here you is got yourself some fine young thing and the best I can do is fall out cross the bed and try to get some sleep."

"O I see," he say, grinnin again, "youre just putting me on, arent you?"

Hard to say myself whether I was or wasnt, so I just let him think what he wanna think and wave him out the room real playful-like. "Listen, you take it easy now. I dont want you comin back here too excessively charged up, you hear?"

I listen to the news over KCBS until it start repeatin and I cant stand it no more. Some dude come on talkin bout this wonder drug that practically cure cancer, only you gotta go down to Mexico to get it because the doctors up here done got a law against it. That make me think about Squirrel and I'd done told myself I wasnt gon do that that night.

By that time, I'm just about finished workin the Sunday crossword puzzle. I usually get em pretty much finished by Wednesday or Thursday, Friday at the latest. It's a letter I been puttin off writin my sister Gladys in Pittsburgh for the longest. I get out my writin tablet, address the envelope and put a stamp on it. Now all I gotta do is write the damn thing. I hold my ballpoint over the page and go to clickin the little stop-go thingamajig with my thumb. Bout as far as I can get is the date, *Dear Sis,* and *I am finally doing okay and hope you are the same.*

When I catch myself noddin off, I inch the dial over past KRZY and land on this station that's got some kinda story goin on. Talk about bein a fan of somethin, I use to be crazy bout them radio dramas. They always made more sense to me than the jive they be flashin over TV mosta the time. I pour me a taste of port—the usual, I still aint drunk none of Marguerite's gift wine yet—and settle back to do a little listenin.

It's a woman cryin and a man tryna soothe her down in a soft voice, only he slurrin his words kinda. *"I'm sorry, Annabelle, I really am, I . . . I dont know why I keep letting myself get in this condition."* After he get thru sayin that, she quit cryin and go, *"Well, I'll tell you why if you really want to know! This is why, this stuff, and I hate it, you hear? I despise it!"* Then she let out a coupla shrieks and I can hear em tusslin and bumpin up into things and after reckly this bottle go crash and the man—you can tell he hot—he say, *"Now look what youve done. I hope youre pleased with yourself, you . . . you—"* The organ music come up real loud and drown em both out. When it ease down, this smooth-voice announcer come on and say, *"From that night on, George Wilson began to fall down in the world. Annabelle took the children and moved west to be near her mother. Two weeks later he lost his job with Mutual General and rented a room in a shabby, rundown hotel in the heart of the city's skid row. And yet, even then, even with poverty and humiliation star-*

ing him in the face, he continued to drink himself into a stupor, night after night, day after day. We'll return to our story and its miraculous conclusion directly following this message from the World Christian Mission."

I gulped another swallow of Eyetalian Swiss anyway and switched to that Albuquerque station you can only pull in loud and clear when it's late at night that dont play nothin but classical.

Sometime what you need to cool your head out so you can think over things is a little Beethoven or Mozart. It's like a mild soporific.

I was worried bout them KRZY commercials comin up.

20

Ed Jason say, "OK, Sitting Pretty, Ive given you just about all the advice I can and now I really do have to get back across town for a meeting with a sponsor. Just relax, be yourself, dont let the cameras or microphones make you nervous. Passionate Patricia will be right there in front of you holding up the cue cards. The messages are simple and easy to remember. Colin Crews, as you can see by now, is a good man—even-tempered, low-keyed and awfully under-standing. Follow his directions and you cant possibly go wrong. How do you feel?"

"Pretty good actually."

"That's the spirit." Then he wink at me and add, "Watch out for that Patricia. She does have a way of being distracting thru no fault of her own, hunh? Good luck, fella."

We shake hands and he cut out. Mr. Crews, a big tan man with recedin light brown hair and a beard, come over with Patricia and ask me if I want any more coffee or a sammich or anything.

"Nope, I'm ready to roll em!"

Patricia reach up and go to straightenin my shirt collar and brushin the wrinkles outta my coat. She a little bitty thing the color of caramel with ink-black hair done up in big ringlets that be fallin all down her neck, and, unless I'm crazy, she smell just like orange extract. I read in some magazine a while back here where women can use vanilla and lemon flavors and all such as that insteada commercial perfumes to make em smell appealin. Whatever she was doin, she was shonuff appealin to *me*. Somehow it wasnt the same as Wanda munchin on that Life Saver. This woman, like we use to say, was built little and low but you talk about fully packed! She got one of them steatopygic derrières on her that come from straight outta southern Africa, the Hottentots. Willie G. call em them spook shotgun butts but I seen em on white people too. Fact, old-time white ladies use to get all hitched up in bustles and things expressly for the purpose of achievin that effect. Patricia she just squeeze herself into a pantsuit and get everybody to pantin.

"Ready?" she say.

"Ready," I tell em both, weakenin a little round the knees.

The scene is Union Square. I'm settin up there on a bench, dozin with my transistor radio mashed to one ear and it's people all around and in backa me doin they little daily thing.

Mr. Crews hold up five then four then three fingers and so on to Patricia and then she point at me to start. Cameras click on and it's a microphone suspended by what they call a boom up over my head.

I know I'm on. I make out like I'm dozin for a coupla beats, as they call em, and then I raise my head up, stretch and yawn and say, "Hi, my name is Sitting Pretty. I always wake up to KRZY Radio. It's got that community sound that cant be found anywhere else on the AM dial. For people on the fly, it's KRZY." Then I stand up with my radio still pressed to my ear and stroll off, you know, like, into the sunset. Some corny continuity if you ask me but, like Ed Jason say, you cant never underestimate the intelligence of the American public. Colin Crews and them probly ran every bit of that rap thru a computer before decidin it was just what they wanted.

The cameras click off and Crews rush over and grab my hand. "Perfect," he say. "That was simply perfect. We wont even have to do a second take. Youre a natural. O I'm so pleased!"

"Dan did a few cutaways," Patricia say, "just in case."

"Good, good," Crews say. "I wish everybody was as easy to work with as you, Sitting Pretty."

The following mornin, Saturday when I didnt have to be worried bout bein on the job with Sam and Wanda later on, we shot two more—one with me steppin inside a phone booth and dialin KRZY. Naturally, the thing is I got my trusty radio with me as usual and I'm callin to tell em what a winner of a radio station they got. It taken us a lot longer to shoot this one than it did the Union Square spot, mainly on accounta all these little kids that kept crowdin around tryna get in the act. We shot it in the Fillmore, I guess because old C.C. got it in his mind to get over to the black audience, the potential ethnic community market as he call it. Well, they sure got a whole lotta colored faces into that promo. He and Patricia ended up passin out one-dollar bills left and right to keep some of the brothers and sisters from clutterin up the set and ruinin everything.

"Yall gon play this flick over television?" one particularly obstreperous teenager come askin Crews just when we bout to do a take.

"That's correct," Patricia answer, runnin interference.

"I wasnt talkin to you, sister," the little dude say. "I was askin this white man that's actin like he in charge."

"I am in charge here," Crews say. "What can I do for you?"

"Yall comin down here in the community, exploitin us to make this picture and we wanna know what's in it for us?"

Crews say, "If you dont mind, sir, I beg to differ with you. Far from exploiting the community, it's our intention to rectify a number of inaccurate and distorted images which have previously been projected by media regarding the community. I should think you would welcome our presence."

"You aint answered my question, faggot. I wanna know what's in it for us."

"You mean what's in it for *you*, dont you?" Crews tell him, noddin at Patricia.

She walk over and hand the joker a five-dollar bill. That's all it took. He break out into a big chesscat grin, rub his

125

chin, cram the money in his pocket and turn to a coupla his buddies and shout, "See, what I tell you? You gotta assert yourself and confront these honkies and bullshit toms. We cant just hang back when our rights is bein violated and have them run all over us."

Kid couldna been more'n thirteen. I couldnt imagine what rights of his was bein violated, but I did catch myself thinkin: *Well, more power to you, son, for loudtalkin the man outta five U.S. dollars!* At the same time I'm wonderin whether white folks that be in commercials have to go thru the same kindsa headaches.

The sky cloudin up and it look like it might rain, so we pack up and rush over to do the final commercial which take place down by the ocean on the beach where Playland use to be before it shut down. I still miss all them rides and amusement machines.

I'm perched up on topa one of them giant rocks with waves washin in and out and breakin all around me. My only lines go somethin like this: "As you can see, I'm Sitting Pretty. Just like KRZY Radio, I'm on the scene wherever it's happenin. Set your dial to KRZY and youll be sittin pretty too."

For some reason, I keep blowin the lines and we have to do retakes. It probly had somethin to do with us being set up in almost the exact spot where me and Squirrel drove to that same stormy mornin I asked her to marry me. Taken five tries to get it just right. Rain started to come down the minute we finished.

"That's it!" Crews holler. "We finally did it. Let's wrap it up!"

I was so glad I didnt know what to do.

"Youve been wonderful," Patricia say, rushin up to lay one of them big juicy showbiz slobs and hugs on me. "We've had more difficulty with some of the other people. I'm very proud of you."

"Your appreciation is much appreciated," I tell her, tryna make her little jive caress hold out for as long as I can.

"Good going," C.C. tell me. "Ed Jason's to be commended for helping us select such outstanding talent. Your cooperation's been remarkable, it really has. It's been a pleasure working with you. I'll bet youre pretty tired by now."

126

"My pleasure, my pleasure," I manage to tell him. "I enjoyed every single minute of it."

"Over the next few weeks we'll be busy editing all the promos we've shot," he say. "I'll have Patricia get in touch should we need you to come in for any additional dubbing or retakes. Personally, I think your portion of footage will be easy to work with. We do have your Social Security number, dont we?"

"I already gave it to one of the secretaries at the station."

"Good, good. We'll be getting a check to you shortly."

Funny what money will do to you. Now, workin for Sam, I'm damn lucky if I can pull down five hundred a month take-home, whereas on this gig I'm spose to be makin two grand for a coupla days' work and already I'm tired of it and flat-out happy it's over and done with. Am I crazy or somethin? I mean, janitorin you can work off all your heavy frustrations thru pure physical energy while you be cleanin up a place and puttin it in shape. With actin, you never really sure how things workin out. You up under all this pressure and supervision, plus it's all these other people standin round whose livelihood depend directly on how well you doin your thing. Damn! You better be good or *else!*

When C.C. and them invited me to join them later on for a drink at some little bar near the station to relax, I declined as politely as I could.

The kinda drinkin I needed to be doin behind all that fidgetin and performin wasnt anything I wanted to get into in the company of people I didnt really know yet.

Didnt nobody in the crew seem to mind much my turnin down the invitation. Not even Patricia and ooooo, lemme tell you, that hurt.

21

"Excuse me," Willie G. say as he stroll away from me up to this expensive-lookin freckleface girl with long reddish hair, "but didnt I see you in here last week standin in fronta this very Matisse?"

"You very well might have," the young woman tell him. "I'm an old fan of his work from way back."

"Now, it cant be from that far back because Ive got a few years on you and you cant possibly be older than nineteen or twenty."

The girl push back some hair from outta her eyes and shift the raincoat she carryin to the other arm. "I'm twenty-three," she say, blushin a little. "Are you a Matisse lover too?"

I liked to fell out laughin.

Here Willie G. is all got up in his little sweetwater security-guard suit, navy blue, no jacket, just a badge, got a gun on his hip and this official cap like the kind I use to have when I was drivin a bus, only it actually do his head a grand justice. He never went in for gettin a afro or anything like that, so when you see his dome you lookin at the original knucklehead. You lookin dead at the Negro's *true* head. Them natchals and afros saved a whole lotta dudes from embarrassment and harassment. Willie's cap the only thing between him and indecent exposure.

128

Anyway, the scene is I'm slouched on a bench up in the San Francisco Museum of Art over in the Civic Center where Willie workin now. I had the KRZY people drop me off here on the way to they studios downtown. It's fifteen minutes to closin time but I just couldnt resist checkin him out on his job.

Willie G. slick. He answer Miss Red's question just loud enough for me to overhear him say, "Am I a Matisse lover? Baby, you lookin at one of the most devoted of the devotees. Shoooot, I been diggin on Henri and Pablo and Juan Grease, Kandinsky, Brock and Salvador Dally and them ever since art turned modern. Want me to name some more?"

The girl laugh and I can tell right off he gettin over to her in that good old off-the-wall manner. This where the joker's pure slickness come in. He continue his rap but proceed to nudge her on cross to the other side of this wing marked "Permanent Acquisitions" solely for the purpose of preventin me from listenin in on the resta they conversation.

I act like I'm not innerested anyway but Willie G. must know me well enough by now to realize I dont let nothin get past me. Quite naturally, I'mo be layin for him.

The older you get the less you excited by the promise of excitement. That might be a fact but it's hard to say for sure. The only person I can really speak for is me. Back when I was in my prime, whatever that's spose to be—teens, twenties, thirties—I'd go steppin out nights with that wild, private, wired-up feelin that some type of thrill was waitin for me just around the corner. All it had to be was night and all I had to do was get out there in it.

Lotsa times somethin different or excitin actually would happen, but mosta the time it didnt. The whole idea was to go on nursin that feelin, ridin it on out till the last hold card was played or the last drink was drunk or the last woman was flirted with in some bar or else you picked each other up and went someplace where the mystery could work itself out. All it take is a little bit of daylight oozin thru the shades and lightin up the sheets.

Even old Humphrey Bogart—accordin to this book on him I picked up used for fifteen cent—said he liked goin round

129

with the feelin that anything could happen at any minute. That's pretty close to that secret surge nighttime use to bring out in me.

It quit bein like that ages ago, for me anyhow, for a man that's done spent too much of his life bumblin around in a rage. And even when I say somethin like that, I still cant help wonderin if I'm tellin the truth. I mean, for the longest time I wasnt really in that much of a rage.

I was mad all right, I was angry, I was always lookin to get even with people for all the nasty little numbers they done on me—evil numbers, insults, lowdown tricks, all of em pulled in the spirit of malice aforethought. When I reflect back on all the dookey that's been put in the game—includin family bullshit and World War Two—I start gettin mad all over again. Here I am livin like some kinda nut or recluse or somethin just so I can be at peace with the world when maybe what I shoulda done a long time ago was to pick up a pistol and blast me a few Americans. Aw, I dont wanna kill nobody or anything like that, just shoot em in the arm or the leg some to show em how I feel and teach em a lesson.

Squirrel and Francesca Corradini, they special. I can see now where they musta kinda loved me at one time or nother in that sweet, aggravatin way people have of showin love. That go for Cornelia and Aristotle too. But the resta these clowns, I dont know. I'm still at my age tryna sort my experiences out so I can figger out who is who and just what the hell is what.

Like, who is Willie G. really and what in the world are we doin settin up here in JoJo's Let's Get It On Club over by Fillmore and Haight?

"How you ever find out about this joint, Willie?"

"Easy, I met the owner herself at the museum one afternoon. We got to talkin art, you know, and she told me she painted a little herself and laid her card on me. That JoJo, I'm tellin you, is a mess. She one of them downhome sisters from the old school but *smaaarrrt!* This place use to be called Slim's and wasnt nothin happenin but a buncha old heads from the neighborhood hunched around slurpin up juice and wearin out the television. Now that she done got hold of it, it's startin to liven up. Sundays she got jam sessions and a talent show. JoJo tryna attract the younger set. Tuesdays is poetry night."

"Poetry?"

"That's right. The kids come in and get up on the platform there and read stuff they wrote. Most of em is a drag but it's a few can kinda halfway get down with it. It's a joker come in here every week call hisself O. O. Gabugah, wear a leopardskin dashiki and one of them little African caps and got a silver crescent pinned in one ear. Sit, the brother is outta sight and I mean that in the real sense of like you be runnin a race with somebody, startin out side by side, and the next thing you know you look over and the dude done *gone!* As far up the trail as you can see aint nothin but footprints and dust. He outta sight!"

"O. O. Gabugah, hmmmm. Now, that's a pretty peculiar name."

"He blow some peculiar poetry too. Even inspired *me* to start dashin off a few lines. This security-guard-museum gig the best thing ever happened to me. I'm over there round culture and cultured people, my head's openin up and my hands stay clean. Now, that's where you wanna be comin from."

"Where you learn all that jive you was layin on that redheaded gal about paintin and stuff you was tryin your best to keep me from listenin in on?"

Willie laugh as he guzzle down the lasta his second double bourbon and 7UP. "That wasnt no jive I was runnin to that broad, Sit." He say this with a straight face. "I really have got off into that shit. I study them paintins they got up round there and I even picked up a coupla books on great art masterpieces. It's gettin to be one of them subjects I can come in early on and stay way late."

"Yeah, OK, but how come you had to screen me outta the conversation? I never pulled nothin like that on you. If anything, you usually be raisin your voice a few decibels when we out together in a public situation. Like, I dont hear you tryna keep too quiet right now. What was that action back there all about?"

131

"You wanna know what it's about, just wait till we leave here and get over to North Beach."

"North Beach? Sound like you got some kinda schedule lined up."

"Nope, aint no schedule. I just would like to see you loosen up a taste. We both stay down there at that Blue Jay Hotel and, to tell it like it is, I think we both could do with a little freshenin up. I'm even thinkin bout movin up here where all the action's at."

"You call this action—settin around drinkin, listenin to a lotta loud jukebox music with people crammed in all on topa one nother, breathin all this noxious air?"

"What kinda air?"

"Noxious."

"I'mo have to start writin down some of these words you use, Sit. Is that anything like *ob*noxious?"

Willie look dead at me and break into a grin after he say that. I know when somebody signifyin and I can take a hint. I lean back in my seat and take a look around. It's a few white faces sprinkled in among the darker ones. Somebody musta punched up on the jukebox every record Al Green and Marvin Gaye ever put out because that's all we been hearin from the minute we set foot inside. JoJo's Let's Get It On Club aint too much bigger'n, say, if you was to combine five or six of our Blue Jay rooms, but between the bar that run down long one side, the midget stage, the jukebox, the teeny area where folks that feel like it can get up and dance—between all that plus the artwork on the walls, it's not a bad little place if you in the mood for that kinda thing.

"Come on, man," Willie say, "smile a little bit. You mean to tell me you on the verge of bein some type of television star, them people done paid you all that easy bread and you still got to go round makin out like you just lost your last friend? Have another drink. I'm payin. Hey, JoJo!"

He wave at this tall darkskin woman in a African-lookin gown and gold headdress. She settin at the bar kinda checkin things out but smile real friendly when Willie shout her name. In no time she at the table askin, "William, my dear, what can I do for you? And *who*, may I ask, is—" She trail off just like that, step back and grab her own head with both hands. She lookin at me so hard I can even feel her eyes runnin up and down my body. "Who's your friend with the irresistible face? O Ive just got to paint him, Ive just *got* to! Drinks are on me. What is your name? Just promise that youll sit for me."

Willie go to snigglin and coughin smoke, then he get hisself together and calmly say, "Ahhh, JoJo, you somethin else, you know that? As usual you hit the nail on the head. JoJo McBee, I want you to meet . . . Aw, what can I say? . . . The man's name, believe it or not, *is* Sitting Pretty. Betcha anything you wasnt ready for that."

"In this place," she say, smilin and shakin her turbaned head, "I stay ready for anything. What's your pleasure and mind if I join you?"

Talk about a scary night that didnt wanna end, this was one that took the cake and all the icin with it!

We no sooner get thru guzzlin up JoJo's on-the-house drinks—with me promisin her I'd get in touch about posin for a paintin—than Willie G. jeck me up out my seat and rush the both of us thru Saturday night traffic over to noisy North Beach. By now we half drunk and we know it.

Aint no place to park except in one of them skinny little Chinatown alleys illegally. I warn him bout that shit—which I found out the hard way—but he tell me I'm bein too jiggedy and let's just do it and forget it. I'm countin on if push come to shove I can always make that last Greyhound run outta Seventh Street and Market on down the Peninsula even if it do take forever gettin there. I just *know* I'mo slip clean free of this mess before one o'clock in the mornin.

We wobble thru the crowds and past all the tit-and-ass joints got these obstreperous dudes in front tryna hook you inside by rappin at you all loud. "Show's goin on right now, folks! Got a new act tonight—Miz Goldilocks Head, dye-rect from Australia, dye-rect from Down Under, goes *all* the way down and comes up shakin! Catch the whole show for the price of a drink! Seatin right now! C'mon in, gents, and have a look around, whaddaya say?"

Willie G. say, "Hmmmph, Sit, dont know bout you but I kinda would like to stare at some of that Aussie pussy myself."

I just reach out and push him and say, "Aw, man, keep movin. Aint nothin you gon see you aint already seen enough of."

"I dont never get tireda lookin at *that!*"

We finally get to Vesuvio's where it's a sign in the window read: BOOTHS FOR PSYCHIATRISTS. This a place I aint been in since Kennedy was President but the atmosphere pretty much the same as it was then, even down to some of the people I use to see in there back when me and Black Buddha was doin our maintenance thing on the Beach and makin it. People still lollygaggin around, talkin that talk and drinkin them drinks while KJAZ play on the P.A. system and the after-the-rain breeze blow in from off the street every time somebody walk in or get up and walk back out. Anyway, it's still Saturday night and, everything considered, the atmosphere at Vesuvio's is cheerful, neutral you might say.

It's one particular chair in there that face the bar, one of them basketlike seats, wicker they call em, only the back is wide and curved like a shell and fan out over your head when you settin in it. I use to call it the throne. Well, we come in lookin for someplace to plop down and there Miss Red is, the museum gal, laid back like some queen in that very spot. She splittin a pitcher of beer with a brownskin chick kinda favor Diahann Carroll if you dont look too close.

"What the hell's all this," I ask Willie G. as we head toward they table, "some kinda double date you cooked up?"

"Be cool," he groan way under his breath. "Just relax, OK? You can cut out whenever you feel like it."

I didnt feel like leavin yet and I didnt feel like foolin with no women younger'n my daughter either. Be bad enough if I was sober but what was I spose to say to em with my head already messed up?

Miss Red, I have to admit, is lookin awfully good. Her freckles dont show as much in the toned-down light or else she done worked a little powder room magic on em. Anyway, I like the fact that both the girls relaxed and kinda dressed up. You get tired, or at least I do, of dealin with kids dont know how to make theyself presentable. I mean to say this youth kick that everybody been on done got to the place where it's way outta hand. A kid is a kid and a grown person is somethin else. Gimme somebody you can get down with and relate to in that happy-go-lucky quintessential way without havin to stop and examine the whole universe or the way the world work every time you wanna make some simple-minded point. The Professor, as much as I go for him personally, is bad about gettin on my nerves like that. Does man exist or doesnt he? Well damn, hell yeah, man exist all right and that's the biggest problem we up against!

Quiet as it's kept, when it come to women I like them well-seasoned types that's been thru it all, all bent outta shape and you can tell they just holdin on. If so ever the word *love* come tumblin off they tongue, I know it's got more'n a coupla decades fulla meanin behind it. Even if they never mention the word, the wallop they pack just by still bein innerested in bein in the world is pretty much enough to innerest me. Marguerite, Squirrel, dont care who you name, every woman got somethin every man need to experience and reflect upon.

"Hey, it's good to see you," Miss Red say, all bright-eyed. "We didnt know if you would remember or not. In fact, youre a little early. Adele here was betting me you'd be arriving on C.P. time."

Adele, the colored chick, who I can tell just by lookin at take a pretty cautious view of everything, she scoot her chair up close to the table and scrutinize me and Willie G. with the grandest of cool.

"Hello," she say when we bein introduced, "I'm very pleased to meet you both. Sandy's been telling me about you, Willie G."

"Yall good friends, hunh?" he say, wavin for the waitress at the bar in her micro-miniskirt.

"We're roommates," Sandy say, Miss Red up till now, "and Adele's quite involved with the art world too. She's a print-maker and writes a little poetry on the side."

"Well, how do you do," Willie G. say just as the chunky

135

little waitress arrive in time for him to order another pitcher and a coupla glasses. "I write a little myself and I'm crazy bout art. My man Sitting Pretty here is in the arts as well. This dude, you wont believe it, can act his posterior off. He just got thru doin a series of TV commercials that it wouldnt surprise me if they turned the whole industry around."

"O yeah?" say Sandy and Adele simultaneously as they let down they defenses and focus all they attention on me.

"Well, facta business," I say, "it really isnt any big thing. I just struck lucky, that's all."

"Let's hear about it," Adele say, beamin. "I once was thinking about breaking into television myself. Is it fun?"

Right up over the bar on the wall they were runnin old-time 1910-style picture-postcard slides of nekkid women which is one of the little side attractions they been featurin in there for as far back as I can remember. Quaint, I reckon you might call it. Aint nobody payin it no mind but me and mosta my mind is zoomin in and outta the Squirrel problem.

With my attention split every whichway, I get to talkin and the girls start listenin. Willie G. make out like he listenin too but all he really doin is waitin for a pause where he can break in and take things over.

All night now it's a parta my head that's been attemptin to get quiet, aint got nothin to do with drinkin, like it's gettin ready to receive some message somebody tryna send out to me. I figger I better watch it.

After while, all of us get to yakkin and halfway listenin at the same time. Nothin I like better'n a crazy, lowbrow, free-associatin type of conversation where everybody can say anything they feel like sayin, dont care how off-the-wall it is.

Under the table, while Willie G. and Sandy holdin forth on somethin call Abstract Expressionism which sound pretty unreal to me, Adele brush the toe of her boot up against my shoe and then move in with her knee which she brush upside my leg only she dont pull back and we stay like that till I look at her funny and she smile.

22

So after takin our time talkin that talk and puttin a coupla
more pitchers away, we finally wind down a little and head
out for Green Street up the way where Sandy and Adele live.
I mean, both these gals was beer *drinkers,* baby! Set there
battin they eyes at you all sweet and petite, waxin all knowl-
edgeable and sophisticated, but if you aint careful they will
flat out drink your butt clean under the table faster'n you can
say Jack Johnson.

Green Street right off Union, round in there, my goodness! Time keep doin numbers on you and doin em faster
the older you get. Like, I use to drive both the 30 Stockton
and the 41 Union bus on routes that run thru North Beach,
the only parta town where I really felt relaxed even when the
bus was loaded up in the afternoon with fifty thousand
Chinese kids makin it on home from school. The 15 Kearny
line's another one. I use to love workin that run that also
take you thru North Beach which, far's I'm concerned, *is* the
heart of San Francisco—and yall can go tell Tony Bennett
I said so.

I'm feelin pretty mellow on the surface and just groovin
with things by the time we windin up the four flights of stairs
it take to get to they apartment door. It's three flights too

many, you wanna know the truth, but I try to conceal the fact that my breath's runnin short. All my life it look like everybody I go to see for the first time live on the very top floor of some steep apartment buildin aint got no elevator. I cant handle these damn walkups like I use to could. The girls all sprightly and playful, runnin up the steps, skippin two and three at a time. Me, I'm more like back when Aristotle and Cornelia was babies and we'd go up and down stairways in slow motion, one step then the next, countin one-two-three-seven-five as we go.

Willie G. got such long legs and so dead set on *coppin* a little leg, he proceed right up, no pain, no strain, steady rappin trash all the way. "Sandy, you know what? You really do kinda put me in the minda Marcel DuChump a little bit."

"How's that?" she call back, climbin on ahead, leadin the way.

"Aw, you know that masterpiece he knocked out before he got off into layin back playin chess—*Nude Descendin the Stairs?*"

"But, Willie, take note, I'm technically *ascending* this staircase."

"Plus she's fully clothed," Adele say.

"Details, details," Willie tell em. "I'm just talkin bout the general overall effect, you know what I mean, heh heh."

When we do get inside—it's a large comfortable-lookin place—the first thing everybody got on they mind is breakin for the bathroom all at the same time. Everybody got to pee and that certainly include me. Thirty years ago that mighta been humorous but now, as overworked as my poor system is, it's about as funny as a tumor. For all they talk about women's rights, we end up lettin the girls go first. But when it come down to just me and Willie G., I cop out on age and seniority and rush right in on ahead of him.

Goodtimin? Well, I'll tell you. You can talk about it all you want to and maybe I'll even join in with you, but unless you in the right mood, unless you feelin good as the time you tryna have or wanna have it just aint all that much that's gon happen.

Willie G. grab up some old James Brown and Aretha Franklin records from out the collection they got lined up on the floor there in one corner of the livinroom and stack em on the record-player. Then he drag Sandy out to the middle of the floor and start tryna get her to dance.

Now, what he wanna do that for? Next thing I know—while they out there bobbin and bouncin, grindin and groanin, shimmyin and shakin and flailin they arms—here come Adele, look like she bout three-fourths gone, yankin on me to get up out my comfortable seat and boogie a little bit too.

Lemme level with you. Dancin one of them activities I dont engage in much, at least not round here lately. O I use to could shake em down with the best of em but it's somethin you gotta keep up or else you can forget it. I can still jitterbug a taste or do the Hucklebuck. I can even, when I'm pushed, get into a passable version of the Chicken, the Watusi or the Jerk. The one they call the Hitch Hike I never could really get with even tho I did manage to work up halfway decent imitations of the Twist, the Mash Potato, the Hully Gully, the Swim and the Monkey which all came out round the same time, give or take a few years here and there. Matter of fact, when the Monkey come out I was seein this crazy lady name Jessica Watkins, live in Redwood City, and one time we even made a trip out to the San Jose Zoo just to check out the real monkeys and see how they move. Jessica was forty-five but looked around thirty and was the original party goer and giver. We lasted six months. It felt like six years. I done been thru maybe twenty trips like that, some of em fizzlin out in just a few days.

The Slop and the Slide, now, them's my specialties along with the Cha-Cha and the Pachanga which I dont think gon ever come back. I can keep that stuff up all night long. As for the Funky Robot and all that old do-your-own-thing mess the kids be doin on TV, like on "Soul Train," my personal response is you got to be jivin. I mean, that aint dancin, that's group therapy.

In the end the youngsters gon have to find out that, when it come to gettin over and relatin to each other on a one-to-

139

one basis, aint nothin can compare with a good old Fox Trot
—right-wing as that might sound—where you can squeeze
hands, if nothin else, and press up tight against one nother
or sneak a little handfulla back or butt or tit even, whatever,
providin the lights turned down low enough.

So me and Adele—people somethin else with they wants
and needs, aint they?—we out there poppin our fingers and
clownin down right long with Willie G. and Sandy. Them
gals puttin me and him both to shame. Lemme tell you, they
can dance they modern little boodies off! I'm floppin round
there feelin like a wholesale sacka potatoes the Lord done
breathed some life into. I'm sweatin too and Adele she studyin me like I'm some relic of a bygone era she been assigned
to do her term paper on.

The main thing that's on my mind is callin Squirrel and
gettin back to Palo Alto. The last train leave at twelve thirty-
five and it's already pushin eleven, plus I gotta figger on givin
myself a good half hour to get to the SP Depot on the bus.

After fumblin my way thru three dances, I ask Adele can
I use they phone.

"It's out in the kitchen," she say. "Come, I'll show you.
We've got a coupla sixpacks and a gallon of Red Mountain
Burgundy stashed back there too."

She taken me by the same hand I'd been wipin sweat off
my forehead with from jumpin around so much. I wanted to
pull away but she held on and led the way. The squishiness
didnt seem to bother her none.

"Over there," she say, pointin to a bright red wall telephone before goin to the icebox for the beer and wine.

While I'm standin there by the phone gettin my little address book out, I cant help noticin all the stuff they got
tacked to the cork bulletin board right next to it. It's two
things I zero in on right away.

One is a picture of this light-haired broad—a black and
white photograph, a little outta focus—and she workin out
with this athletic-lookin colored dude. I mean, like, they actually in the act of conductin sexual intercourse. Pinned up
next to that is the fronta the Ivory Snow box somebody done
cut out, got the same broad in color snugglin a little baby
and grinnin the way people tend to do in them ads, like I had

140

to do in them KRZY commercials. Underneath the picture
is a little strip, artistically lettered by hand, that say: STILL
99 44/100% PURE.

The other thing is also printed up by hand and all it is is
a sign that go like this:

I KNOW THAT
YOU BELIEVE YOU
UNDERSTAND WHAT
YOU THINK I SAID
BUT
I AM NOT SURE
YOU REALIZE THAT
WHAT YOU HEARD
IS NOT
WHAT I MEANT

I try gettin Squirrel on the phone and was just about to
hang up when a man answer. I thought I had the wrong
number till I realize it's Frazier's voice that's comin at me
kinda deep and sleepy-like.

"She's in the hospital, Sidney." Frazier and me aint never
got past the formal stage with one nother.

"How she doin?"

"Not bad, considering. I was with her this afternoon for
about four hours. She's pretty cheerful but doesnt talk too
much. She's got cancer of the colon *and* the lower intestinal
tract. It's terrible. I havent really slept much in weeks."

"I knew about the lower intestinal track thing but—"

"Well, they found out about the colon just the other day.
I dont know what the hell's the matter with doctors these
days, the goddam American Medical Association. With all
their fancy equipment and training and instruments, they still
cant diagnose cancer from acne unless the patient points it out.
Squirrel had to tell them she'd been having all kinds of
trouble with her bowels, so finally they decide to run a check
on that region too. She's been operated on now and her bowel
area's been sealed off. She has to eliminate everything thru
a tube. Now there's a blockage in one of her entrails. Gas
cant get out and her stomach's been producing this liquid
that can only be drained off by means of tubes protruding

141

from her nose, and there's a machine that regulates the flow. Sidney, I tell you, I never was much of a prayer man but yesterday I got drunk in a bar and beat up another drunken man pretty badly. Half an hour later, if you can believe it, I'm in this Roman Catholic church—and I was raised Baptist—"

"I know, me too."

"—asking God to forgive me and to see after Squirrel. I was trembling, Sidney. Where're you calling from anyway?"

"From right here in San Francisco. I'm visitin some friends. What hospital she in and when can I visit her?"

"She's at Kaiser but the staff there is pretty touchy right now about her having visitors. I suppose they wouldnt mind an old friend like you coming to see her but—"

"Old friend? Frazier, I was *married* to the woman!"

"I know, Sidney, I know—and I didnt mean anything by that. It's just that Squirrel isnt up to seeing anyone for longer than twenty to thirty minutes at a stretch—not even close relations, not even me."

"Well, I think that's enough time for me to get over. I'll go by tomorrow. Maybe I'll see you there."

"Maybe you will. Listen, Sit . . . We should maybe, you know, really sit down and talk with one another one of these days. Go have a drink together or something like that."

"I'm game if you are. Just let me know when."

"We'll work it out. Glad you called."

"Be seein you, Frazier."

I hang up feelin out of it.

For one thing, that's the first time me and Frazier ever even came close to havin anything that halfway resemble a conversation.

For another thing, he called me Sit and he aint never done that in all the ten years Squirrel and him been shacked up together.

It's kinda like the time I was on this 707, jettin back to Pittsburgh to see my sister Gladys. Settin cross the aisle from me is one of them old-time I-aint-gon-never-change shonuff crackers outta Alabama, Indiana, Michigan, California or someplace. I could tell right off he just flat out resented my bein on the same plane with his sorry, prejudiced ass, dont

142

care how much he done laughed at Flip Wilson or Redd Foxx on the tube.

All of a sudden, just outta Denver, the plane go to jeckin and flip-floppin and carryin on. "Make sure your seat belts're fastened," the pilot say. "We're in for a bit of turbulence."

Next thing I know, this very peckerwood got his long red neck—bald head and everything color of a radish—stretched over my way, talkin bout, "Hi, how ya doin there?" He grinnin like a sheep with his dyed-in-the-wool racist self. "This here's enough to make a fella take back up with the Good Book, aint it?"

Frazier, Squirrel, the girls, Willie G., me—it plenty times I just rare back and wonder just where in the world must God be comin from.

I get back to the livinroom and it's smellin like a opium den. Willie G. and Sandy still busy dancin, only by now they doin it real slow and all up against one nother, got they arms round one nother with her head on his shoulder and stuff. As I'm easin on past em, Willie flop his head my way and gimme a big red-eyed, slow-motion wink.

Adele curled up in one corner the couch, puffin on a reefer and drinkin that wine which make me think of Marguerite and wonder what she and Desirée been up to.

"Sit," she say.

"That's my name."

"No, I meant why dont you come and sit down and relax your mind. I'll drive you to the train station. Youve got a few minutes yet to just float. If you miss your train, I'll drive you all the way home to Palo Alto, promise. I'm a good driver and I love to drive at night. I'd like to hear more about how you broke into television."

"Aint too much to tell," I say, settlin down beside her but at the same time makin sure we a respectful distance apart. The younger a woman is the more nervous she make me feel.

"Would you like some of this?" she ask, holdin the reefer up.

"No, thanks, I quit foolin round with that stuff way back in the fifties."

"The fifties? Why? That's when I was born."

143

"That's what I figgered. It just didn't do all that much for me, that's how come. Beside, I dont even smoke cigarettes."

Funny how sometime you can find yourself in the perfect situation for gettin it on but yet and still your mind be off someplace else. In spite of mister johnson's unpredictable stirrins, I really never have been much of a cockhound. Like, while I'm checkin Adele pour me out a generous libation of Red Mountain, my mind is on stuff such as what if she was Cornelia and I was just any old rusty wino she'd done picked up off the street and brung home?

I knock back the burgundy in a coupla quick gulps and ask her, "Adele, is it feasible that I might could spend the night here?"

She dont even give it a second thought. "Why not? I mean, it's cool with me and, unless my judgment's off tonight, I cant see where Sandy'd have any objections. There's a mattress in my workroom at the end of the hall and we've got extra blankets and a pillow. Of course youll just have to put up with all my printmaking equipment and junk but that shouldnt be so bad. Ive slept there myself and found it rather pleasant, a change anyway."

Sandy and Willie G. done disappeared to another parta the flat. Way off in the distance I can make out the sounda they voices and laughter. I figger he done just about Picasso'd him some pussy. Or, to look at it another way, they done jabbered each other into bed—my friend from the wreckin yard and the chock fulla culture museumgoer, hmmph!

"Sure you wouldnt like a hit off this before I put it out?"

Probly on accounta I'm tired as I can be and wanna go to sleep petrified like a zombie so I wont have to even think about nothin or dream about nothin, I give in and smoke up what's left and down a little wine on the side to boot.

I look at Adele and she look at me. She settin there in her long bright gown but I can see the outlines of her big legs and warmlookin, soft, brown body underneath. Mister johnson sayin yeah but I'm sayin unh-hunh, no, it's lines you gotta draw and this here's one of em. Like with a lotta pretty people, it's a good deal of ugliness I can see in her chocolate Anglo features. With ugly people, I can pretty much always read some beauty into how they look.

144

I stand up wonderin what she see when she gaze at me, but all I know for sure is it's a lotta us both hangin out there in the curlicue smoke that's fillin up the room like fog with a smell and driftin on back toward the parta the house where I'mo bed down for the resta the night.

After readin in the *Chronicle* Sportin Green bout all the football and basketball hi-jinks, I click off the light in Adele's studio and pull the sheet and army blankets up over me. It's a drag to have to try and blot out all that groanin and whinin and howlin and whimperin goin on cross the way in Sandy's room but such is the nature of nature in the raw, you know. I start fallin off to sleep with everything on my mind—Squirrel and, for some reason, Miz Duchess, plus the fact that Marcus been workin on some project with Marguerite's old man. Then I focus in on them TV spots, Ed Jason, Colin Crews, Passionate Patricia, and how I coulda done more better if I'da had just a little more time. Then come the best parta dozin off where what's spose to be for-real commence to mergin with feelins and fantasy and then, just as I'm groovin on nuttiness and foolishness, sleep slip up on me sooo sweet I wanna start all over again at the beginnin but *mmmmmm* it's too late, I cant wait, it's too *zzzzzz* . . .

In the middle of what's left of the night—clock time dont mean nothin no more—I wake up and feel somebody slidin in next to me under the covers. Couldnt be nobody *but* Adele. She got a thin nightgown on. My arms wrap round her automatically as she jut her pantied butt back up against my belly and turn her face to mine and whisper, "Dont worry, my friend. Go back to sleep. I just felt kinda lonely listening to all that lovemaking commotion coming thru my bedroom wall. Oooo, you can hold me like this all night if you want. I wont do anything. It just feels so lovely. Besides, I'm in my period."

Bitch, I thought to myself, you must think I'm made outta ice!

I had to struggle to be as matter of fact and avant-garde about it as she was, but right off she get to snoozin and snored somethin awful. Taken me forever to get back to sleep.

WINTER

23

Actually it's spose to be cold and damp and actin like winter, but the rain's done subsided, like the weather people say, and aint no more coastal fog movin inland because overnight the sun's come out, *way* out, so that in the space of a few nervous hours the temperature done shot up from forty to seventy.

Now, that's a number that dont happen too often noplace else. Far's I'm concerned, it's one of them phenomenons that help contribute to the image this country got of being a little, you know, funny. California *is* a country—and it's a south and north to it in case yall misunderstand me—pretty much all unto itself like Texas, Oregon, Washington, or any other funnystyle state that's on its own trip and damn what's goin on in neighborin territory.

For the time bein, everybody and they mama outdoors doin they own version of soakin up the sunshine, hoggin up the heat, crawlin round in cars and steppin out in style.

Any direction you wanna look in it's traffic jams. Down on Fisherman's Wharf, the Ghirardelli Square part, what pass for the tourist section of town—which, strictly speakin, include every incha San Francisco—is where I find myself late that Sunday mornin, down on the sandy pier, this nasty beach really with stone steps leadin down to it, to the broke-up glass and popsicle sticks, beer cans, dangerous poptop metal thatll cut your sand-crossin short right quick you crazy enough to walk out there barefoot. Yet it's plenty little kids out doin just that and lovin every minute of it.

I set on the bottom step and stretch my legs out, lookin at how my poor shoes need shinin as the heels disappear down into the sand which is still pretty wet from the rain.

Adele and Sandy got up and fixed scramble eggs for breakfast with toast, grapefruit juice and coffee. I'm full as a tick and just settin there restin, hopin maybe the walk over from North Beach done helped me work a little of that food down. That cholesterol'll getcha shonuff at my age if you stuff yourself and lay up and dont get no exercise. You talk about Cardiac City!

Beside, I had to get outta that place. Willie G. and Sandy was lookin all wore out and actin like they didnt have too much more to say to one nother or anybody else. Adele still tryna be tight with me in that peculiar way she got. Her remark from last night when she slipped in bed with me still playin on my mind. I mean, it's like that sign they got next to the phone. I know I believe I understood what I think she said but I aint so sure what I heard was what she meant.

Be that as it may, I still enjoyed her bein close to me all night—and I suspect she did too—mostly, I think, because it's times when people—and more especially strangers—need to touch in a way that aint got much to do with gettin in one nother's pants. Sometime all you need is a taste of that easy, simple kinda contact that help you blot out—for a few hours anyway—how painful the stupid world is. It's definitely done helped me keep my act intact.

It's a white boy with a goatee and no shirt on down long the beach to my right, got his saxophone strapped round his neck, a tenor, I think, and he listenin to his transistor radio and blowin his horn off tunes it's playin. He blow awhile and listen awhile and just diggin on hisself and the sun. He aint half bad neither.

Off to the left, in backa me, way up topa the steps at street level, it's a scene goin on remind me of stories my great-grandmama use to tell about *her* daddy who was there in New Orleans back in the days when Congo Square was happenin, when the Negroes would gather together to beat on they drums and do they strange dances and get off into them trances we famous for. This was back before the white folks finally peeped what was goin on, all that voodoo action, and banned both the niggers *and* Congo Square which, accordin to Sadie Jeanine—that was my great-grandmama's name, Big Mama we use to call her—caught fire and burnt down.

Anyway, maybe I exaggerate, but the Negroes up there topa the beach steps, poundin on drums and playin they flutes, *was* causin a whole lotta excitement this mornin. They aint like the other musicians round the area that's got a tin cup or pass the hat for donations. They aint like the concert violin player, or the folksingers with they guitars and harmonicas, the little family bands of three to five pieces, or the slick trumpet player call hisself the Human Jukebox that stand inside this big tall colorful box with a lista all the selections he play tacked to the front. No, these brothers aint playin or performin for nobody but they own self. And, I mean, they *doin* it! Got white folks and every other nationality you wanna name up there crowded round em, movin and shakin and cuttin the fool.

It's even one big afro'd Jewish-lookin gal up there with em, jumpin round in a crow-shayed minidress, wigglin her ass, singin and sippin Coors beer outta all the drummers' cans, carryin on somethin fierce and so downfront with her shit until all I can figger is she tryna be Sheela, Queen of the Jungle, or *somethin* with her handsome, horsey self.

What I dig about em is they interminable spirit and the good feelin they bring out in me. Like, there I am, shot to my toenails, workin up the nerve to go see Squirrel again and at the same time wonderin how long I'mo last janitorin with Sam and Wanda when here I got a coupla grand comin in I hadnt ever counted on and still got my doubts about.

For the hell of it, I tip down to the ocean, take off my shoes and socks, and stand there lettin the cold water wash up over my big rusty feet.

What was the meanin of all this anyway? I was tireda com-

151

mittin experience, as the Professor say, when all that really seemed to matter was makin peace with my own soul and dyin happy.

A little girl come up to me. She look to be around seven and Mexican, you know, a Chicana. She say, "Mister, could you hold my kite up for me while I run down the beach and try to get it off the ground?"

Of course I would. It taken a few tries but we finally do get it to sailin, way up in the air, but nowhere near as high up as all the other fancier-lookin kites that grown folks is standin around flyin all proud. People tickle me with they little hobbies and pastimes and the way they get to ego-trippin over em.

It turn out to be the most constructive project I been involved with since I helped Miz Duchess move outta her room on the third floor of the Blue Jay upstairs to the fourth a coupla weeks before I got to foolin with Marguerite. Made me flash back to my long-gone family-man days when I actually got some sense of accomplishment outta undoin knots in the kids' shoelaces.

24

Who should be settin there in the waitin room but Frazier hisself, got on a light blue seersucker suit with a coffee-color shirt and a white bow tie—the cleanest dude I done seen all day right down to the bottom of his flared britches and bright white shoes.

I have to stand back and look at the nigger before I stroll over and shake his hand.

"You know somethin?" I say. "Frazier, I gotta tell you, you clean on back! I feel like some kinda stevedore or somethin, standin up here in my outdated rags. How come you gotta come showin me up like this?"

Frazier gimme one of his careful smiles and close his *U.S. News & World Report,* motionin for me to take a seat.

"Squirrel will never even notice the difference," he say. "Glad you could make it. What's been happening on the Palo Alto scene?"

"Not all that much. I'm still pullin down a check doin janitor work. Any new developments here since I talked with you last?"

"Not really. They say she's improved. They removed the machine this morning, the one that was set up to suction out her nasal passages. She's lost a lot of weight but the nurse was telling me a few minutes ago when I arrived that she's doing better and appears to be in a pretty good mood."

I'm lookin at him again, at the hair turnin gray that circle his black bald head, at his white mustache and the gold teeth at the backa his wide mouth, the way he comport hisself with confidence and properness like I tried to keep doin for years after I got out the service—shoulders back, head held high.

This human bein trip—or life, as they call it—aint nothin to play with, dont care what anybody tell you. It's been turnin me around ever since the night I tipped past my daddy and mama's bedroom and overheard them arguin bout some children he'd had outta wedlock, way before he'd married my mama. This was forty-six years ago and I still aint got over it.

I aint never got over Frazier neither. I mean, just think about it. Here we both set, two men pretty much the same age and size, side by side, one a successful small businessman, the other'n the biggest failure *out*—and we both waitin to see the same woman we done loved and lived with and slept with.

"Pretty warm day, isnt it?" he say, takin out a coffee-color handkerchief to match his shirt and dabbin at his forehead with it. I know he just doin it to have somethin to do because the whole inside of the hospital is air conditioned.

"Yeah, but it just might snow before the afternoon's over. You never can tell anymore."

"That's right, youre so right."

"Unh-hunh."

"Uhmmm, Aristotle, Cornelia and even Squirrel have been telling me about what a big hit youre making on some radio talk show around town here. I'm sorry to say Ive never gotten a chance to hear you."

"Aw, it's no big thing. You might just say I'm a little compulsive, that's all. I do enjoy gettin my opinion aired, you know. Save me from havin to deal with psychiatrists."

"I understand. I imagine those programs provide an emotional outlet for an awful lot of people who're in the same boat."

I had to lean back and think about that one because I aint

so sure how to take it. What is it he sayin exactly, that I'm some kinda nut—which I know I am—that need some forma transfactual therapy as they done taken to callin it lately? The best thing to do, I decide after lettin a few moments slip by, is to ease in on *his* case and put *his* ass on the spot.

"How's the real estate business these days, Frazier?"

"Pretty rough, pretty challenging. It's a tough line of work to be involved in here of late."

"Is that right? Just the other day I was readin bout where the average American cant even afford to buy a house since the prices on em done shot so sky high. Sound like to me it's a seller's market."

"True," he shoot back, "the outlook for prospective home buyers is grim, to say the least, and I wish it were otherwise, but that isnt my field. We're dealing strictly in commercial properties and rentals."

"You mean, you aint sellin homes?"

"No, never did. We sell and rent mostly to people in the market for office space or storefronts although we do handle a sizable number of apartment rentals as well."

So you probly one of them slumlords, I think to myself, but all I say is, "So you doin all right?"

"I'd say business was fair to middling, considering the state of the economy which, I dont think I have to remind you, is discouragingly chaotic."

The nurse come out and tell us it's OK to go in now. As foolish as I feel about our dumb conversation, it's still the furthest I ever got tryna communicate with Frazier. Then too it really didnt seem to matter as much as what was comin up.

We both get outta our seats to walk in, but Frazier turn to me and say, "Why dont you go first, Sidney? I think it might be easier that way."

He take a hard look at his watch and that's when I definitely understand he tryna tell me somethin.

She done lost so much weight until it's hard for me to even recognize her at first. It's Squirrel all right but it dont look like Squirrel which send me trippin off in all kindsa directions that aint got all that much to do with the fact that facts is facts.

She say, "Is that you, Sidney? Bend down a little closer."

I do like she say and she lay one of them looks on me so tender and innocent, so much the old Squirrel, in fact, I like to broke down and cried. Aint no way in the world to describe a look like that. Bout the closest I can come would be to say it put me in the minda Mama back before the war broke out when somethin round the farm'd be done gone down wrong—a mule say, or a cow done jumped the fence somehow and trampled up her vegetable garden. Everybody'd be all hot and bothered but then Mama'd all of a sudden turn her face my way in the middle of all the fuss and shoot me one of them dont-yall-worry-bout-a-thing kinda glances with so much stored-up secret happiness in backa it until I'd feel like I was lookin dead at the sun shinin down thru the eye of some horrible hurricane.

Them old Squirrel ocean eyes can still do that, eyes that know everything, plus that special smile she can get together whenever she want to. Put em together and you got one unbeatable combination that'd make the president of General Motors turn over his annual take-home salary to the Sickle-Cell Anemia Fund.

"How come you havent been to see me before now?"

"Sweetheart, I just now found out you were in here."

"You coulda called the house at least."

"I did. Frazier answered. He the one filled me in. How you feelin now that the worst is over?"

"Who says the worst is over. I feel fine up here," she say, tappin at her temple where the gray hair turnin nappy from not gettin pressed. "It's my body. That's the hangup. Frankly, I never thought I'd live to experience the day when my health and strength would snap like this, all of a sudden. You know the type of person I am."

"You always did like to get up and do. Even when you were low sick I practically had to beat you down to get you to stay home in bed."

"Well, that's just me. I have to be up and around, seeing after things that have to be done. Now here I am laid up like a vegetable, unable to do for myself, a burden on everybody. I cant take it, Sidney, I really cant take it!"

Her eyes go to fillin up with water again and overflowin all down her face. I set there tryna take it without lookin off but it's hard not to put myself in Squirrel's place. Just the notion of it get me to feelin so awful and depressed and hemmed up, I wanna crawl cross her bed to where the window is and kick out the glass so some fresh air can get in. I'm so choked up by now tho until it's all I can do to get my head and mouth to move much less force the words up past my throat that's tremblin in my belly.

"Listen," I tell her, wishin to God I could believe it myself, "the day gon come when youll be lookin back laughin at all this. I know it's rough but you done overcome and outlived so many catastrophes, baby, that, well, you know, thisll just be one more hurdle you managed to get over."

The minute the words ooze out my mouth I realize how phoney and goofy they sound.

Squirrel just lay there, lookin at me all sad, then she reach over and brush her fingers along the backa my hand, tracin out teeny circles at first and then loopin her fingers with mine and doin that squeeze.

"I'm glad youve still got a little bit of faith," she say. "There're moments when I feel that way too, but then I'll do a turnaround and dont see anything but the dark side."

She pull my arm over closer to her so our hands can rest on her stomach which is covered up with a thin blanket and a sheet. When I start imaginin all the tumors and decay and stuff that's takin place underneath the skin and tissue of that parta her body, my head go to poundin.

"Dont be so nervous, Sidney. I could feel your pulse doubling up just now."

"Aw, dont pay me no mind. I'm just goin thru changes, that's all."

She lift my hand to her lips and commence to kissin on my fingers, knuckle by knuckle.

She say, "Lately Ive been praying a lot. I know you never went in for that sort of thing but, well, I was brought up to believe in God and the older I get the more I find myself moving back in that direction."

"Now, you know I was raised up close to the Baptist

church too and grew up scared to even look a preacher in the eye, much less a picture of Jesus. But I never did want my children to have to grow up totin all them other people's guilt and sins on they shoulders which was how come I told you we oughtta should teach em to do unto others and all like that without necessarily encouragin em to rush out and hook up with anybody's congregation."

"Do you ever pray?"

"Sure," I tell her—and meanin it too—even tho the only time I actually get down on my knees the way you spose to do is when somethin happen that's so awful I get scared I just might not be able to carry on. I done a lotta prayin durin the war and when Papa died and Mama died and back here when I was kinda tryna drink myself to death after me and Squirrel had the partin of ways. Reckon I'm like most people. I pray at the last minute after every other possibility done gone up in smoke.

Squirrel shoot me one of her who-do-you-think-you-jivin? looks and say, "Well, take time out and pray for me. Would you do that, Sidney? Do you promise me youll do that?"

She coulda asked me for anything and I woulda promised it but all she actually requested sound so simple until I'm already rehearsin a few prayers in my head while we settin up there lookin at one nother.

Well, after that it got quiet for a spell and that just wont do when you visitin with sick folks. True, I can only speak for my own self but that silence really gets to me and I feel like I gotta say somethin, anything, just to generate a little bit of exchange.

"You know I'm bout to bust out and make my television debut, dont you?"

"Television debut? How do you mean?"

"Mean it just the way you heard it. I'mo be on TV over Channel Three."

"Channel Three? That's KRZY, isnt it? What in the world're you gonna be doing?"

"Aw, nothin much. Just pluggin the station."

"You getting paid?"

"Yes I am, believe it or not. You remember Ed Jason, that dude with the radio talk show I use to call up all the time?"

"*Use* to? I heard you on there just a few days ago talking about the people on the San Francisco City Council. I even got a little mad about it because there you were bad-mouthing our representatives and you dont even live here. In fact, Jason even got a little hot about it himself and informed you that he had another call on the San Francisco line."

"Yes, that's right, you still got a good memory all right. I was just tryna get my two cent in on the subject of politicians in general. You know me, Squirrel, I aint really liked none of em since Roosevelt passed on. For a while back there I thought Jack Kennedy was gon straighten things out but then after he went and got us in that Cuban Missile Crisis and that Vietnam mess, I kinda had to back off from him too."

"Listen," she say, settin up a little, "JFK was only doing what he had to do. I loved that man. I did a little research on Vietnam myself, you know. Come to find out these people were already plotting the Korean War and this Southeast Asia stuff way back around the time you got discharged from World War Two."

"Humph! That's what this boy call hisself the Professor that stay down to my hotel was tellin me. They dont waste no time, do they?"

"You better believe they dont. You know how a lotta the groundwork for the atom bomb was worked out by all them egghead professors and experts in the hills up behind the university where you live? Well, a lotta the Vietnam strategy was worked out by those very people years before it got into the media, the same way the government gave the contract to the polly sigh specialists out there in Ann Arbor, Michigan, to do research on how to track down that joker Ché Guevara who, as you know, got shot up and silenced like both the Kennedy boys, Malcolm X and Dr. King."

Squirrel gettin a little excited and worked up and I'm glad to see it happenin since it taken both our minds off the heavy business at hand which, to tell the nekkid truth, aint nothin but blues. What make it all go down so bitter is it's a situation I cant do much about. The woman's in pain! I can tell just by lookin at her she aint got no business havin a lotta company or talkin too much in her condition.

She thin, she wore out, she done been operated on and

tested on and still aint got no guarantee all this modern medicine gon do her any good. I hate doctors almost as much as I do politicians.

Aint too much else to talk about after that except little things—the weather, Frazier, things we'd do different if we had em to do all over again, my little upcomin TV spots as they call em, her plans for the future, the kids again.

"Something tells me," Squirrel up and say outta nowhere, "that Cornelia and Marcus've been having a few problems here lately."

"What make you say that?"

"Unnngh," she groan, clutchin her side all of a sudden and screwin up her bony, pretty face like she feel some kinda spasm comin on. "Please excuse me, Sidney. Would you mind pressing that button by the table there for me?"

"This one?"

"Yes, thank you."

A voice come outta the little intercom and ask what she want.

"Request for pain medication," Squirrel say, "in room two-thirteen please."

"Thank you," the intercom say. "The nurse will be with you in a moment."

I figger it's time for me to be cuttin out, so I lean over and give her a peck on the jaw.

"I know I'm gonna conquer this thing, Sidney," she half-whisper, squeezin on my wrist. "I just *know* I am. The Lord is with me. I can feel Him or Her or whatever that power is—you know you have to be kinda careful about sexism nowadays and I'm trying my best to break some old habits—I can feel it inside me, stirring around." She manage to work up a little smile to go with her frown.

"Makes me feel good to hear you talk like that, honey. I'mo be pullin for you too. You can count on it."

"Just say a prayer."

"I'mo do that, Squirrel, I'mo definitely do that. By the way, you think I oughtta give Cornelia and them a call? You mentioned they wasnt doin so hot."

"Well, I dont know. That's just my intuition, that's all. I

160

mean, I think I know my daughter pretty well by now. I dont think Marcus has been giving her much attention lately. He's all wrapped up in this urban systems project with that specialist on the Peninsula."

Specialist on the Peninsula? Hmmm. The big dinner up at Cornelia and Marcus' flash past the backa my mind and make my stomach tighten up a little the way thoughts'll do you sometime for no discernible reason. It's like this loneliness flash I been gettin a lot of lately where it feel like your whole past is chasin after you and crumblin to dust at the same time. You reach out to touch what you see, to give it a hug or to knock it back away from you only—only it aint nothin there. It's done pretty much gone up in thin air and smoke.

Here Squirrel is the one sick yet and still I'm driftin off into one of them dont nobody love me moods make you wanna just tiptoe unnoticed outta everybody's life you ever knew. It's a monster emotion and I feel guilty bout havin it come over me right in fronta Squirrel.

"Well, here's the nurse with your medication. I'll check back with you again soon, hear?"

"It's always good to see and hear from you, Sidney. You have been in my prayers for some time now, you know."

That cause me to do a complete turnaround. "No, I didnt know."

"Well, now you do."

25

"Youve been looking awfully solemn here lately," Sam tell me one night while we takin a break. "Is there anything the matter?"

I put my can of 7UP down and look across the aisle where he havin his coffee. Sam love that coffee. Aint nothin he like better'n hunchin over a table or desk with his porkpie hat pushed back on his head, sippin on coffee, smokin his pipe and rubbin on his jaw with his eyes half-shut like he fixin to doze off. He be wide awake dont care how sleepy he look. Taken me a long time to piece that fact together.

We just got the contract to clean up this real estate office, Ripley and Steele, on University Avenue. It's a big job which mean it's bringin in Sam a lotta new revenue. He worked em in without droppin any of our other clients, so we been workin our tails off goin on a coupla weeks and everybody beginnin to feel the strain, him and Wanda in particular since they on full-time and I'm still holdin down that Monday-Wednesday-Friday slot.

"Aw," I say, "to tell you the truth, Sam, I'm still up against a lotta the same old pressures—what I'mo do with my life, how long can I keep on like I'm doin now."

Wanda out grabbin herself a snack at the pizza joint up the street, so it's just the two of us for now.

Sam say, "Well, all I can say to that, Sit, is if you want to change things in your life youre gonna have to put forth a little effort."

"Now, Sam, you not gon lay one of your Sunday mornin deacon specials on me, are you?"

Sam aint one to do much smilin but his lips do kinda curl upward some when I tell him that.

"No, no, never. I havent preached to you yet, have I? I dont believe in getting mixed up in other people's problems and I dont go around handing out advice unless it's asked of me. All the same I have been impressed with the way youve been trying to keep on the right track lately, here on the job anyway, and I hate to see you looking so down. I know about your ex-wife and all—Wanda's told me—and I'm sorry. I lost a brother a year ago and I can sympathize with what youre going thru if that's any consolation."

"Cancer?"

"Yeah, the Big C, as John Wayne called it. I still havent gotten over it. We were pretty close. But the reason I brought up that business about making an effort to help yourself comes right outta my own experience." Sam take his hand away from his jaw and turn his cheek to me, pointin at the long scar. "You see that? You know how I got it?"

I hate it when somebody be askin me a question they know I dont know the answer to, so I just look at him and shake my head.

"Well, I'll tell you how I got it. There was a time when I hung out, gambled and drank heavy, had a woman on each arm and would still be trying to get next to another one. I carried on that way for years, getting into fights, wouldnt have a dime in my pocket one day and next day I'm carrying enough to pay cash for a brand-new Lincoln. Then one day a little business I'd put a good deal of money into, a chili parlor up there in East Oakland, burnt up—I mean, burnt to the ground!—and me and my partner hadnt taken out a drop of insurance. You know what I did? I sat down the next morning and started drinking. Before the afternoon was over, come to look up and see I'd polished off a fifth of Seagram's Seven Crown. Well, that got to me, it scared me really. Then I went and got into an altercation with one of the women I

163

was fooling with and, by her being the jealous type who didnt like the fact that I was something of a rounder from in front, she was out to hurt me. I mean, *physically* hurt me. She came at me with a butcher knife. I was too drunk and wasted to fend her off. She laid my cheek wide open with that blade. Pretty little thing too and real quiet-like. Those're the ones youve got to watch out for. It took seventeen stitches over at Highland Hospital Emergency to close the wound. They released me and I broke off with her and all my old so-called friends, but I went on drinking until one night, high as a kite, I'm weaving along on the Nimitz Freeway, on my way back to Oakland from a poker game in San Jose, and scraped up against the road divider at seventy-five miles an hour. Even tho I'd tore up the left side of my car, I was still able to somehow get back on the road. I pulled up along the side of the freeway, cut the engine, laid back and went to sleep. When the highway patrol woke me up and asked what the matter was, I just leveled with the man, told him I got a problem, a very serious problem."

Sam stop talkin while we both look up at Wanda comin thru the doorway with what's left of her snack wrapped up in aluminum foil and some coffee in a plastic cup.

"I quit drinking after that, just quit it cold. Decided I was still a young man. I was thirty-four then. I'm pushing sixty now, same as you, right? From that day on, Ive been busy making up for lost time and seeking peace of mind. That decision saved my life and Ive never regretted it for one minute."

"That's a heavy story all right, Sam, and I'm happy for you. It's somethin to think about, I can grant you that. I think my problem might be just a little bit different tho."

"What do you think your problem is, if you dont mind my asking?"

Now, if anybody'd asked me that twenty years ago, last month or even yesterday, I probly couldna answered em without stumblin and stutterin and takin all night to do it. Sam put the question to me straight and simple with no monkey business affixed and so, without even givin it a split-second thought, I come right out with what was to me the most satisfactory answer I ever uttered.

164

"Trouble with me," I catch myself sayin while Wanda waddle past us on her way to the back, cool enough not to interrupt our conversation, "is I never truly made up my mind as to what it was I wanted to do with my life."

I hold off a minute, waitin to see how Sam gon take that, halfway expectin him to break out into a sermon for real this time. But he dont. He just smoke on his pipe and nod his head. I reckon he a man of his word and got sense enough to know by now how I cant stand to be proselytized by nobody, dont care if it's the Salvation Army, the Vegetarian Party or the Easter Seal people. Whatsoever it is you hustlin, leave me alone until I get it in my own mind you just mighta stumbled up on somethin I might wanna sample or look into or even get behind.

"Even at my age, Sam, I still think about gettin married again or goin back to school, dramatic jive like that, and you know I'm too old to be entertainin such thoughts."

"Are you?" is all Sam say, standin up with that serious look which I know mean it's bout time to get back to work. "Whatever you decide, I want you to know that, far as I'm concerned, youve proven yourself to me as a good worker. I like you. The full-time slot is yours if you want it. I'll even give you a raise in pay."

"You cant be serious."

"Dead serious. Ive made up my mind to buy another van and build up another crew."

"Well, do tell! Is business really all that good?"

"I'm playing a hunch that itll be getting better in spite of all the talk about the depression coming up. Are you willing to come on full-time?"

"Can I have some time to think about it?"

"Let me know in a month's time."

It's scrubbin and dustin and polishin time again. We get to workin and sweatin so hard until aint nobody got a minute to even joke with one nother which is somethin we usually do a lot of.

"Hey," I tell Wanda later on that night while we finishin cleanin the bank, our last stop, and mellowin down since it's yeahbout goin home time. "That brother of yours is all right, you know?"

165

"You mean you just now done got around to findin that out? He ask you to stay on five days a week yet?"

"He sure did."

"You gon take him up on it?"

"We'll just have to wait and see. Thing I like about Sam is he aint like a lotta these churchgoin folks that's out to save your soul so they can stand on your head and rule you."

"I go to church too," she say, gettin that jolly, mis*chie*vous look while she wringin out a mop, "and I aint like that."

I ease up and squeeze her waist with my arm round it. She poke me away real soft with her elbow. It's done got to be a game we play.

"Could I stop by and visit you sometime if I behave myself?"

Wanda look away from me, tryna act shy, I guess. No, I think *coy* might be a better word.

After she done cleared her throat, she say, "Well, maybe. We'll just have to wait and see. Frankly, I didnt think you was ever gonna ask."

26

It musta been right around the first of the year that things started lookin up for me and at the same time lookin kinda down. Which is pretty much the way it usually work out. You do win a few. I think yall know how the rest of it go.

I got thru the holidays on Portuguese wine and 7UP. Both Cornelia and Aristotle had me up for Christmas dinner. I was cool and didnt eat or imbibe too much at either of they places. I was very proud of myself—a gentleman at least if not exactly perfect.

They released Squirrel from out the hospital, let her go home for the holidays. She was lookin right pitiful to me but seem to be in fair to middlin spirits, considerin what all she'd been thru. I gave her a bottle of expensive brandy, even tho I knew she wasnt spose to drink, and a big rhododendron plant I picked out personally which I thought she and Frazier might enjoy. It was one of the heaviest and slowest Christmases I ever had to struggle thru.

It was sad too, like, watchin Squirrel and Frazier tryna get back use to one nother. She wasnt quite the same woman he'd taken up with and he wasnt the same man she'd been diggin on before she contracted all her medical problems.

Aristotle and Izetta was too much off into keepin up they

image as professional Negroes, if you ask me, and poor Cornelia and Marcus doin the best they can to see after the twins and to say hi to one nother, much less work at stayin in love which use to be a real big number with them.

I look at my kids and see how hard they strive to be successful, sophisticated and with it, but I always end up racin back home where I can soak my feet in some Epsom salt and listen to the people and the music on the radio.

Finally it happen. I go saunterin thru the lobby one afternoon, a Saturday, on my way to meet Willie G. at the Ocean Cafe. We spose to have lunch together.

"Mr. Prettymon, Mr. Prettymon!" I spin around and catch Frank, the baldhead dude with garlic-smellin breath that work the Blue Jay desk on weekends. He wavin me over. "Got some more fan mail for you from that radio station up in the city. Jeez, youre getting to be a regular Paul Harvey, arent you?"

"Hey, thanks, Frank. It always picks up my day when I get a letter. Dont look like anybody ever think about me unless I jump on that phone and start soundin off over the air."

"I should have such problems. Any day you name I'll trade you some of my mail, all bills, for yours."

I look at the envelope and slip it in my inside jacket pocket to look at later on.

"You actually answer all that stuff?" Frank ask me, got one hand at his mouth like he tryna hold back one of them belches.

"Nope."

Now, in reality, I do scribble out a postcard every once in a while to some of them nuts and cranks that take the time to write me but that aint none of Frank's business. As a general rule tho, I tend to keep pretty quiet bout what I do and dont do, specially with white folks who, it's been my experience, look like they wanna know all your business.

I get to the Ocean Cafe and Willie G. settin at the counter with a beer and one of the longest faces I seen since Buster Keaton quit makin pictures.

"What's the matter, man?"

"Aw, aint nothin," he say, scratchin hisself down under the stool. "Must be goin on a coupla months since I seen you last."

"At least. How's the museum gig goin? You started paintin yet?"

"Naw, just a few pencil sketches in a little notebook I keep. I been meanin to take a night course of some kind in basic drawin. Poetry seem to be my thing right now. I'm turnin it out like it's goin outta style."

"I never even knew it was ever in style. What type of themes you writin about?"

"Uh, you know, the political situation, women, freedom, still lifes, problems, Africa."

"Africa? What you know bout Africa?"

"Much as anybody else that dont live there, I reckon. You just kinda generalize and put in a lotta your personal feelins. I been goin over to see my man O. O. Gabugah, that poet I told you bout comes in to read at JoJo's, remember? He say my shit is pretty good except I got to work more of the black perspective into it. I really like old O.O. Joker never writes down a word. He thinks the stuff out in his head and then dictates it to this other writer—forget his name—who types the poems up for him. Now, that's a good way to work, dont you think?"

"I'm sorry, Willie, but when it come to poetry all I really care bout is the classics."

"O yeah? Like *who*, for instance?"

"Well, like Emerson, Thoreau, Omar Khayyam, Paul Laurence Dunbar—folks like that."

"Hmmph, well, I cant say I'm as well-read as you make out like you are but I have been known to turn a page or two. I never heard tella any them people you talkin bout. But, here, lemme drop one of my latest numbers on you for, you know, a little test reaction."

"Aw, Willie, cant we order first? I'm hungry."

"Yeah we can order. I'm hungry myself. Just take a look at this, it aint all that long."

"Do I have to?"

"Sit, I thought you was some kinda frienda mine."

I put the menu down—with great hesitation, if yall know what I mean—and try not to look too bugged while Willie G. go fumblin in his wallet and bring out a wad of three-hole

169

lined notebook paper which he unfold and hand me. It's got bacon grease stains on it and the ink kinda smudged but I can still make out the words wrote in ballpoint.

OH SAY CAN YOU SEE?
By William G. Jenkins, Jr.

Oh say can you see?
Say hey can't you see?
Filth and oppression and poverty
Does not fill my heart with glee.
For the Caucasian bringeth misery
Fraught with exploitation and discrimination
    every place that they be.

Oh say can you see?
Well then listen to me. . . .
Pimps and players sellin' pussy honestly
    on Ghetto streetcorners
While the relentless honky pimps and
    fucks over our minds from
        The WHITE house! ! !

Oh say can you see the wet red rain
Of pain that will drive us all insane
Until we put a bullet in the Motherfucker's
          b
          r
          a
          i
          n
And drain his cruelty to nought. . . .
For we are of Love and of Blackness;
Brothers and Sisters, Ms. and Misters
Engulfed no more in the dawn of past regrets
That blinds our rat-infested Souls with
        lonelyness.

Oh yes we can see!
But can you see me?

"Well, what you think?" ask Willie who been settin there all this time lookin over my shoulder at his own composition.

"Uh—uhhhh—I'd really have to study it some more to familiarize myself with all the little subleties."

"Aw, forget that, Sit, just gimme your gut reaction. I mean, does it do anything for you? See, I worked a long time on that

170

one and you might say it's a radical departure from my usual style. That's what O.O. told me anyway. See how I spell the word 'brain' straight up and down like that? Now, that's one of them hip modern licks. I'm tryna experiment more. Could you relate to the symbolism in there?"

"Symbolism?"

"Yeah, like, the part about the *white* house, get it? And here where I say "the wet red rain of pain'—that stand for blood, you see?"

"Hmmm, right, I see but—"

"But what?"

"Well, it do have a sorta strong dramatic ring to it."

"Hey, thanks, man, that's what I was aimin for—drama, the inner drama within ourself that dont too often get expressed. Glad you could see that in there. I read it to this little sister come in JoJo's every week for the poetry readins and she like to flipped! Couldnt wait to mash some of that good nookie on me. Tell you one thing. I might not cant make no money writin this jive but I can sure use it to talk up on me some leg, betcha that!"

It's depressin bein captured like that havin to put up with Willie G.'s diarrhea of the mouth, but at least I done got him off my back about that sillyass poem of his.

"Now," I tell him, pickin up the menu again, "it's my turn to read you one."

"I'm listenin, Sit. How it go?"

"One roastbeef sammich on a French roll, easy on the mayonnaise. A bowl of navy bean soup, hold the crackers. And a glassa 7UP with plenty of ice. How's that?"

"You call that a poem?"

"Call it anything you want to. It's just somethin I can sink my teeth into. How's your art-lover partner doin these days? You still seein her?"

"You mean JoJo? Who, by the way, still want you to come pose for a paintin."

"No, I mean—what's her name?—we spent the night at her and Adele's place."

"Sandy. That's who I was afraid you meant. Well, Sit, to make a long story short, I had to cut the girl aloose."

"You run outta painters and stuff to discuss?"

171

"Naw, that pretty redhead with her innocent-lookin freckles and sea-green eyes up and gave me the pure dee clap!"

"You sure it was her?"

"Had to be. I tracked it back to her anyway and told her to go get herself checked out. Had to ask two or three other young ladies to go check in too, much as I hated to, but Sandy the one I was jammin the most. I'm to the place now tho where I'm ready to go back usin Trojans like back in the old days. Them San Francisco women outnumber the men now, you know, and they too damn liberated for me. I done even stopped kissin broads on the mouth too much anymore. No tellin where they mouth done been. You subject to pick up almost anything! Man, you talk about itchin! I havent been thru nothin like this since Korea. Escuse me while I go to the head. Tell em I'm havin the special."

While Willie off in the men's room, I open up the letter I got. Good golly Miss Molly, my heart go to racin and I got to lean down closer to make certain I see what I think I'm seein!

There it was all right. A check made out for two thousand dollars payable to Sidney J. Prettymon for Talent Services Rendered from KRZY, a Division of Amalgamated Media: A Communications Corporation.

I musta been grinnin like a cretin. Willie come back and say, "Whoever wrote you that letter you puttin away musta been sayin some awfully happy shit."

"O no, no," I say, straightenin up and tryna act serious and matter of fact, "it's just another letter from somebody out there in Radio Land."

"Well, I sure could use some good news like that. I'm thinkin bout tryna get back on at the wreckin yard if theyll have me. This pressure from that security-guard job is gettin to me."

"What pressure? I thought you loved that job."

"The job's all right, I guess, if it doesnt bore you to death. I never woulda thought that standin around like that could get on your nerves."

"You think you might be expendin too much energy tryna hit on every woman that walks into that museum?"

172

"Every young woman, Sit, every young woman. You might have a point. I thought about that. At least down here on the Peninsula it's a little harder to get to know people. What's your life like these days? Hey, when they gon play your commercial over television? I been kinda lookin out for it."

"I dont know."

"You gon tell Sam to kiss your ass after all that good bread start rollin in? I sure as hell would."

"I dont know."

"How much they pay you for that? C'mon, man, you can tell *me*."

"I dont know."

Willie gimme one of his special-occasion belligerent looks and say, "All right, nigger, I wont ask you nothin else, you wanna be like that, but I'mo be watchin you. It'll all come out by and by."

Maybe Willie G. was right. On my part, however, I got it in my mind to be bout as aloof and tight-mouthed as a right-wing mortician in a health-food store.

27

"What happened? Did somebody die?"

"Beg pardon?" I say to the big-bosom brownskin bank teller.

"Two thousand dollars is a lot of money, Mr. Prettymon."

"Yeah, well, so it is."

"I thought perhaps someone had passed on and willed it to you."

"O I see. Well, we all entitled to our thoughts, I guess. It just so happen I earned the money."

"Is that right? What doing?"

"Tendin to my business and leavin other folkses affairs alone. Would you mind enterin the amount in my bankbook and stampin it for me?"

She get a little hot behind my attitude and quit lookin directly at me. She say, "Excuse me, *sir,* but any deposit in check form over fifteen hundred dollars has to be cleared by the supervisor."

"What's there to clear, *madame?* Ive had an account here for years. The check's legitimate! You can see it's been made out to my name!"

"No need to go raising your voice, Mr. Prettymon. I'm only following bank regulations."

It taken a little red tape to get it straightened out, but finally I get the damn money deposited, catch my breath and walk back out in the windy afternoon, wonderin when colored people—black, brownskin and yella people—gon finally start treatin one nother with the kinda respect we all been strugglin to get from white folks.

It's that funny time of day, a Monday, when most people lookin forward to gettin thru that last hour or two on the job. Here I am tryna get in my last free-time licks before reportin to work. I done already taken Sam up on his latest offer on what he call a provisional basis—meanin, lemme test it out and see how I like workin full-time. Maybe by the end of six weeks we can reach some type of final decision. I'm figgerin that oughtta gimme enough time to figger out what I'mo do.

The majority of people my age got they eye on retirin in a few more years. Me, all I'm hopin is I can keep my raggedy act together long enough to qualify for Social Security and Medicare.

In Woolworth's—which I always cut thru on my way from the bank to University Avenue—who else do I spot but Marguerite. She lookin at datebooks and calendars at the stationery counter. I hang back so she wont notice me. It's fun sometime to trail somebody you already think you know just to observe what they like when they be doin they everyday thing.

She buy a coupla items, then I follow her into the Penny Lane Market a coupla doors down—known for its expensive food, like, plums in the summertime, twenty cent apiece—where she pick up some grocery and charge em.

Now she stridin along with two bags, steppin up the street like she some twenty-somethin-year-old thing. You can still make out her generous butt and other shapely attributes in spite of the long leather coat and stylish boots she sportin. I can even tell she still managin to keep that weight down which mean she must be done cut down on booze and now tryna get more exercise. The woman got class. I will say that for her. She move down the sidewalk like she the young Jacqueline Kennedy Onassis or somebody. She aint payin them peasants and riffraff no mind, aint got no time for trivia. I'm thinkin, wow, can this be the same tipsy lady I been rubbin up against and kissin on and gettin squeezed back by and a whole lot more?

At the pet store, she stop and stand gigglin at the little puppies in the window, then she strut cross University which the city done recently had beautified and look in a shoe store window. She go in there and try on shoes for ten minutes but dont come out with any new packages.

From my side the street, I follow her up to Baskin-Robbins 31 Flavors where she buy herself a doubledip cone—hmmm, cant be doin all *that* much weight-watchin after all—and walk back to the corner, bitin and nibblin and lickin on the ice cream so slow and juicy-like until I can yeahbout hear mister johnson groan.

Then she just stand there on the corner, lookin up and down the block like she waitin on somebody. I do a fast turnaround so she dont recognize me. I can feel her eyes gazin at the backa my head seem like.

When I ease on round real cautious this time, the Mercedes pull up, that very Mercedes-Benz 220 sedan I drove her home in the night we hooked up at Adamo's Liquor Store and she was too wasted to function. It seem like just a few weeks ago and it seem like years done gone by. It was only last summer, late last summer, but long ago I came to the realization that time and feelins got a way of contradictin one nother.

At the driver's wheel is a grayhead white dude with one of them peculiar-style stickin-up beards like Fuzzy Q. Jones use to wear in cowboy pictures goin *way* back. Marguerite climb in between him and another dude, colored. Both the men wearin turtleneck sweaters and jackets, only the black one look a lot younger'n the other one. Fact, in fact—when I squinch my eyes and focus in right close—hmmmph!—I can see that the youngest man my own son-in-law, Marcus.

I watch her give em both big kisses on the mouth which make em grin. They wait for a bus to go by, then they pull away and motor on out toward El Camino.

For a minute or two or maybe a lot longer, I stand where I'm at with my hands in my coat pockets, tryna make sense of just what it was I done witnessed. Trouble is I cant think too good in the afternoon, only late at night, so it would all have to wait till that little inner drama, as Willie G. put it, worked itself out inside me.

Beside wantin to get to work on time, *my* little wish—not to be confused with mister johnson this time—is to rassle with that Creole charmer just one more time, commencin, say, at four in the afternoon and wrappin it up round midnight—the perfect swing shift.

I catch myself feelin pretty cheap and lowdown even thinkin anything like that when here Squirrel was back in the hospital for another operation and aint too much anybody can do bout it except cross they fingers and hope for the best.

28

God, this is Sidney comin at you again, Nebuchadnezzar's boy of the Missippi Prettymons. What with all the evil that's inundatin the world, I know you probly got better things to do with your time than to fool with me and my problems, but I would be much obliged if you were to favor my ex-wife with a blessin or two.

I'm levelin with you, Lord, since you must know by now the type of person I am. I'm no churchgoer. Mosta my prayers get said in emergencies. It's been times when I caught myself wonderin if you ever even existed. Goin by all the misery and hatred and injustice in the world which seem to be growin worse, it's no wonder people like me have a hard time keepin the faith.

Like, how come you continue to allow all this sufferin and ignorance and bloodshed to go on? When I use to ask my mother this, she'd tell me it was things we never was meant to understand; higher truths that's hid from us. Well, that could be. I do notice that the older I get the more I find out and the better I get at piecin stuff together. Maybe if I was to stick around, say, a good thousand years everything might start fallin into place, only by then I'd be too old to benefit from the knowledge I'd be done gained. Is that how it was with Methuselah and them?

All the same, I still get pretty riled up seein all these slick

178

preachers and religious gangsters takin folkses hard-earned money in your name. Fact, it's been my observation that every place where the white man went in, wavin that Bible and mashin that cross up in everybody's face while he talk about heaven—Africa, Asia, North and South America—the people who was already in them places didnt catch nothin but natchal hell.

I was brung up to be fearful of you but somewhere down the line I got it in my head that if you spose to be all that mighty and merciful then maybe we oughtta could talk and listen at one nother sensible-like. For all I know, it just mighta been you helped me outta some of them tight corners I got backed into when I was messin up bad. Maybe not. Anyway, all that's irrelevant now. I'm still on my feet and still in the world some kinda way. Sequoia, my former wife, is not on her feet. No tellin how long she gon be around.

All I'm askin is for you to look after her if you will. I dont ask for no miracles since, for one thing, I dont believe in em. I do believe in keepin my word, and I promised her I'd pray for her, so—do what you can if it's anything can be done and we'll all of us be thankful, Squirrel in particular.

Please forgive me for takin so long to request this one little favor.

Amen.

The first I seen of the TV spots was at Wanda's. I got up round noon that Saturday with everything on my mind, the way you do sometime. Started out with me wonderin what God done made of the prayer I'd whispered in the middle of the night. One thought led to another so that by the time I'm fixated there lookin at myself in the bathroom mirror, tryna decide if I oughtta cut my gray mustache off, the only thing really on my mind is women—Marguerite, JoJo McBee, Passionate Patricia, Adele and, yes, even Wanda who at least live right within walkin distance.

It's been a long time since I got together last with Marguerite, my old Creole ace down in the hole, or with anybody else far as that's concerned.

The tip-off to when you really gettin worked-up, horny, randy, however you wanna call it, is when you start thinkin back over and speculatin bout all the poontang you *coulda* had but, for one reason or other, either passed up or let get away. I dont know if you women, specially you liberated women, feel that way with respect to us men, but that's exactly the mode I get into sometime when me and mister johnson team up and be tuned in on the same wave length. Every time Adele flash up in my mind, I wanna kick myself with hobnail boots even if it *was* the wrong time of month!

So I take off walkin down University Ave, stayin out the way of all the Blue Jay folks I know which include quite a few V.A. Hospital, uh, outpatients they call em. Aint no tellin what kinda number they subject to break into any given minute. Me and the Professor one time got to talkin bout how it's a lotta these college kinda towns got a big mental institution closeby. I told him I'd probly be in one myself if Palo Alto was just a little bit bigger and a lot less quiet. Just might be, come to think of it, I been one of them outpatients all my life, only I got better sense than to go get myself tested.

It's another side to this town, you know—the real suburb side where you can walk for blocks and blocks on end and dont see nothin but big kept-up houses and little kept-up houses and lawns and flowers and trees and more trees. And cars! You liable to glance over your shoulder while you steppin past somebody's magazine-ad dwellin and see a brand-new Mercedes-Benz and a beat-up Volkswagen or Vega parked in the same driveway. Aint nothin for me to set there over by the post office, pretendin like I'm waitin on the bus, and count maybe fifty-sixty Rolls-Royces, Bentleys, Jaguars or Porsches roll by in a hour's time.

I'm walkin out University, thinkin bout my two solid grand socked away in the bank and how maybe I'll just up and kick down some of that new money for a good used car, when this old Calvin Coolidge-lookin dude go to wavin and limpin cross his lawn toward me.

"How're you doing?" he say.

"Fair to middlin and yourself?"

"Not bad, not bad. I see you dont remember me."

"Well—no, not exactly. You not one of Sam's clients, are you?"

"Sam? Who's that?"

"Runs a janitorial service here in town. He's my boss."

"Ah, so that's what youre doing now. No, I know you from years ago—San Francisco. Didnt you once drive a bus up there?"

"Yes, I did."

"And weren't you for a time driving the number 30 Stockton from the SP Train Depot cuts through North Beach on out to Union Street?"

"You remember me from way back then?"

"Hell yes, I was one of your steady riders, always the first one to board the bus while you were parked at the station taking your mid-morning break. We used to joke and talk about the fights—Sugar Ray Robinson, Rocky Marciano, remember?"

"Did I win ten dollars off you in a bet one time?"

"You doggone right you did and I havent forgotten it yet. That Marciano–Ezzard Charles heavyweight rematch, September of fifty-five. Man, what a fight! I figured Marciano had lucked out in defending his title in that fifteen-round June bout when he got the decision. I just knew Charles was gonna slaughter him in the comeback. You didnt think so and that struck me as being a bit odd—you being a colored guy putting money on a white guy. But damn if you weren't right!"

"Well, Marciano, as I recall, did knock Ezzard out in the eighth round."

"Yep, and there I was out of ten bucks to you and a good hundred bucks to all the other guys I'd made bets with."

Listenin at him say all this, I break out grinnin since I myself'd done placed some funny bets on that fight. With some dudes I'd bet on Ezzard to win and with others I'd said it was gon be Marciano. All told, I musta come out maybe thirty bucks ahead. That's how I am—play all the possibilities and stagger your bets.

"But didnt we make another bet before that?" I ask, still tryna recollect the man's name. "Seem like I can remember some other big fight taken place long around the same time, right here in San Francisco."

"We did make another bet, yep, but called it off before the

night of the fight because both of us kept going back and forth, trying to make up our minds which way to bet."

"Was that that Bobo Olson–Kid Gavilan middleweight championship bout?"

"Nope, but youre close. Gavilan and Olson fought in Chicago that spring. Technically speaking, Gavilan was welterweight champ challenging Olson for the middleweight crown. Olson took a fifteen-round split decision over the Kid."

"I remember he talked right funny with his Cuban accent."

"That's right, but personally I always thought Gavilan was the better fighter, handled himself beautifully, beautifully. Then three months later—and this is what youre thinking of —Bobo went up against a challenger named Rocky Castellani that summer right up here at the Cow Palace, got the decision, lost me fifty bucks."

"Yeah, that Carl Bobo Olson was a fightin fool that year. Whipped Castellani then turnt around and scored a TKO over some up-and-comer, a Frenchman, I think."

"Pierre Langlois. That was in December of that same year, nineteen fifty-five, also in San Francisco, but I managed to pick up a cool half-grand in bets on that one."

"I know who you are. It just now hit me—Mr. Donovan, Jack Donovan! You use to run this antique shop over on Union Street."

"Close, damn close, except the name's Donahue, Mack Donahue. What the hell're you doing with yourself these days, Sidney?"

"My God, you even remember my name!"

"Sure do, and I remember when you were custodian for a while here at the Greyhound station right here in Pali too."

"*For a while* is right. That gig sure didnt last long."

"What happened?"

"Got tired of it. Well, it was a draw actually. I got tired of them round the same time as they was gettin tired of me. Did a little short-order cookin after that."

"You move around a lot, eh?"

"Ah, it's a long story, Mr. Donovan—"

"Mack, if you dont mind. I mean, after all, we have been bumping into one another going on twenty years now."

"Well, all right, it's a long story, Mack. I broke up with my wife, stayed on drivin for the city for a while, quit, took up partnership with another guy and formed a maintenance service there in North Beach, did a lotta odd jobs, fell apart, moved down there to Palo Alto and after that it's been touch and go ever since, mostly *touch*, altho here lately, *just* here lately, it look like I might be gainin on the *go* part a little."

Mack Donahue look at me and smile kinda. I can tell he wearin dentures now cause his teeth all even and white and they use to be snaggly and smoky from them cigars he use to mash out right before he'd get on the bus and set right backa the driverseat and commence yakkin.

"It's a hard world to beat," he say. "I thought I was on top of things for years. Had three businesses going in the city and one down here, this house and a summer place up in British Columbia, real estate properties, three fine kids and a lovely wife. My oldest boy, the one I thought would become an MD, he took up with some fool swami and moved to Calcutta. My second son came back from Vietnam with a heroin habit. Now he's on methadone—which is still the shits if you ask me, certainly no solution to the problem—and it looks as if he might turn gay besides."

"And what about your daughter, the baby you use to show me pictures of?"

"She's finally finishing up her junior year at Hunter College in New York, majoring in English. Why New York and why English, search me, but I'm worried about her too. Never seemed to date anyone except foreign students—Arabs, Latin Americans—and now she's talking about marrying some Puerto Rican."

Mack shake his head and tug at the collar of his turtleneck sweater, then he ask me if I wanna come in and have a drink. I explain to him I'm on my way to see a good friend I work with and I'm late.

"Sure you wouldnt like a little pick-me-up of some kind? I'd sure like to chat with you."

"No, thanks, Mack. Gotta get to steppin. How's your wife doin?"

"O," he say, lookin down, "she passed on a few years back, heart disease."

"Sorry to hear that. My ex-wife isnt doin so well either."

"I hope it's nothing serious."

"Yeah, it is but—I'd rather not talk about it right now."

"Well, anytime you feel like dropping by and having a drink, just give me a ring. I'm in the book. I saw you on television a couple of hours ago."

"You jokin."

"No, really, right there on Channel Three. Got a big charge out of that, seeing this guy doing a spot on TV after I havent seen him in how many years now? Then I'm fooling around my yard and look up and there he is again walking past the house. I hope they paid you well for that appearance. You did a good job, I thought, added that homey touch."

"Thanks, thank you, Mack. I havent even seen it yet."

"Well, I'm certain you will. Enjoy yourself. Dont let any of this celebrity stuff go to your head."

We shake hands and I mosey on, wonderin if it's any real answers to anything anymore.

By the time I get to Wanda's place on Cooley Street in East Palo Alto, my corns and bunions throbbin somethin fierce. Gettin harder every day to hack these long walks like I use to. I'm thinkin I shoulda stopped and rested at Mr. Donahue's palatial estate and had me a nip. Probly done us both good. He aint got but a coupla years on me yet and still he whiter in the head and lookin lonelier and old.

I no sooner buzz the doorbell than Wanda jeck the door wide open and come slammin into me with one of them bear hugsa hers, like to knocked me down and cracked my ribs.

"What's the matter with you, woman?"

"You just in time, you just in time!" she say, all outta breath. "They playin a commercial over television with you in it! It's on right now! Hurry up, come on!"

She race in fronta me back to the livinroom. I'm hangin back a little, tryna act like it aint no real big thing. But when I finally see myself on her color console, laid back on that bench in Union Square, got my transistor in one hand while the camera pan in for a close-up, talkin bout, "Hi, my name is Sitting Pretty" and "It's got that community sound" and "For people on the fly, it's KRZY," then my heart go pumpin and thumpin shonuff and I start lookin for someplace to light.

Wanda push me into this plastic-wrapped easy chair but by the time I get set down good, my act is over with and up flash all these dancin white kids with one Negro in the middle, singin bout how I deserve a break today so get out and get away to McDonald's.

Whew! Rushin back thru my mind now is the quotation I come across in the Sunday paper once where this New York dude that make a livin outta borin people to death said the time was comin when everybody was gon be famous for fifteen minutes. Fifteen seconds more like it if you ask me.

Wanda lean over and pat me on the cheek and say, "I'm so prouda you. How come you didnt tell us you'd made some commercials?"

"Awww, I reckon I just wanted to surprise yall, that's all."

"Well, you sure surprised the wee-wee outta me, you dont mind my sayin so. I always did suspect you was up to somethin but I never figgered it'd be anything like this. Where you learn to play-act and talk and carry on like that?"

"Been doin it all my life, sweet thing, only wasnt no mass communication outlet for it."

"Mass communication outlet my big toe! Hey, what's this?" She run the backa her index finger cross the topa my lip and say, "You cut your mustache off, how come?"

"That's somethin I do every coupla years just for the hell of it. I think it makes me look younger, dont you?"

"Goll-lee no! Least not at your age. I mean, you dont even look like you. I went for the way you was lookin on television, the way I always liked to think of you as lookin. Now you done gone and goofed your image all up."

Image all goofed up or not, I can still yank her down on my lap and whisper in her ear all slobbery-like. "I know you wasnt expectin me," I tell her, "but didnt you once tell me you had a coupla kids?"

"That's correct," she say, lookin at me all quizzical. "So what is it you wanna know about em?"

"Where they at? I dont see nobody round here but you."

She nibble on my nose kinda playful and say, "Well, if you must know—and it seems as if you do—Leonard and Glorietta both gone to the show downtown. They wanted to see this double bill—*Nigger Charley's Revenge* and *Shaft Meets*

185

Superfly—so I gave em bus fare. Dont worry, you gon meet em all right."

I start kissin on the wishbone of her neck, her double chin and work up to her lips. By the time I'm fixin to explorate her mouth, the phone ring out in the kitchen.

She get up, go answer it and ramble on for fifteen minutes while I'm settin there tryna fake interest in *Whatever Happened to Baby Jane?*—a picture I done seen on TV at least five times, waitin on the part where Bette Davis bring the cooked rat in on the dinner tray to serve to poor Joan Crawford.

When she come back, she say, "Listen, I been tryna put up these shelves in the kitchen, the kind where you screw these metal supports in the wall and then you fit in the wood shelves? By you bein a man, you probly know more about how to do it right than I do. Think you could help me out?"

So after I put up the shelf, clean up, take out the trash, help fix a leaky toilet and put up hooks for some hangin plants, she finally offer me a glassa beer and set there at the kitchen table goin on and on bout what a good-for-nothin so-and-so her former husband is or was. From the way she tellin it, it's hard to discern if he still livin or if he done died.

"If he was all that bad," I take a chance and ask her, "then how come you got married to him in the first place?"

"You know how men are," she chuckle and say. "You a man. Henry got to me early while I was still in my teens, before I'd woke up and come to my senses. A woman dont really come to her senses, you know, until she reach twenty-nine or thirty, round in there. Whatever he told me to believe, I believed it. You want some more beer? It's plenty in the icebox."

"No, thank you, I still got some left. But tell me—did yall break up or finally get a divorce or what?"

"To tell you the truth, Sit, we just went our separate ways. Even tho I thought I was in love with the Negro, after he'd done dogged me around and dogged me around and gone upside my head a few times, it got to the point where I had to ask him to please leave. I'd call the law on him and he'd

186

straighten up for a few weeks and then I'd have to get the man out here on him again. Then he got to drinkin and stayin out all night, missin work, got fired from his job, a good city job drivin one of them street sweepers. I pulled a gun on him one night after he almost broke my jaw. We got scareda one nother and it was time to get out from around each other. Sam got a lawyer frienda his to handle the divorce."

"Well, where's he at now?"

"Aw, he over there in Hayward someplace but he know to leave me and the kids alone. In fact, he behind six months in his child support and I been thinkin bout jackin his butt up legally again."

Squirrel had been such a goodhearted person by comparison. Sure, I'd missed a few child support payments after we split off, but it never woulda entered her mind to sic no law on me. What a fool I was, what a goddam fool!

"You got to be tireda listenin at me runnin off at the mouth bout Henry," she say. "I know you didnt come all the way over here for that. Why dont we go back in the back and relax a little before Glorietta and Leonard get home. Shit! I sure wish them kids next door would cut out some of that racket sometime!"

It sound like some kinda soul rock band warmin up for a practice session next door. The drum thumpin, the organ grindin, and the guitar screamin, plus, by us bein in one of them plasterboard and stucco apartments slapped together by some greedy contractors that just jumped up off the toilet and went to buildin, any type of noise seep right thru the walls. This particular noise got the whole unit tremblin like one of them small-time earthquakes you wake up in the mornin and can feel sometime.

Wanda say, "Sit, would you do me one more favor? Would you go next door and ask em to lighten up some? They think I'm some kind of a nut by now. You might be able to get over to em."

I step out the kitchen door which slide open and look off to my left down the cement balcony. Shonuff, it's a youngish dude with long conked hair leanin up against the concrete railin, got his electric guitar cross one knee, pickin out them sounds that's screechin like a speedway fulla cars doin ninety miles a hour puttin on brakes for a red light.

Now, he out there on the second-floor balcony pickin out notes and I can see the electric cord plugged in the guitar that lead back inside the apartment where the other musicians, so-call, is fiddlin.

"Hey!" I shout. "Hey, man! You playin so loud you bout to drive us deaf, dumb, cripple and blind next door! Think you could maybe ease up a little taste?"

"I hear you, brother," he holler. "I know where you comin from. Figgered the shit musta been gettin outta hand cause I couldnt hardly stand it myself. That's how come I came out here. Dont yall worry bout a thing. We got it covered."

They eased up after that all right, but so did everything else. I mean, I ease up offa Wanda too, and got ready to kiss my sexy Saturday good-bye.

We no sooner get laid down on the bed good, back up in her room, still dressed and fumblin, than the kids come bustin in.

"Hey, Mama, Mama, what's goin on?" The boy's voice sorta high-pitch. I can tell he at that stage where it's bout to start breakin.

"You gotta go see these movies, Mama," I hear the girl say.

Wanda gimme that last peck on the mouth and whisper, "I know you probly drug behind all this, but straighten up and act correct and dont let nothin slip out to Sam about this, OK? Next time it aint gon be like this, I promise."

As I'm gettin myself together to meet the youngsters and split, all I wanna promise her is it aint gon be no next time, not if I can help it. But all I say is, "I'll see you on the job. Dont worry. Everything'll be groovy as a ten-cent movie."

"You wanna be a TV star you better let your mustache grow back in."

That's the last thing she say to me in that cluttered-up, lonesome-smellin bedroom of hers.

29

Wanda offer to drive me home but I kindly decline for a number of reasons. For one thing, I got this funny feelin that get worse the older I get bout bein old as I am and livin in a hotel. You know, at my age I'm spose to be doin better'n that. I oughtta should at least maintain some kinda private residence even if it's just a studio apartment or walk-up room.

I dont want Wanda to know where I live and, beside, I feel like bein by myself, off alone with my thoughts again. So I decide I'll try to make that last number 50 run outta East Palo Alto into the main parta town.

Settin on the bench at the bus stop, waitin, I check out all the little kids walkin by, cussin like sailors, they transistor radios blastin all that ignorant music as Sam prefer to call it.

Two little girls round ten, I'd say, clip-clop by with lipstick on. It's been rainin a lot but today it's clear and the lasta the sunshine dwindlin away, so they decked out in pantsuits—one purple, one pink—with the pants so tight you can actually make out the cracks of they skinny little butts.

Miz Purple, she wavin a lit cigarette and saying to Miz Pink, "Hell yeah, I'll play on a muthafucka that come on like that *any day!* Pissed me off, shit! I didnt wanna be bussed to that honky school nohow. I was doin all right over here with my friends. Damn President back here, rip off the whole country and go scot-free, and all I done was slap some silly little stringy-haired white bitch around in the lavatory for tryna take Leroy away from me. Now the principal wanna kick me outta school—*unh-unhhh!*"

As they reach the corner, I go against my better judgment and shout, "Is all that bad language really called for?"

"The fuck you say?" Miz Purple ask, jeckin her head around and lookin at me all evil with her fresh-fried, greazy hair.

"Hey, dont pay no attention to him," Miz Pink say, makin little circles at her temple with her finger. "He crazy."

Crazy! Well, maybe I am. Maybe the ideas I got about how you comport yourself in public went outta style a hundred years ago. It's true, like I say, that it aint too much that faze me anymore, but to hear youngsters cussin—specially such babies—still grate on my nerves.

So now here I am gettin famous overnight, spose to be some kinda personality or celebrity. Well, I still dont believe it. I still gotta find me some TV set I can set down in front of for a few hours at least and see for myself just what KRZY's been up to since I watched it last.

Betcha yall wont believe who come toolin up right about then in a dark blue Volvo sedan, got jet black hair and a bright suede coat on, and lean over to roll down the window and say, "Sidney J. Prettymon, as I live and breathe, do you need a ride?"

"What you do to your hair?" I ask.

"What you do to your mustache?" she say, talkin niggerish and flat to make fun of me, I guess.

"I'm tireda people askin me bout my mustache. I was shavin and on the spur of the moment figgered it was time for it to go."

"Same with my hair," she say, pattin her head with one hand. "I was dying to get it dyed. It ended up black because I wanted to look natural and not like one of those Mediterranean types with phoney blonde locks that clash with their coloring. Do you like the way it's cut?"

"Little on the short side," I say, takin a closer look, "but it's becomin, I think. Do you like it?"

"I did for the first couple of days, but now I cant wait for it to grow out again. I do rather like that indigo patina, however. It suits me better than red, dont you think? Sidney? Sit? Sitting Pretty?"

"Uhmm, I was just thinkin bout somethin you said—patina."

"Patina, yes, what about it?"

"Like, I dont mean to come on stuffy or anything, but—you sure you was usin that word the right way?"

"Well, yeah. How do you think I shouldve used it?"

"O let's just forget it, OK?"

"No," she say, pullin up to a stop sign, "if I stand to be corrected, then correct me. Fair is fair."

"Baby, you used the term *indigo patina* where I personally think it mighta been better if you'da said indigo sheen or indigo luster. See, I been up against the word *patina* before and had to look it up and get it drilled good into my mind."

"And what does it mean?"

"As I recollect, it mean somethin like the shine you get when you polish any type of old furniture or metallic object, like antiques, say. Now, that certainly wouldnt apply to you or your hair, would it?"

All she do is laugh and laugh. She even reach over with her free hand and squeeze my thigh and keep on laughin.

"In this case," she say while little bitty tears commence to formin in the corners of her eyes, "it just might apply. By the way, where you going?"

"Got any ideas? I got the whole weekend off and I'm subject to take off even more, dependin."

"In that case," she tell me, still chucklin and carryin on, "I think I know just where to go."

"Where?"

"Trust me."

After drivin round up behind Stanford, we end up at this little brown shingle house, a cottage really. What a beautiful drive it was with trees and windin roads and every once in a while I glance out thru the twilight and see somebody ridin long on a horse or some cows grazin on the side of a hill. Make me kinda homesick for Missippi days back down on the farm when it was my job to help get the livestock rounded up before sunset.

"Yall own this place too?" I ask while we standin at the back window which look out over a creek.

"No, it belongs to this woman I know, Carlotta McKay. I knew her back in my New York days and we've kept in touch all these years. She's heading up a women's studies program at one of the colleges in this area, but right now she's on leave for a quarter at the University of Chicago. I drive out here two or three times a week to water the plants and pick up her mail. Quiet and pleasant, isnt it? Let's sit down and catch up. Would you like me to make coffee?"

"How bout a drink?"

"That's what I was afraid you'd want."

"You back on the wagon or somethin?"

She stand there lookin off into space and then she say, "Well, sort of. I think that over the past couple of decades Ive really drank my share, you know. I smoke a little dope now and since I saw you last I have sniffed cocaine once or twice. Have you ever experienced that?"

"What?"

"Coke, cocaine?"

"Nope, but I can remember back when I was a boy down-south the big thing was to drop a coupla aspirin or some BC Headache Powder and wash it down with Coke Co-Cola."

"Hmmm, I see," she say, lookin at me all funny. "Well, I suppose I could treat myself to a Dubonnet on the rocks with a twist of lemon. Carlotta's got plenty if youre agreeable to that."

"If it's sweet and drinkable, then I'm agreeable."

It turn out to be a pretty good little drink, not bad, not bad at all. I make a mental note on it and ask Marguerite, "Say, how's that dog of yours doin, and what's it like with your old man back on the premises?"

She take a sip off her drink and say, "Sit, it's been strange. The whole scene's been strange. I wouldnt even know where to begin."

"Start anywhere. I aint in no hurry."

"I'm not even sure I want to talk about it."

"Talk about what, Marguerite? All I asked you is how was things goin in general. You dont feel like tellin me nothin, fine, solid, OK, that's your business and we'll drop it."

I guess I musta come on a little strong and jiggedy myself sayin all that because all Marguerite do is slit her eyes and frown for a second, then look off down into her drink, shakin her head from side to side. So I get up out the armchair I'm loungin in and walk over to the little do-fold where she at and ease down beside. I put my arm around her and pull her over to me real tender-like.

"I'm sorry, Sit," she say, snifflin a little like she fixin to bust out cryin. "It's just that . . . It's just that Ive been so confused about everything for so long now. Confused about my marriage, confused about myself, confused about—"

"Hey, hey, hold up a minute. We didnt come out here to shed tears and get into true confessions, did we?"

"No, of course not. But there are some things Ive been wanting to talk with you about for weeks and weeks."

"Well then, let's pour out another round of Dubonnet and proceed to converse if that's what it take."

"Help yourself," she say, pullin away from me. "I'm fine. Are you comfortable?"

"I'm all right. Sound like it's fixin to start rainin again."

We both get quiet for a second and listen at the raindrops thunkin on the roof.

"Ahhh, I love that," she say. "A good rain always takes the tension out of me."

"Well, you must be pretty relaxed by now, all this rain we been havin this year."

She smile and snuggle back up next to me again while I reach over and replenish my refreshment. When I take a sip and try to sneak in a little peck on the jaw, she casually move her head to one side which cause me to end up kissin on the backa her new hairdo.

"You know, Sit," she start out sayin, "Ive been thru a lot of crazy trips but Ive always managed to stay on top of things. Over the past couple months, Ive really hit bottom. First I met you and—"

"And as if that wasnt bottom enough."

"Come on, man, listen! I'm serious. Can I just get my two cents in first and then I'll be ready for cross-examining and questions from the floor, OK? So I got together with you and even tho we drank a lot and our relationship, such as it was, has been largely of a sexual nature . . . now, dont get me wrong. There's nothing wrong with sex and I'd be the last person to condemn it as the basis for any human relationship. All I'm trying to tell you is that, in spite of that limitation, I still felt deeply about our friendship and still do for that matter."

"But!"

"Give me a chance, Sit, for crying out loud! So Harry comes home after ninety days abroad—the longest we've ever been apart in one stretch—and I start missing you. What can I do? I cant really telephone you. I dont dare write. I start listening to those silly talk shows which Harry detests, just hoping your voice will turn up on one of them."

"Did you ever get to hear me?"

"Lots of times, and I didnt always agree with your point of view either."

"O yeah? Like, on what issues?"

"Never mind that. We're all entitled to our opinions, right?" She cross her legs and stick her tongue out at me, making a nasty, wrinkled-up face child-style. "But to get back to the point—"

"Which is?"

"Which *is* I never imagined I'd ever get as involved with you and your family."

"Involved with me and my family? If you dont mind my interruptin you one last time, just how do you mean that?"

She straighten up and take a super swig of that drink she only been foolin with up till now. I just set there, twiddlin my thumbs and watchin her drain the glass.

She pour out some more, take a righteous sip and go, "Ahhh, whew! It's really been a long time, you know. But maybe I need to get soused every now and then just to vent a little steam. Maybe I should just come on out and say it."

"Say what?" I ask, tryna hold back a belch.

"Harry introduced me to Marcus, your son-in-law. Theyve been working on some project together. Harry brought him to the house for dinner. I made a play—without even meaning to really—and he reciprocated. Are you listening? Sit?"

"I hear you. And then what?"

"Well, we checked into a few motels around here and in San Francisco. That was his idea. I hate motels. It was awful. It never really worked out. Marcus is sincerely devoted to his family whether you know it or not. I felt terrible, disgusted with myself and sorry for him. I still admire the man. Strangely enough, I suspect Harry of having known all about it right from the beginning. He seemed to be getting some sort of secret kick out of it. That's what I meant when I said the whole scene's been so strange. I couldnt take it. I'm trying to change. As a matter of fact, after Marcus got to talking one night about his hospitalized mother-in-law, somehow your name came up. I felt so guilty I even made out a check and mailed it off to your ex-wife. What's her name? Rabbit? Possum?—"

"Squirrel," I say calmly since aint no other way to say it. I'm still tryna act all detached and shit. "But in order for you to do all that, he musta told you her real name and where she been laid up and everything."

"That's right. He talks a lot, that Marcus, when he's in the mood or under the influence. I'll bet he never gets assigned to any top-secret project." She rear back and look at me long enough for me to study the nervous little grin on her lips. "So now," she say. "So there. What do you have to say? What do you think of me now, Sitting Pretty?"

Lookin back on it now, I reckon I was shook up some, but either too liquored up to show it or else too ornery to let on how I was feelin. It's true too that sometime when you get hit with so much unanticipated jive at one throw, all you can do is just hunch up and take it. Aint no time to figger out how you spose to react.

What I do is kinda dive on topa Marguerite. Not sure if I oughtta smack her cross the face or bite her in the neck or kiss her on the mouth or what, I start tryna tickle her round the tit which get us to rasslin all over the couch. Then she get to laughin real low and start cacklin. She blow in my ear. Mister johnson get the message and rise to the occasion. All of a sudden, she haul off and clamp her big legs around me, squeezin at my pockets with her wobbly thighs. Now, what you gotta remember is we both still got our clothes on, plus she wearin one of them long-ass all-the-way-down-to-the-ankle dresses.

Tell you, them gowns is a mess! They a whole lot sexier'n these micro-miniskirts and short-shorts and shit. I get the same sorta turn-on lookin at these women outta India boppin round town in a sari. It's like, hey, remember how it use to say on the old Cracker Jack box that the more you eat the more you want? Well, with these cover-up fashions and getups, the more you look the more you see.

And the more she squeeze the more I feel. We get to tusslin and fall off the couch but the rug so hairy and thick we land real soft and roll round and roll round to where I wind up with my hand on her whatchamacallit.

That's when she draw back, all the way back. That's when, in fact, she get up on her knees, crawl away from me and say, "Goddammit, Sidney, I'm sick of this shit! Cuss me out or knock me down or whatever the hell you really feel like doing! But *please* dont put me thru another round of these changes! Ive had enough, dont you understand? Ive had enough. I'm tired, I'm tired of it. I'm too old to be getting swacked and interfering with other people's lives when I know better. I like you but I'm trying to change, I really am. Does that make sense? Ive got my own conscience to live with. Does that make sense? Do you understand?"

"I understand, baby," I pull myself up and tell her. "Aint no needa you jumpin all salty and cryin and carryin on. I understand."

"Do you really?" she ask me again, blinkin her eyes that's got tears in em.

I tell her I do. We both get so quiet until all you can hear's the rain pourin down. I'm ready to get out and walk home in it.

30

For days after that, for a whole week in fact, I have the hardest time sleepin and dont eat too mucha nothin. What I do do is get pretty heavy off into guzzlin wine up in my room after work. Take me two-three aspirins and a coupla Alka-Seltzers to get back straight after I force myself up outta bed mornins, straight enough to function anyway and put on some kinda jive front.

Tell you, I was gettin on my own nerves bad and know this bullshit gon have to come to a halt if I'mo hold down that job, stay halfway sane and keep from slidin back into the sad shape I was in durin them years when I thought I might be better off dead.

One night, after I get thru knockin back a few slugs of that wine Marguerite gimme, I even go out and ring up old Judd Jenkins who run the midnight-to-four show over KRZY. He one dude I never did too much go for on accounta his stick is to come on like he everybody's friend which, to my way of thinkin, is impossible. But I guess you get to be like that from year after year of workin the graveyard shift where you mostly be dealin with old folks, drunks, nuts, shut-ins, grouches, and other people like me that be up all night and aint got nothin better to do.

197

The best thing for me to do, I figger, is to disguise my voice—or try to at least—since everybody up at the station probly know who I am by now. I pick a deep kinda proper-soundin voice and test it out on myself right there in the Blue Jay lobby phone booth with the door shut tight, got my little transistor radio with me turned down low. Then I get out my money and commence dialin, knowin doggone well I aint gon have to wait long since Jenkins hisself done just now announced he wanna hear from somebody in the South Bay and the line is open. Just like clockwork his producer come on, put me thru them preliminaries and ask me to stand by till he finish with a commercial.

"Good morning, this is Judd, and *youre* on the air. Who am I speaking to?"

"Uhhh—" I clean done forgot to dream up some kinda name in advance. "Uh, this is, yes, this is—"

"You dont have to give your first name if you dont want to, you know."

I'm fallin all over myself tryna scoop up the phone book and flip to some name. "This is, hrrrmmph, this is National, I mean, Nash, Paul Nash calling," I say strugglin like all get-out to maintain my composure and keep up my fake voice which mean I gotta be careful bout droppin my g's or soundin too flat and country.

"OK, Paul," he say. "Now that we've established *who* you are, just *what* is it you'd like to talk about?"

"Well, this transactual analysis thing you been discussing for the past hour. I wanna know more about it. Like, without coming on like some type of spoilsport, just how would you deal with a situation where, say, you know a close relation of yours was having relations with another friend?"

"I'm afraid youre going to have to clarify that one a bit more for me, Paul."

"Hunh?"

"Specificity for the sake of clarity is what's involved, I'm afraid. In brief, just what is this close relation's relationship to the other friend?"

"Hmmm, well, all right, I can relate. The close relation's my son-in-law, my daughter's husband, and the friend's what's called an older woman, someone Ive been knowing for a number of years, a married woman, if you just got to know, who *has* been involved with me. For the record, Ive been divorced going on, O, many years now."

"That certainly puts the problem into more lucid perspective."

"Lucid perspective, indeed. I should smile. I'm the one being perspected."

"Paul, tell me this. Do you own a car?"

"I dont at present but I once did."

"Very well, that's pertinent enough. Now, let me say this. Take that battery youve got. It charges and it gets charged, right?"

"I guess so, but what's that got to do with transitional analysis?"

"Trans*actional* analysis, if you don't mind, Paul. And to return to my analogy—that battery is *you*. You can either be one of those people who take and take and take, or one who's constantly discharging. *Or* you can be the rare type who gives and is simultaneously given to. That's the type I'm trying to become—the person who gives of himself or herself and who, by the very act of giving, gets recharged at the same time, do you see?"

"Hmmm, well, it is not all that easy to follow, but I think I get the general idea. Now, tell me this. How would you go about handling the situation I was running down to you about this son-in-law of mine that's been seeing this same married woman I have been knowing?"

"Let me get this straight again, Phil."

"Paul."

"I'm sorry. Paul. Your son-in-law is seeing someone whom you say you have known. Now, just how do you mean that?"

By this time, I'm gettin pretty sicka goin round and round with this Judd Jenkins with his no-comprehendin ass. I fold open the phone booth door to let some air in, at the same time figgerin it's bout time to hang up. That's when Broadway strut by, see me settin in there, do a double take and start lollygaggin around, lookin at his watch like he got some urgent call to make at one in the mornin and why dont I wind up

199

my solo and give him a crack at what he call Mister Bell. Now the shit get tense.

"I mean *knew her* in the biblical sense," I tell Jenkins, carryin on in my same low off-the-wall voice. "Like, the same way Adam *knew* Eve and all like that."

"I see," Jenkins say, "but I do think youve come to the wrong radio program with your problem. I truly believe you'd get more significant response, and possibly more insightful advice, by phoning the fellow who runs the sex-talk show on another station which I'm not about to mention. I think his name is Chuck Chambermaid or something like that if he's still on the air."

"Thank you kindly, sir," I say, peekin out at Broadway who givin me this head-shakin grin like he aint been too long finished dinin out in some public restroom—if yall know what I mean. "I just might phone in to that other show because this one's been putting me to sleep."

"Glad to be of use to you, Paul. You strike me as being a somewhat distressed individual who could probably benefit from some sound sleep and rest. Other callers are waiting, so I must say good night."

We both click off at the same time. I set there for a coupla seconds, turn the radio up and wait to see what he gon say over the air after that. All I hear is the end of our so-call conversation played back over the delay tape, then he go right into another call from some old biddy that open up with: "Boy, that last fella you talked with really sounded like he was awfully mixed up, didnt he?"

"Yes, he did," Jenkins say, "but I'm not a licensed psychiatrist."

I tune em out after that, wonderin why in the hell I waste my time and money callin up them programs in the first place. Look like they damn sure cant do you much good when you really got a problem and need some copasetic feedback.

Broadway jiggle over to me as I'm gettin up to go and ask if I got change for a quarter, still grinnin, his eyes all red and squinched up. I count out two dimes and three pennies in the little sucker's hand which he have to accept cause that's all I got. I'm gettin such a big kick outta that until I even act friendly when I flash on him and say, "How you doin, Broadway? Long time no see."

"Yeah, it's been a good spell, brother," he say, jeckin his eyes the way he do, remind me of a mole or a possum or somethin you catch in broad daylight and play with awhile. "But hey!" He stick out his other hand which I grab without thinkin. "I caught your act on the telly up in Oakland the other night. Not bad, Sit, my man, not bad at all. As one old trouper to another, congratulations is in order. You had your shit down! Told this little tequila-sunrise–drinkin, wig-headed woman I was watchin with, 'That's my man Sitting Pretty. He talk more talk than Radio Free Europe and probly lay more pipe than PG&E or any other gas company for that matter.' That's what I told her."

Then he go to jeckin on my hand, fumblin with my thumb, squeezin my fingers, boppin my wrist. I wanna take my fist and bip him over on his behind.

"Whatcha been up to, Broadway?"

"You know—goin and comin, comin and goin. I got a A-1 top-priority call to make, that is, if you dont mind, my man."

I tell him I dont mind at all and get out his way. It's a pleasure, believe me. It's time to start dreamin and schemin.

31

Just the sighta Miz Duchess settin down to dinner at the card table in her room is bout enough to make me sadder'n I already am.

What's she havin for dinner? Alpo. Alpo Dog Food warmed up on the hot plate, that's what.

"Sure you wont join me?" she say, wipin off her fork with a napkin and diggin in. "It isnt bad, you know. In fact, it's about the meatiest stuff you can buy for the money nowdays. They advertise it on the Johnny Carson Show. You ever look at that, where Ed McMahon comes out with this big old cute dog and talks about Alpo?"

"What's the world comin to," I say, "when people gotta resort to eatin pet food?"

"O heck, it could be worse. Of course, I have to spruce it up a bit with a little chopped onion and pepper and sometimes I'll even stop by the Stardust Market over here on Lytton and pick up some potatoes and carrots to add to it. Penny Lane's got the best produce, if you ask me, but I simply cant afford their prices, even on food stamps."

"Maybe I will try just a little bite, Duchess, if it's all right with you."

"Go right ahead, help yourself."

"I aint all that hungry but wanna test it out anyway. You never can tell bout nothin till you tried it."

"Well, so what do you think?"

"Taste bout good as can beefstew to me."

"See, what'd I tell you? People think it's peculiar to be getting by on Alpo but I can remember back to times when there wasnt even anything like this to tide you over. Now, you take us—me and my folks back in Oklahoma during the Big Depression when we had the Dust Bowl, you know—we'd be happy to bite into air sandwiches whenever we could get the bread to make them."

"I know all about air sammiches, ketchup soup and miss-meal colic too."

"I'll bet you do. Ive been saying for years that dogs and cats eat better now than we use to. Why, back in those days, pets and critters had to fend for themselves. You see these little lap dogs and poodles yipping and yapping all over the place now? Well, there was a time—and it might come again—when we'd just as soon skin and roast one of those jokers as look at him. Hey, tell you something else that isnt half-bad—this Kal-Kan tuna dinner for cats they put out."

"Now, Duchess, you didnt invite me up here to your room to just talk about chow, did you?"

"Not on your life, brother. I got a problem I thought you might could give me some advice on."

I take another nibble, make a face I hope she dont notice, and sink back against the foldin chair set up cross the table from hers.

"Sit, I think by now I oughtta be able to lay it on the line with you. We've been knowing each other for a long time. Basically we're in the same boat right now, doing time at the Blue Jay which is nowhere, except youve got more to look forward to than I do. I dont really know about your past, but I can tell you I sure dont have much of one. My people got off the reservation by marrying up with white folks. And a lotta good it did. The Cherokees wouldnt have us, not the full-blooded ones anyway, so we all ended up Okies. Ive been thru two husbands, both of them Okies, the second one a half-breed like me—and you know what?"

Miz Duchess fork up another gob of that Alpo, cram it in

her mouth and keep right on rappin and chewin at the same time, gravy splish-sploshin every whichway. I just set there takin it all in, figgerin this what I'mo probly be like if I can manage to hold out long as she have.

"My first old man got shot up right there outside Tulsa back in the thirties by the law because they thought he was some small-time bank robber they were looking for which he wasnt. Left me with a boy to look after. My other husband, Bennett, he got called up for World War Two, even tho he was pushing forty at the time, and got knifed in a crap game before he even got outta boot camp."

I wanna tell Miz Duchess somethin good that's strong enough to last her thru the week, but I cant think of nothin, so all I say is, "What's this big decision you want me to help you make?"

"It's simple, Sit, it's very simple. Ive been thinking of moving into an old folkses home. What with Medicare and Social Security and the little money I get from Bennett's death being service-connected, I oughtta be able to check into a pretty good one, dont you think? My son, he up and moved to British Columbia over twenty years ago and took out Canadian citizenship. He's the only person I write to. Answers about one letter to my thirty. So Ive got four granchildren Ive only seen a few times over the years, and two great-grandchildren Ive never seen at all in the flesh. But Ive got some snapshots if youve got a little time to do some looking."

"No, thank you, Duchess. I'll have to check em out some other time. I have to be at work in forty-five minutes. Tell me this. Do you really think life'll be any better for you if you put up at some convalescent home?"

"I'd like to be comfortable and looked after," she say. "I'm tired of dragging these old bones around, wondering if I'll even live to see another bedtime, much less morning. Comes a time when you just get flat out tired of splashing around in this flood all alone. The burden gets to be too much. You wanna be taken care of. I wanna be taken care of. Pretty soon I know it's gonna be time to move on in with the Great Spirit and celebrate, but Ive had it for now. I know this all sounds foolish but you are one of the very few people who've been good to me since Ive been at the Blue Jay. Youre always pleasant. You help me up these goddam steps sometimes when I cant manage them. There've even been times when Ive thought of running up them as fast as I can just to see what'll happen. Maybe I'll have a heart attack and get this misery over with."

"Now, Duchess, dont talk like that. Dont nothin you sayin sound foolish to me. I understand, but you hittin me with some pretty heavy stuff and I'mo need a few days at least to think it over good. That's a big responsibility you puttin on me, askin me what I think you oughtta do with the resta your life."

"I know it is, Sit, but Ive been thinking this way for a long time now. You can put things off and put things off but it's hard to shut off that voice inside you that tells you when it's time to make some kinda important move."

As I'm movin toward the door—picturin myself in her shoes a few Thanksgivins from now or maybe a few Christmases— the smell of that dog food catch in my nostrils and I wanna be someplace where it's a high wind risin, blowin so strong until all I gotta do to be set free is to let myself float right long with it.

"I'll catch back up with you in a few days, Miz Duchess, you hear?"

"You do that," she say, wipin her chin with some of that bathroom tissue she use for napkins. "I'll appreciate it because I respect your opinion on things. Just remember Ive gotta make some definite plans soon. I'm getting too old to be strolling these streets, even tho Dr. Meyer at the clinic keeps telling me all that walking's what's keeping me alive."

Awwwww, here come that breeze again bout to whoosh all the edges clean offa my corners!

Every time I take this Bay Cruise they call it which you buy your ticket for and board right there at Fisherman's Wharf, I'm like the little boy that use to ride up front in the wagon next to Papa when we'd be on our way into town. Sometime, just to make me feel good, he'd lemme take over the reins and tell the mules what to do—*"Haw there, old*

Jenny! Now, gee! Whoa back, Jack!" Then too, I aint never got over the time I spent kickin round Gulfport and boodlin round Biloxi and Ocean Springs, workin my boodie off tryna prove to my family I could make it on my own. Them was good times shonuff! Then I had to leave the Coast to go back home and get called up for service.

All the people—more especially the girls and kindhearted women—all the good times and bad times, pumpin gas and deliverin grocery—it's all like a long ago, faraway dream to me now. Life's like that. You ramble thru all these funny, ridiculous, complicated changes that's enough to set anybody dead against the whole idea of bein alive, then you turn around at the damndest times and catch yourself wonderin if any of it ever really happened. Like, for all you know, maybe you did make it up, or it's somethin somebody told you bout further back than you can remember but you liked the story so much until you started goin round thinkin you the one it happened to. You that very joker the joke done been played on.

What's happenin now is it's Saturday again and I'm bout to meet up with Cornelia and Marcus to go pay Squirrel another visit. In the meantime, I'm payin myself a visit by sailin out here on the water in the cold, lappin up every windy minute of it. You *can* lose tracka yourself, you know. You can even get so far outta touch with yourself until you can look in a mirror some mornins and find it hard to believe that that's you you lookin at. Sometime it's wine that bring me back around to seein who I really am. Other times it's a good workout with somebody of the opposite sex'll do the trick and then again— you never know—that just might make it worse. Playin, prayin, walkin, talkin, sleepin, workin—you never can tell what it is that's gon give you that jolt you need to snap back into your original right mind, that special parta you that's always been there runnin all the way back to when you was just some ignorant kid, settin up in some chinaberry tree lookin at a lizard zip along a branch a little at a time, wonderin what the hell he gon do once he reach the tip where it aint no more limb and it aint no more leaf, just sky for bout as far as you can see.

O lemme tell you, when I'm out here on the water feelin all right, I can just natchally *do* some philosophizin! Land or sea, if I'm in my right mind, I can pretty much tell you everything it is to know bout the world. I know, for example, that it aint no use in me gettin all pushed outta shape about that little thing that went down between Marguerite and Marcus when there I was monkeyin round with the woman in the first place. I'm grown, she grown and Marcus might be my son-in-law but yet and still he a man same as me.

Now, Mama use to would get mad at everything masculine on the face of the earth and say, "Sometime I wonder if it's gon be any men in heaven!" Which is all well and good except you gotta look at that from both sides. I mean, Pearl Bailey wasnt just whistlin Dixie when she put out that record Squirrel use to be so crazy bout. After all, it do take two to tango, dont it?

All right, Cornelia just happen to be my own flesh and blood, but Marguerite some other man's daughter too. Am I makin any sense? So maybe I wont see things all this clear after I get up tomorrow, whenever, but this the way my better mind is workin right now. I wouldnt want anybody to go holdin any such mess against me, so why should I hold it against Marcus?

All of a sudden, I catch myself feelin like some tired old man that's in love with his daughter. This cause me to snap back into real life and look around to see if anybody watchin. It shonuff aint nobody studyin me. They all leanin on the railin, drinkin pop and beer and coffee, smokin, laughin, takin pictures, foolin with they friends and kids and grandkids, yakkin, snackin and havin what pass for a good time.

It's a coupla young people pitchin woo out here, and a considerable number of my people, elderly folk, bundled up, starin at the water that's older'n everybody in the whole world put together—starin so hard out yonder in space until we dont even hardly notice when the excursion boat go into a turn and the trembly taped voice over the loudspeaker say, "We're now approaching Alcatraz Island . . ."

I drift off thinkin bout how that health-gym dude Jack La Lanne got out there and swam from Alcatraz to shore with chains on his legs at the age of sixty. The shape I'm in, I probly couldnt even *walk* it if I was Jesus of Galilee.

Actually, facta business, I never really did ever learn how to swim, but I can look and I can think and thatll just about carry you any place you wanna go or be, specially when you lonesome and kinda likin it for the time bein.

Comin down the gangplank, fulla fresh air, I see a young-ster—look to be round nine—do a double take when he see me and run up and say, "Mister, can I have your autograph?"

His mama look down at him and say, "Danny, why on earth would you want this gentleman's autograph?"

"He's famous," the boy say, "Ive seen him on television. Isnt your name Sitting Pretty?"

"Son, you hit the nail right on the head!" I tell him while Moms still standin there lookin consternated and stupid. "What you want me to sign?"

"Your name, please."

"I already *know* that. What you got for me to write it on?"

"Right here," he say, pushin this old beat-up copy of *Mad* magazine up at me. "Why dont you write it on this?"

I take the book, whip out my five-dollar ballpoint I found in the street the other day, and stop for a second tryna figger out what to write. Sidney J. Prettymon? Sidney "Sitting Pretty" Prettymon? "Sitting Pretty" Prettymon?

By now it's other people comin up lookin, probly wonderin what's goin on. The little boy's mama gettin nervous. So finally I just commence scribblin on the front cover, right up long-side old What Me Worry's head—that joker Alfred E. Newman who to me is kinda what Broadway'd look like if he was white and had good hair and freckles.

Best of luck
from me to you,
yours truly,
"Sitting Pretty"
(of television fame)

When I hand it back to the boy, he take one look, turn red and say, "Thank you, sir. Youve made my day."

"Quiet as it's kept, son, you done made mine too."

Then his mama snatch him by the arm and drag him on off down the Wharf.

One teenage Negro turn and say to the other'n, "Is he supposed to be famous or something?"

I spin around and give em both the peace sign *plus* a power salute which blow they minds and mine as well.

32

I'm lookin at Cornelia now, lookin at the way she hold her head when she walk, the way she got of tuckin her lips in and holdin her beautiful nose in the air that she got from her daddy; lookin at that broad back and them big feet she got from Squirrel. She walkin cross the floor in the hospital cafeteria to the hot food machine to get herself a can of chili.

How she manage to work off all that chili and junk and still keep halfway trim is beyond me. When aint nobody home but her and the kids, she steady be's nibblin and munchin on stuff like that. Course, now, when Marcus get there she switch straight into all that *savwah fair* fifth-generation San Francisco jive—"Darling, would you like a martini or a tequila sunrise before dinner this evening? I have the most scrumptious dinner simmering—all French. Julia Child would turn green with envy, asparagus green. O, which reminds me—youve simply got to listen to this new Al Green album I picked up this afternoon. He really does get down!"—and all such carryin on as that.

Now, lemme tell you, Cornelia wasnt brought up that way. That's jive she picked up outside the house, hangin out with niggers like Marcus in fact.

I aint never gon forget the afternoon I come home from work and found her settin on the stoop with a book open in her hand. She musta been round eight and was all the time drawin these way-out pictures of people look like they come from Pluto or someplace. She look up at me when I hit that front step and she say, "Daddy, you know what? I dont like the way we live. The minute I get grown—you wait and see—I'm gonna leave this place. I intend to get so far away from here that it's gonna cost a thousand dollars to mail a postcard back home."

Now, that is heavy and that's Cornelia. She never did get outta San Francisco really, not yet anyway, but she shonuff didnt waste no time in gettin bout as far from how we raised her as she possibly could. That little girl had her act together from the minute she got here seem like. She never was one for just talkin just to be talkin. She never did say much but once she said it she flat meant it—*period*.

But you take Aristotle—he started jabberin early on and aint stopped since—and you talk about *slick!* He slicker'n Dick Nixon tried to be and then some. I just hope to hell he know what he doin in this lawyer racket, up there defendin all these rascals round here. Next time I see him, just for the hell of it, I'mo tell him, "Take it easy, greazy, you got a long way to slide!"

Bein a daddy or a mama's got its moments, you know. Aint no way of tellin how your kids gon turn out, but no matter how they do—and even tho they wouldnt believe it—you pretty much know em like you do your own heartbeat.

"Squirrel's doing a lot better than she was a week ago," Marcus say to me.

"What's different about her?"

"She's awfully jolly, laughs a lot, makes fun of everything, herself in particular."

"How you doin, Marcus?" I ask while Cornelia still gettin her chili.

"Been thru a lot lately, Sit. I'll have to tell you about it one of these days when youve got a little time."

I can tell by the way his eyes keep cuttin from me cross the cafeteria and back to me again that the boy got somethin pretty serious on his mind.

Cornelia come struttin back ready to chow down now, even if her somethin to eat dont come from no doggone France.

"I really go for that Shelley Winters," Squirrel say, got the television on. Evidently she bout well enough now for them to let all three of us be in her room at the same time. Up there on the tube is Shelley Winters in some kinda Western with Ossie Davis and Telly Savalas, that bald-headed dude. "She'll play anything—housewives, gun molls, nurses, secretaries, rich old ladies, whores. Doesnt matter what role it is, Shelley gets on out there and does it."

Well, aint nobody bout to argue with that and Squirrel know it, so I ask her to click the set off with her remote control. Then, foolin with the knot on my tie, I say, "What is it in the world you want most?"

Marcus and Cornelia go to lookin at me funny and Squirrel raise up on her pillow and say, "Exactly how do you mean that, Sidney?"

I stick to my guns and take it from another angle. "Now, let's pretend like I'm the Question Man or the Question Woman that write for the *Chronicle*. I'm out there interviewin people in the street and my question for the day is what is it you want most outta life. Just how would you go bout answerin that?"

"Wouldnt take me any time to answer that one," Cornelia blurt out. "I'd like to be able to travel all over the world."

"And I'd like to be able to work with my hands," Marcus say, "like, build my own dream house myself from scratch."

"But wait a minute," I tell em, "I aint talkin to yall. I'm askin Squirrel."

Squirrel shut her eyes for a minute and say, "Peace of mind. That's all I want. Peace of mind. No way you can beat it. Ive got two lovely children, a man who loves me, a pretty good home and property and income. Ive got the Lord's blessings, so what could I possibly want except peace of mind?"

Cornelia, she uncross her legs and say, "But what does it mean when you say peace of mind, Mama?"

"All it means is being able to sleep well nights and get up in the morning without worry the first and move thru the day with the knowledge that I'm completely in control of things and then lie down and go back to sleep as happy as when I got up."

"Whew!" I whisper. "That's askin a lot."

"No, not really, not after youve been down like Ive been. People run around vexed about this thing and that thing, forgetting how lucky they are just to have their health and strength to fall back on. Since Ive been laid up here, everything I think about's a wonder to me—everything that crosses my mind, the good and the bad. Does that sound funny?"

"Unusual perhaps," Marcus tell her, "but it doesnt sound at all funny. I'm envious, if you must know, captured as I am in the prime of life yet lacking both the sweep and depth of experience which you must certainly cherish."

Squirrel put her hand up in fronta her mouth and yawn and peep over at Marcus and say, "Well, I dont know about all that. All I know is when you got God working with you, life can be wonderful, filled with wonder. I know there're people in bad shape right here in town much less in Africa, India, South America and throughout the rest of the world. I would like to be able to help all the needy on the face of the earth but I cant. So the best I can aspire to is being an individual who helps other individuals. That's what it finally comes down to in the end, isnt it, one individual helping another? That answer your question?"

She say all this in the clearest voice that sound so for real and sincere until all we can do is do her the honor and pay her the respect of bein quiet for a minute or two.

"It's too much silence for me around here," she say, lookin at me. "Would yall mind if I snapped the TV back on just to provide a little background commotion?"

"No, no," everybody say. "Do whatever suits you. We're *your* guests, remember?"

When the picture flash back on, we look up and see all them technicolor stars packed inside one nother come racin out at you from the center of the screen as the man say, " 'The Saturday Night Movie of the Week' will continue after station identification." Another voice come on and explain how it's KRZY-TV we lookin at. And then while everybody still watchin—they couldna timed it no better—up pop my genial, smilin face again. It's like I'm the man in the moon.

33

Sweatin out the next ten days was like hearin one of them psychics predictin when the next earthquake spose to take place. Dont matter whether they say it's gon happen in a coupla years or a coupla weeks, you kinda wanna believe *in* em but somehow you just cant believe em. All the same, you wind up takin long trips inside your head, too scared to put it outta your mind.

I'm draggin round, hopin Squirrel's doctors is right, yet and still I'm steady tryna reconcile myself to the notion—this strong inklin I got—that they probly wrong, dead wrong. In this case, so help me God, OK, I'm hopin they right.

See, I aint never forgot the time back here—only seem like day before yesterday—when all the forecasters and sooth-sayers and witches and warlocks and O Cult folks was cashin in, warnin everybody to get the hell clean on outta California, the Bay Area anyway, because it was gon be a giant quake that April the likes of which aint never been seen before.

Poor old gullible Jessica Watkins, that crazy lady from Redwood City I was seein at the time, she went and got a real estate agent to sell her home so she could move back down to Little Rock, Arkansaw. Dudes and women I use to hang out with up in the City, Oakland and Richmond, they just up and disappeared.

I even sat down with Aristotle and one of his law partners

214

to discuss what they called the *feasibility* of my makin out a will. What a joke that was. Outside of a coupla rings and a watch my daddy left me, all I had to leave to anybody wouldnt amounted to more'n a pile of Goodwill–Salvation Army rags with maybe three dollars and seventy-five cent in cash plus a unopened bottle of Chivas Regal Scotch I'd been savin up for some special occasion but, in five years, hadnt come across no occasion that struck me as bein special enough.

I keep on callin up the hospital every coupla days like I been doin all along, hangin up relieved she aint been sufferin no setbacks.

One night while I'm bent over, squeezin out a mop, Wanda slip up from behind and goose me then start cacklin when I just about fall over headfirst in the bucket fulla water.

"What the hell you do that for?" I struggle up and turn around and ask her.

"Just a little token of my affection, honey. You been walkin round here all worried and lost in your own thoughts for so long now, I figgered somethin like that might give you a little jolt and let you know it's people you work with every day that be's thinkin bout you even tho you dont be thinkin bout them. How's your former wife gettin along these days?"

Since I dont wanna get nobody's hopes up, least of all mine, I just smile at Wanda and tell her, "OK. We still pullin for the best."

"Yeah, I know, it's awful. I wish I had some ex-old man cared as much about me as you do your ex-wife. That rascal come by the house last week to pick up the kids and take em to Marine World. And all he could think to say to me when I open to let him in was, 'Mind if I bum a coupla cigarettes offa you and use the bathroom?' That's what that Negro come askin me! Aint said 'hello,' 'how are you,' 'excuse me, dog!' or nothin! I was so got off with I yeahbout told him to leave both me and the kids alone and dont never call or write or come back round any of us no more. But I was cool, I was cool, Sit. I put the kids' needs in fronta my own humiliation, like Sam's always tellin me to do, and let him take em out to Marine World. Do you think I did right?"

"Well, I aint got nothin to do with it, Wanda, but seem like to me you done the best thing."

"So when do I get a chance to see you again?"

"You lookin at me right now, aint you?"

"Aw, c'mon now, Sit. You know what I mean."

I know what she mean all right but insteada sayin anything I go to sloshin the wet mop round on the floor.

"What's the matter with you, Sit? You got another one of them old used-up devil women you seein after you get off work?"

"Hey, back off, child! You gettin on my nerves and I already got enough real problems to worry bout without you addin to it. If I'm seein *anybody* that's my own damn business, and so far as *seein you* again's concerned—itll happen when I'm good and ready if it happen at all!"

It wasnt my intention to have to come on so evil but Wanda been ding-dongin me and tryna get in my business for too long now. She one of them worrisome bitches—excuse my language—that keep on harassin and pickin at you till you finally steam up and get em told.

"Well, excuse *me, Sit, Mister* Sidney J. Prettymon! I never woulda thought you cared enough about me to get hot and go to hollerin like that. That's a compliment whether you know it or not."

"Watch out for that patch of water there," I shout as she turn tail and waddle off. "Wouldnt want you to slip and break a hip."

That's what I mean about Wanda. You cant win. If you act nice and grin in her face, she gon put you down. You put her down first, she go for that. Either way it go, there she is, somebody you got to cope with whether you like it or not.

What she really want—and it's plenty women like her—is for you to take your fist and knock her straight cross the room, fight her like a man so she can call the law on your butt and put you in your place, then wipe them tears away, throw them big old luscious legs round you and wear you out by daylight.

I got wise to that jive a long time ago, and that's how come I try to stick it out alone. Bein married one time was enough for me and too much for me. I just couldnt handle it even tho, lookin back, much as I love Squirrel and the kids, I still catch myself wonderin what things mighta come to if I'da never come back from overseas.

216

34

"Lie on your side," the doctor tell me. "I have to make some recordings of your heart."

"Make some recordins of my heart? You mean, like, you gon tape my heartbeat or somethin?"

"That's entirely correct, Mr. Prettymon. It's a relatively new technique we've adopted for use in our volunteer heart study program here at V.A. Hospital. In fact, it's essential that you lie absolutely still, as still as you can. Breathe normally and please try not to cough or move around. You see, the equipment we use is so sensitive that it's easily thrown off by random, extraneous interference factors."

"You just want me to play possum, right?"

"Precisely, play dead. While I'm setting up—itll take a few minutes, I barely know the procedure—I want you to just relax on this table, breathe in and breathe out—and—and—think about anything that crosses your mind, so long as it's peaceful, peaceful things. Youre serene, quiet, totally free of tension, laid back. Have a dream on me. I'll be right back."

So far it's been a pretty strenuous examination mornin. I got here at nine and now it's goin on ten-fifteen and before I go to work I'm spose to get back and check with Miz Duchess bout *her* big problem.

First this wide-butt college girl assistant—she little but she qualify and got what it takes—go to pastin all these little nipplelike electrodes to my chest, remind me of suction cups. Now, I know you know I liked that. She cant help but touch me while she stickin em on. We talk a little. She say she got the feelin she done seen me someplace before but cant think where. I dont say nothin. She shy on the surface but I can tell deep down she probly wouldnt mind *me* doctorin on *her* a round or two.

Next, with all type of wires danglin offa me, they put me on this electronic treadmill and tell me to start walkin while the doctor and the girl get they clipboards out and commence to foolin with these dials and buttons and things. They start me off at a right comfortable pace. I'm holdin on to this bar and steppin bout the way I do down the street when I aint in too big a hurry. Then they speed it up a little bit at a time and ask me to tell em when the pace go to gettin too rough. Ever now and then the girl'd come over and pump the band round my arm real tight and take what they call a readin. Pretty soon, however, they got the damn thing cranked up so fast until I'm runnin and sweatin and breathin hard.

"Too fast for you yet?" the doctor wanna know.

"No, nope, I can still take it all right."

"Are you sure, Mr. Prettymon? This isnt the same as an endurance test. All we want to find out is how your heart responds to physical exertion for a man of your years and condition."

"I'm—I'm really OK," I tell him, pantin and tryna catch my breath.

"All right. Margene, we'll track it for another sixty seconds and then shut him down and take a final reading."

Well, behind goin thru all that plus gettin weighed, measured, a blood test and a urine sample, I'm ready to go home now and get back in the bed. But while I'm waitin on the doctor to get back to me, I try to do like he say do.

I lay back and close my eyes and just breathe and let my mind roam. Before I know it, I catch myself slippin off in and outta that private zone where this world start gettin mixed in with other worlds, where it feel like you wide awake and got everything covered except your mind's on vacation and the

218

parta you that's made outta dreams and pictures done gone on automatic. It dont take long to get there.

Like, it's Itly in the springtime, May of 1945. Mussolini been iced a coupla weeks back but it's warm outside, night comin on. There I am in my khakis and cap—no tie, thank God—layin up in bed with Francesca, only it's somethin funny bout the whole scene which, when I pay close attention, is due to the fact that the bed situated in my daddy's cornfield right there in Missippi. Pasquale, Francesca's little bug-eyed brother, he standin in the door and sayin to her, "You think it's gonna be long now, Big Sis?" Then it dawn on me I got some forma cancer and got it bad. I go to rubbin at my belly. Francesca, when I look dead at her, favor Squirrel except she lighter complected and done undone her bun to let her hair drop. It's all down round her shoulders and back. She pull the covers up round her, then she take holda the cross round her neck, reach round with both hands and unhook it. Now it's all bunched up in her teeny hands. She kiss it, press it up against my forehead and then whisper somethin that sound real serious in Eyetalian—

"Cant tell you how pleased we are, Mr. Prettymon," I hear the doctor say. "Youre only about the seventh person to respond to the ad we placed in the local papers. What made you do it?"

"I'm gettin old and run down. Anyway, I figgered it was high time I got my heart checked out."

"Well, this is only an experimental program. We're mainly concerned with combating heart disease by making people aware of factors which contribute to it—high cholesterol and triglyceride intake, excessive weight, lack of exercise. Was it difficult for you having to fast for twelve hours before coming in so that we could get a clear blood sample?"

"I just turned myself off and went to bed early."

"Do you drink?"

"O, maybe a coupla cocktails before dinner and a few afterward."

"I see. Could you hold that position, Mr. Prettymon? Hold it right there and relax, breathe easy. This is going to take a few minutes."

I freeze while he mash this little microphone-lookin thing in and outta my ribs, bendin his head down to listen while he operate the dials on the machine. He keep fumblin round forever look like.

They got Miz Duchess' stuff and my stuff piled up in fronta the Blue Jay, right out there on the sidewalk, people walkin by and everything. Some of em stoppin to look and pick over it. They must think it's some kinda garage sale. Cant say I blame em. Aint nothin there worth much except maybe for sentimental reasons. Suddenly, oozin out one of the hotel windows, is somebody's loud radio with Nat King Cole's record "For Sentimental Reasons" on it. The Duchess cryin. I'm fightin back tears. Willie G. drive up in one of them big-ass campers cant nobody but the Teamsters afford, got a motorcycle hitched up to each side, his and hers, with a California license plate that read RIP OFF. He open up the back and start throwin all our belongins in, aint asked our permission or nothin. Miz Duchess ease on round and take a good look up inside. "Why, there's two men and a woman in there!" she shout. I walk back and take a peek myself. Shonuff there old Marguerite, Marcus and Broadway is, scrounched up and screwin like it aint no tomorrow. When I ask Willie G. what he think he doin, he say, "You gotta be jokin. When somebody die, it's customary to divvy up the leavins. Yall been dead for bout as long as I can remember and I just now got me a vehicle big enough to haul away yall's trash for cash"—

I open my eyes and see the doctor still hunched over me, sayin, "I'll only be a few more seconds, Mr. Prettymon. I must say, you're the first patient Ive ever had fall asleep on me under these circumstances. If you could only relax that way more of the time, perhaps those readings we got on your blood pressure would be a bit more encouraging."

Miz Duchess done got the jump on me. She already got a few boxes packed. What's left in her room—aside from furniture that come with the place—is all jumbled up and spread out. Look like she fixin to throw a rummage sale or somethin.

"Hey, what's all this?" I ask while she foldin up blankets and puttin em in a big plastic garbage bag.

"Quilts," she say, "the real, authentic, old-timey crazy quilts you make by hand. Grandma used to make em and my mother did too. I made this one myself. I was the only girl in the family that kept up the tradition." She undo one of em and hold it up for me to look at. "How's that for fancy patchwork? Pretty professional looking, eh? People're just now starting to appreciate this stuff again and ready to shell out good money for it too. I was over at this crafts show at the shopping center the other day and seen for myself what theyre getting for homemade quilts. Hell, this one bag here—if I was crazy enough to put it on the market—would snare me a coupla thousand dollars."

"Lookin mighty good to me, Duchess, I must admit. Musta taken you a whole lotta nights to stitch that one together."

"A coupla dozen months might be more like it. Made this for my oldest grandchild to pass on down to her children and grandchildren. By then, something like this'll really mean something, even more than it does now. You like the design?"

"I'm crazy bout it."

"Those colors and pattern—that's Injun stuff. I copied the design off one of my grandma's quilts but worked in my own colors, you see. This here's green for new leaves, and that's reddish for berries. This part's golden yellow for the sun and for happiness, and all this portion through here is pale blue."

"Representin the sky, right?"

"You catch on fast, kid. That's right—the sky and also the color of a clear, flowing stream with sky shining in it."

"And what about all that brown in there, Duchess?"

She chuckle and snort. "Why, that's the earth, Sit, the ground we walk on and plant things in and get laid to rest in. So what do you think?"

"I think it's beautiful."

"Well, I do too. The white man thinks he invented abstract painting and designs and all that. We were doing all that stuff as far back as you wanna go and, I suspect, your people were too."

"My people?"

"Back there in Africa."

"Duchess, it's somethin I wanna get straight. Are you really a fullblooded Cherokee or what?"

"You mean you dont believe me?" She try to look stern but

221

cant help crackin a smile. "Ive only explained it to you a hundred and one times! I'm fullblooded Cherokee but, like I say, there's a couple other strains leaked in there somehow. It's what you *feel* you are that matters in the end, isn't it? Well, I feel like a Cherokee. All my life Ive been treated like one. I *am* Cherokee! That answer your question?"

"Yes it do," I tell her while she puttin that mind-blowin quilt away. "But I got another one for you. What'd you finally decide?"

"About what?"

"About movin out the Blue Jay."

"O," she say, settin down on topa this big rusty trunk got ribbons and strings and sleeves stickin out from under the lid. "To tell the truth, Ive sorta been waiting to hear what your thoughts were on that."

Me, I'm driftin back out there on the water again, takin the boat ride with the whole sky reflectin offa my brain, groovin on the long-ago way Squirrel use to would cross and uncross her legs, back when just the scent of her sent me. *Whew!* That's how much of a loop Miz Duchess threw me for.

"Now, Duchess," I tell her, "here you done packed and sorted all your belongins, and now you mean to tell me you still want my opinion?"

"You never can tell, Sit. You never know. What you have to say just might be the very thing to help me change my mind which I'm not adverse to doing even at this late date."

"Hmmmph, I see. You sure got a funny way of doin things. But, come to think about it, I reckon practically everybody round here do. OK, for what it's worth, Duchess, I think you oughtta should write your son up there in Canada and tell him the situation. I mean, since it look like you done already made up your mind to get out the Blue Jay, then why not try to put up someplace that's close to some of your kinfolks at least. You see my point?"

"I get your point perfectly, but Ive already done that."

"And what'd your son say?"

"He never even answered."

"When did you write him?"

"About ten days ago."

"You ever thought of callin him up?"

Miz Duchess squint her eyes and sigh. "I suppose I could. It's just that—"

"It's just that what?"

"It's just that it's so godawful expensive to call up there. I can barely even afford to call across town much less British Columbia."

"Awww, Duchess, really now!" I take out my billfold and hand her all the cash that's in it—a five and seven ones. "If it's money that's all that's hangin you up, then take this and go telephone your son."

"C'mon, Sit, I cant accept your money."

"Why the hell not? You really got me innerested now in the whole situation. Like, what's he gon say when he hear it's you, your voice, his own mama that's on the line? Here, take the bread and if that aint enough, just say so and I'll be glad to lay a little more on you."

The Duchess get a look on her face that make me think of somebody that's just been knocked down to the ground and picked up and kissed all at the same time.

"I really dont quite know what to say," she tell me. "For days now all Ive been doing is packing and planning, planning and packing, and now—"

"And just where was you plannin on packin all this stuff to, Duchess, if I may be so bold as to ask?"

"You certainly do come on funny sometimes, Sitting Pretty. You arent going to believe this, but I still hadnt made my mind up about what to do. I was simply going about it my way which is to get on the stick and get moving, you know, *action,* and then just see what happens. That seems to be the only way for me to get anything done. I was all packed and ready for a coupla months up there in South City before a woman I was chatting with in a Foster's Cafeteria talked me into moving down here on the Peninsula. I put in three sad, lonely months in San Jose—that's where she was living at the time, just before she passed on—and then ended up moving to Palo Alto. You know how much I like this place. People know me and seem to care a little something about me here. Like, when I set foot in the Penny Lane Market, the main post office,

Walgreen's or Discount Pharmacy or Woolworth's even, there're people working in those places who know me by name and treat me real nice, not to mention all the walking-around people and Blue Jay friends like you who're always looking out after me. O, Sit, I dont wanna go! You dont know my son. I never could explain. He wouldnt understand."

My nerves on edge. It's that itchy time of day again when I'm up against another countdown, when I gotta get ready to go foolin round with Wanda and Sam on into the night. I can see Miz Duchess fixin to go soggy on me, and I just plain am not in the mood.

"Tell you what," I end up sayin. "You go head and call him. Call him tonight, and then lemme know what he tell you, OK?"

She just stand there all wet-eyed, noddin at me, I think, and grinnin.

35

After four Dubonnets, one Rainier Ale and a good old gin and tonic which I really coulda done without but let JoJo McBee talk me into since she insistin on treatin us again, I'm gettin a whole lot looser'n I'd intended to. This tickle Willie G. Aint nothin he like better'n seein me get drunk, or anybody else far as *that* go.

I aint feelin right and I know damn well I aint got no business messin up like this, specially since the doctor done sent back a report on them tests I taken and called me in for a personal lecture. Told me I wasnt doin too good in the triglyceride and cholesterol departments. I gotta cut down on drinkin and eatin greazy food and butter and eggs and stuff and get a lot more exercise than I been gettin.

That was yesterday. Now here I am again out cuttin the gump with Willie G. in San Francisco at JoJo's Let's Get It On Club in the Fillmore. Squirrel spose to be released from the hospital tomorrow, so I figgered I'd lay out round the city overnight and turn up there Sunday to help see her home. But it's too much goin on.

First of all, Wanda aint turned up for work in three days. She called in sick Wednesday which mean me and Sam been haulin ass to keep everything at work covered and together.

We both of us wore out and now that soft-handed doctor tellin me I need to jog or take up bike ridin or somethin, else my arteries gon harden or my heart subject to start actin up. Here I am so tired and shot I been fallin asleep in the bathtub, yeah-bout drownded myself one night, and I'm spose to pry my butt outta bed and go run track first thing.

Second, JoJo McBee keep comin over and hangin round us every chance she get, still tryna talk me into posin for one of them paintins of hers. I like the woman, least I think I do, but she way too connivin and aggressive for me. Ahhh, but that perfume she wear and all that mess wobblin round and thrustin forth from under them cover-up outfits she be sportin! Plus, the woman so doggone frisky it's enough to make a Muslim even lay his Koran down.

Last of all is Willie G. I know the joker kinda halfway jealous of me but I gotta strain and act like I aint been noticin that. Funny how you can up and achieve somethin most people consider to be a real big deal, such as my TV spots, and then turn round and come to find out how jealous and petty people can be, your so-call friends in particular. Look like dont nobody mean you much good. Human nature is all it is, but up until just here lately, I always thought human meant somethin else.

The whole scene is somethin else. What JoJo done, just to experiment, was to shift the poetry night from Tuesday to Saturday. "For the hell of it," she told us. "I'd simply like to see how it goes over." Willie G. been tryna get me out to hear this dude name O. O. Gabugah for the longest, and, boy, he shonuff in his glory now that I done showed up.

How I got thru the first three poets I'll never know, altho I cant help but think the liquor musta had somethin to do with it.

The first youngster to step and read appeared to be in his middle thirties. Talk about emaciated, gaunt and skinny, this boy looked out and out unhealthy. I kept wantin to tip up there to the platform and offer him some of our potato chips and hot sausage, fatten him up some. In between poems, all he know to talk about is how he a parta the underground movement, whatever that is. And damn if he didnt look like he been draggin round and wallowin all down in the sewage system and stuff, up there in a rough-dried shirt, his ass stickin outta his nasty-lookin britches. He kept rappin bout imperialism and exploitation and racism and revolution in his, OK, let's call em poems. Me, I figgered maybe a little fresh air and sunshine and a few square meals might help him get his writin together to the place where he could come right on out and say what he wanna say without havin to beat round the bush so much. Wasnt nothin he was puttin down I hadnt already picked up from Roosevelt and all them New Deal people goin way back.

Next to come on was this roly-poly pale woman got light brown hair and wearin a rug, I guess you call em ponchos. Her big thing is women, women—we women this, and we women that!—a stone bulldyke if I ever seen one. After rantin on in general bout how women been mistreated and all, she finally get down and show her behind in one of her writins where she tell about makin love to this youngish other woman who I suspect is the one settin two tables away on accounta every time the gal on stage say fuck and cunt and clitoris and tit, the girl in the audience go to closin her eyes and shakin her head and gruntin and clearin her throat and coughin too much. Miz Roly-Poly say she a parta the women's movement. If she'da said bowel movement, I might coulda followed it with a little more innerest.

Then here come this sucker in black. He wearin black everything—boots, britches, shirt, undershirt—and even got a black rag tied round his old bald head. His Vandyke beard is gray tho, and his teeth bout as yella as the paper he got his poems wrote on. He got this peculiar-lookin green thing, a gemstone kinda, hangin round his neck. While I'm tryna figger out what his trip is, he bust out whinnyin like a horse and mooin like a heifer, then, just like that, he go right into a sheep thing, a lion or a tiger thing—hard to tell which—and commence to quackin and cacklin and goin gobble-gobble-gobble. I figger he must be losin his mind and break out laughin but aint nobody in the audience cracked a smile. Fact, all except a few colored folks that's there turn around and look at me real rude.

227

Well, this fool went on belchin in the mike and makin fart sounds for a while, then he put the paper down and say, "Basically, we are all animals, each of us, and I strive to make my poems reach people on that level—the visceral, the blood and bone unconscious level where our animalistic heritage is biochemically stored."

And that aint all! He went on readin poems bout the devil and witches and warlocks and after that put some kinda heavy curse on the President of the United States which I frankly had a hard time followin.

I lean over and whisper to Willie G., "What's he talkin bout? What group do he represent?"

"Represent the satanic movement," Willie say all matter of fact.

"What's that?"

"Well, like, they believe in the devil the way a lotta people say they believe in God."

"And you mean to tell me you actually like to come here and listen at these people?"

"I come to hear my man O. O. Gabugah. The resta these niggers can—"

"But all we been checkin out is white folks so far."

"Dont make no difference. Aint none of em sayin nothin. Beside, when I'm drunk I call everybody nigger. America aint nothin but a nation of field niggers nohow. All these saditty civil servants and p'fessors and engineers and guvnors and salesmen and things—all they are is field niggers. Big Charlie set em up to take care of his little nickel-and-dime dirty work while he busy settin up in the big house, shakin glad hands and schemin with all the oil people that's really runnin everything on the sly."

Willie G. say this so loud until even the dude on the stand stop right in the middle of what he sayin and stare at both of us.

"Shhh," I tell him, "there you go talkin too voluminously!"

"Awww, man, this sissy aint excitin me. You know dont no one monkey stop no show."

"You thinkin what I'm thinkin?"

"Probly. What you thinkin anyway?"

"I'm thinkin that since he make out like he love the devil so much, then why dont he just go to hell!"

Me and Willie slap hands just when the audience is halfway applaudin forget-his-name's act.

Way in the background, thru all the clappin, I hear some shonuff disgruntled boxer-lookin customer turn to his girlfriend and say, "Mycetta, let's get to stepping! Later for all this running off at the mouth. I can get up there myself and bullshit. I thought you told me this was a righteous, together place where we could grab a drink and boogie down some. Every one of these old stiff, corny, off-the-wall deadasses need to be dragged out and cremated!"

"It doesnt seem to be working out," JoJo admit, "like it does on Tuesday nights. I had an inkling it wouldnt. Saturdays are just different. But Ive kept my word. I promised the poets I'd give them prime time and see how it went over."

"It aint over yet," Willie G. tell her. "My man gon come out here and shake em up. You watch. You just watch."

"I hope youre right," she say, pickin up my gin and tonic. "Ready for a refill, Sit?"

"No, thank you. I think I'll just coast for a while."

JoJo herself get up there in fronta the mike and explain to the public how this aint the regular thing that the Let's Get It On Club is all about. And then she tell em, say, "In keeping with our policy here to render unto you what is different, what is unusual, what is—shall we call it *exotique,* it brings real joy to my downhome heart to have the opportunity of presenting once again a witty, relevant, provocative young brother whose out-of-sight writings have graced the pages of such prestigious and outstanding publications as . . ." (she unfold a napkin and go to glancin at it) ". . . *Mwandishi, Holy Moly, Black Junction/Function, Othello's Revenge, Afro Confessions, Bronze Thrills, The Jefferson Davis University Quarterly, The New Commune Nest* and *Yardbird Reader.* He also has books out which you may very well find on sale at the door. What else can I say? Ladies and gentlepersons, Mr. O. O. Gabugah!!!"

Just like Willie G. run down to me, he come out in a animal-skin dashiki, only this time it's tiger insteada leopard. Them silver crescent-moon earrings is there, gleamin in the spotlight. He got a tambourine with him and some I think you call em maracas. He got a huge, blown-out afro with a cornrow plaited down thru the middle.

He say, "I'm just up here for a chat to let yall know exactly where it's at. Yall ready for that?"

"YEAH!" the people yell out, probly glad to be up against somebody with a little bit of zip for a change.

"That's what I wanna hear. Now, I want everybody to get their heads together and their hearts together and their hands together and clap along with me and my tambourine here while I deliver my very first offering of the evening. C'mon now—uh-one-*clap*, two-*clap*, three-*clap*, four-*clap* . . . That's it! Yall got it, *yeah!* Just keep it right there!"

"Hey, what's this joker's trip?" I ask Willie. He busy clappin away like he been told to do. "I'm tireda this mess and wanna go someplace and rest."

"Just hold [*clap*] your horses [*clap*]," Willie G. shout.

Well, like it or not, right then and there I can see it aint gon be no gettin outta there till this O. O. Gabugah go thru his number. Anyway, I aint got no intention whatsoever of clappin and stompin and makin a first-class foola myself like he got all the resta them silly people doin.

This how the first thing he come up with go:

> There were two victims of oppression
>   sittin on a railroad track.
> One of them was very Negro,
>   the other one was black.
>
> The Negro want a handout,
>   the black man want a gun.
> The black man say, "Let's halt the train!"
>   The Negro want to run.
>
> The Negro say he want to cry;
>   the black man want to scream.
> The Negro say things will work out
>   because he has a dream.
>
> The Negro say that what he really needs
>   is just some capital.
> The black man say, "You must be
>   pretty stupid after all."

The black man say, "Hey, ain't you heard
  that capitalism's dead?"
The Negro he just look away
  and then he scratch his head.

"If capitalism's dead," he ask,
  "then what's gonna take its place?"
"Why, revolution," the black man say,
  "to humanize the race."

The black man try his best to explain
  but the Negro won't react.
Just then they both look up and see
  the train comin down the track.

"Only revolution can bring evolution
  to us as a people and nation,
And that," the black man tell his friend,
  "will end situations of exploitation."

The Negro stand up with a white handkerchief
  and wave it over his head.
The black man's handkerchief's all balled up
  but the color of it is red.

The Negro say, "This stand for truce.
  I want to ride that train."
The black man say, "I'm gonna blow it up
  and start all over again."

The engineer he slow the train
  and shoot the Negro cold.
The black man say, "Well, Uncle Tom,
  I guess he got *you* told."

Then as he hurled the dynamite
  wrapped up in his red flag,
The good brother say, "Jig's up, old Pig!
  Papa's got a brand-new bag!"

Aw, it was somethin. I mean, the people break out roarin
and whistlin and stampin they feet and cheerin and applaudin.
You mighta thought he was General Mack Arthur or somebody, talkin bout, "I shall return!" I glance over at the other
spose-to-be poets and they just settin there with they jaws
tight, checkin out the audience.

"Look at old Mr. Satan," I hunch Willie G. and say. "Over
there yawnin like he fixin to doze off."

Willie, he chuckle and turn to me, say, "He need to be yawnin all right. Done got up there and put everybody to sleep with all that dull, whiney prose of his."

"Prose?"

"Hell yeah, prose! Cant rhyme, cant chime, aint even got no sense of time. A curse on the President, my ass! Betcha he wouldnt last five minutes playin the dozens. Betcha if I was to tell him, 'Whomped your mama on topa the house. . . . She thought I was Mighty Mouse!' he'd just shrivel up and couldnt come back with dog-do. President dont care nothin bout some little rootypoot hobo out in San Francisco gettin up in public and cussin him out, puttin some kinda halfass hex on him. The President, he probly laid back right this minute on Scotch and tranquilizers, surrounded by art treasures, contemplatin some new visit to Russia or China or someplace and digestin his filet mignon. But, now, my man Gabugah, he hits you right where you live at! Stick around. I want you to meet him."

I stick around thru I couldnt tell you how many more recitations by the dude Willie say is his A.B.C., his ace boon coon. After while, he take a bow, climb down off the stage, pick up this big Mexican shoppinbag fulla books he tote around and head straight for our table.

Willie get up and greet him with a hug and say, "O.O., my man, that was beautiful, beautiful! Like you to meet a good frienda mine that came up from Palo Alto to catch you—Sitting Pretty."

And, just like Broadway, Gabugah go to yankin on my hand and grinnin. "A pleasure to meet you, brother. I been checking you out."

"You have?"

"Sure. On television. Youve been doing those KRZY commercials, havent you?"

"Well, yeah, but—"

"You dont have to come on all that modest, brother. I understand how it is. You got to put up some show of modesty so people wont peep that youre hip to how good you really are, right? Solid! I dig what you do and I hope those spots youre doing'll lead to an opportunity for you to promote some right-on black causes in the future."

Frankly, he makin me nervous and I'm havin trouble figgerin out what he talkin bout, but meanwhile Willie G. cut in
with, "Yeah, old Sit, he somethin else! I think he'd make one
helluva commercial for Geritol or Ex-Lax if they ever let him
and—"

"What you mean—Geritol or Ex-Lax?" I'm hot and hip
to Willie and wanna make sure he know it. I give him my
evilest look. He aint gon wiggle outta this one. "Just exactly
what is it you signifyin bout?"

"Heh, look at that, O.O.," he say, fakin. "Got old Sit's goat,
I guess. Sit, you know I'm just playin with you."

"I dont know nothin of the kind. You think you slick with
your barbs and asides. You think everybody was born yesterday."

"Barbs and asides," Willie G. say, lookin at Gabugah to get
out from under my ruthless gaze. "This brother, O.O., is a
potential poet hisself, come up with stuff'll crack anybody up
they listen at him long enough. Don't worry bout it, Sit, I wasnt
puttin you down or anything."

"The hell you wasnt!"

"Hey, now, wait a minute, Sit! You awfully on edge tonight
for some reason. You know that?"

"On the edge of gettin somebody straight and up offa me.
I'm tireda people signifyin and tryna low-rate somebody and
do you in, and then turn around and act like it was all a joke.
Now, can you comprehend *that?*"

"Hold on here, hold it! You mad at me or somethin? Just
come on out and say it then. Dont be pussyfootin round, actin
all indignant and puttin shit on me without no explanation."

"Explanation, *nothin!* You know you—"

"Brothers, brothers!" Gabugah bust in and shout. "Now,
why dont we all let's sit down and cool down and quit talking
down to one another. We can resolve this misunderstanding
rationally, I'm sure, no? No sense in two honorable gentle-
men such as yourselves—and good friends at that—falling out
over such a trivial matter. First of all, I got something to present to each of yall."

We all sit down even tho I aint yeahbout to cool down. One
way or nother, I'mo break Willie G. up from his bad habit of

233

woofin and stylin at my expense. But right this now I'm tryna act sensible while I watch O. O. Gabugah pullin copies of his books from out his bag and writin in em.

"This here's an autographed copy of my last book, *Slaughter the Pig and Git Yo'self Some Chitlins*. Actually, it's my first book but it just in a special twenty-fifth printing edition, hardcover. And this is the Australian edition of *Love Is a White Man's Snot Rag*, just brought out last week in Melbourne. O yes, and I want yall to be the first to get signed copies of my latest which hasnt even been released yet. Pub date isnt until April first."

"Hmmm," Willie say, pickin it up and lookin at the cover that's got a picture of Butterfly McQueen on it. "Innerestin photograph. Isnt she the sister played in *Gone with the Wind?*"

"That's *her* all right," Gabugah say, glistenin.

"And this title," I say. "Now, lemme get this right. *Ghetto Buddha: Modes, Odes & Coal Train Roads: A New Hoo-Doo Autumn*—that's really what you callin it, hunh?"

"Yeah. See, I believe in rolling right along with what's happening." Gabugah look around and dont seem to pay much attention to all the folks that's lined up to talk with him or get his signature or shake his hand. "Tell you. This strong-arm stuff is going outta style. By that all I mean is—check back with me and see if I wasnt right—this racket of playing with the honky, calling him all kindsa pigs and devils and mother-fuckers, that's going the way of the Deuce and a Quarter, stacked heels, reggae and being a nigger. This depression got it so a whole bunch of people're experiencing hard times. Theyre no more interested in getting whipped round the head by how-tough-it-is-to-be-a-nigger niggers than a drowning man is in lemonade. The new lick is being yourself—love, roots, nostalgia, superstition, well-bred bitchiness, getting by on a shoestring, the economy. As a good Marxist Pan-Afro-Muslim Cultural Nationalist, I'm a firm believer in the efficacy of Dialectical-JuJu."

"What time is it?" I ask. "I got this appointment."

Willie say, "What kinda appointment you got this time of night?"

"It's a private appointment. Oh yeah? Yeah, that's right. O, I see."

By now I can tell by the way he squintin his eyes Willie G. bout ready to leap cross the table and go round and round with me.

"So anyway," Gabugah go on, "with this new book, I dont intend to take no chances. I'm branching out into unexplored territory. You might even say *Ghetto Buddha* is sort of a concept album—you know, like Marvin Gaye's been into—except in printed form. We got to get the brothers and sisters to reading more. Of course, having the pictures in there and the short poems in big type helps."

"So you still intend to stick with the community," Willie say, "but youre changin your approach somewhat."

"That's right, there you go," Gabugah say. "Eventually, see, I'd like to stretch out into doing LPs and concerts, maybe even singing my message with a band behind me like that other brother from Harlem is doing—Phil Scott-Seagull. We're both from the same neck of the woods, you know. Did yall know I was born in a taxicab right there at 125th Street and Lenox Avenue on Lincoln's Birthday?"

"That's what the write-up say on the backa this book," I tell him. "Nice meetin you, man, but I gots to cut out. Thanks for the autographed copies. I'll carry em home and give em a good goin over. Take it easy, Willie."

"Be checkin you, Sit. Hope everything go all right tomorrow. How you gettin home anyway?"

"Who said anything about goin home? Dont worry, I'll get to wherever it is I'mo go."

While Willie G. frownin and shakin his head, JoJo slip up behind me and go to whisperin somethin. It's hard to make out what she sayin with the jukebox blastin and all the resta that racket. She step in front and motion for me to follow her toward the door. After we get there, she stand oozin fragrance by the cigarette machine a second and then hand me this envelope that's all sealed up.

"What's this all about, Jo?"

"Read it when you get home. I just want you to know I'm really serious about doing your portrait. And I'll do it for

235

nothing. Not too many painters around who're willing to make that kind of offer, in case you didn't know."

"That's awful nice of you, JoJo, but—"

"But nothing. Give me a ring any weekday morning, but make it soon, will you? There's something about you, a certain something that fascinates me, that I like, and I'll bet I'm not the only one. Those TV plugs you did are going to make you lots of friends. Read my note. Youll call me?"

"OK, I'll do that."

"You wont be sorry."

"Never thought I would be."

"Tell me something."

"What?"

"Have most of the women in your life had to come on to you as aggressively as I have?"

"Damn, JoJo! Do I have to answer that?"

"Nope, not at all—but I'll bet it's been a long time since youve made any real effort to win a woman, hasnt it?"

36

It's like old times. I'm three sheets to the wind but yet and still my mind feel clear as cold water. I mean, I come bustin outta JoJo's joint just like I know what the hell I'm doin. Actually, like most people when they aint on no hard-and-fast schedule, I'm not sure if I'm comin or goin.

Course, I can drop by Cornelia and them's place and stay the night, or bus over to Aristotle's in Oakland—but it's kinda late for all such as that and I aint in the mood to try to straighten up and play sober.

Now, what I'd kinda like to really do is another matter. I wouldnt mind backtrackin after all this time to Green Street in North Beach, Adele and Sandy's place. Been thinkin a lot about that silly night I spent with that girl with her sweet, slinky, fine brown frame. If any of yall old enough to remember Nellie Lutcher's record, youll know what I mean by that. Then too, I wouldnt mind callin Marguerite up—husband or no husband—and gettin her to drive up here and do a quiet Holiday Inn thing with me, talk all that unsettled mess out sensible-like. For once in my life, I got the money to pay for it right there in my pocket. Be worth it just to have her wrap herself up round me so cozy again I cant hardly tell my toes from my earlobes. Wanda? That's some too much *way* too bossy woman for the easygoin man I am! Jessica Watkins, she done moved back to Little Rock *but*—if you dont mind bein round somebody that's crazy and talk a whole *lotta* old off-the-wall first one thing and another, which I dont mind, and then go out and get all liquored up and cut the fool the way it aint never been cut—then she the one can make my love come splatterin down like rain down a drainpipe the same way Maria could when I use to get to kissin and feelin on her in the dark.

But it's another aspect to these women and women in general. I find they make better all-round companions than men do if you a man and can keep that TV–Hollywood fairytale that's spose to be what men and women is all about out the picture. Sex, that's OK. Romance aint nothin to play with. All I'm sayin is it's a lotta romance that go with just likin somebody for who they are and what they stand for or wont stand for. Like, you really like somebody and they like you in a hit-and-run kinda way that aint connected up with kids, family, holdin down a job or buyin a house and fixin it up or botha yall's future and you got a good friend that aint gon try to control you because they damn sure dont wanna be controlled! That's pretty much how I been dealin with it lately.

Inside my drunk old tired head, I flash on myself in North Beach, Broadway, hobblin round thru all the fast action, halfway expectin to run into Adele. Market Street done got real weird since it's been all beautified. Polk Street and Union Street aint my thing and the Tenderloin's realer and colder'n Broadway—Broadway the street and Broadway the dude.

I end up at the Mars Hotel down on Mission below Market where the people pretty down and out and out-there too, but at least they for real. The floors creaky and the plumbin work funny and the overall atmosphere bout the same as the Blue Jay.

First thing I do—before even takin off my coat and shoes—is take all the money out I'm carryin and count it on the bed. Stacked up in fives, tens, twenties, fifties and hundreds, it's shonuff a beautiful sight. Remember readin someplace where Muhammad Ali use to do the same thing after he cashed a big check from a fight. Course, now, that was back in the early days when he was just playin round with thousands in-steada the millions he later started knockin down.

Layin in the bed with my trusty transistor plugged in one ear, a half-swigged bottle of Dubonnet right there where I can reach it, readin bout the economic decline of the United States in a rumply *Examiner* somebody left behind, I feel perfectly at home. Hell, I been practicin up for this big depression ever since the last one. It's good to see all these bourgie, arrogant, greedy self-righteous folks gettin hit in they ass pocket for a change.

I know that sound cold but that's how I feel as I snap off the light, click off the radio, stretch out and pull the covers up over me, ready to fall off and dream till the year three thousand.

37

Well, there Frazier is in a sharp tweed suit and a fancy raincoat look like it was sewed right on him. Frazier aint studyin bout no so-call depression. Cornelia and Marcus, they lookin kinda sad. Aristotle, he a gentleman too, aint a speck of dust on him noplace and he the cheerfullest of all. Now, Izetta, poor Izetta, she fightin hard to keep from cryin, almost as much as my daughter is. I cant really look at either of em for too long.

We all stand around the hospital room, packin stuff up, makin small talk and congratulatin Squirrel who still lookin better'n she did even a coupla weeks ago but I can tell she gon have to do some doin to gain back all her weight and looks.

Outta all the days for her to come home on, the doctors would have to pick a stormy Sunday where it's lookin like Noah bout to go raid the zoo.

"How you feelin?" I ask Squirrel.

"Pretty good," she say, "and yourself?"

After she say good-bye to all the nurses and personnel who been figgerin pretty strong in her life of late, we help her down the elevator to the backa the hospital where the three cars is waitin—Frazier's, Marcus' and Aristotle's. I ride up front in the lead Chrysler and the kids all follow behind.

All the way home, Squirrel keep sayin stuff like, "I cant tell you how much those people back there mean to me. Theyve been absolutely wonderful, all of them—doctors, nurses, attendants, all the other patients."

"Yeah, I can see you was pretty popular."

She glance at me in the back seat and go to cryin real soft. Frazier take one his hands off the wheel and pat her shoulder and say, "Wont be long now, sugar. We'll be back home where we'll try and continue the good service and hospitality and you wont have to worry about anything."

What we do is talk all that sweet nothin that people slip into when it's a tense situation you dont wanna be reminded of. Out in the livinroom it's records playin and food bein served in the dininroom. Neighbors droppin by and even Cornelia and Izetta busy tryna be jolly while we take turns, one at a time, slippin back to Squirrel's room where Frazier, bein thoughtful, done gone to the trouble of settin up one of them adjustable hospital beds for her to feel comfortable in.

Marcus come out lookin funny and troubled. As I head in, I stop and ask him, "How she doin?"

"O, you know, she's fine. She's making a lot of religious pronouncements, however, which I frankly dont know how to deal with."

"Like, for instance?"

"Youll see. Go on in. She's been asking about you."

"Well, I'mo see if I cant get her to laughin a taste and trippin out, as the hippies use to say."

"All I can wish you is the best of luck." We standin in a little kinda hallway-like and Marcus all of a sudden do a pause and jeck his head around. Then he stretch his neck out toward my face, lift his pipe down outta his mouth and say, "Hey, Sit!"

"How come you whisperin?"

"Listen, I may not get another chance to talk to you."

"Bout what?"

"Now, you know as well as I do, Sit, that men are men and women are women. As a matter of fact, contrary to what's believed in some quarters, women are far earthier than we are.

241

But we can level with one another, right? Both of us are well aware of the little games we've been involved in."

What's crackin me up even tho I dont so much as smile is the fact that Marcus—who got this strange look in his eye—is talkin all this frantic man-to-man stuff in the loudest whisper I ever been hit with. And while he hissin and gruntin and carryin on, I'm driftin on back to that embarrassin phone call I put in to Judd Jenkins bout all this that dumb night Broadway walked in on me fakin my voice. Add to this the fact that right now I'm so fulla salami and cheese, chips and chip dip I wanna burp—and you might get a fairly reasonable idea of how I'm feelin. I mean, I definitely am *not* ready for *any* of it.

"We're friends, right, and relatives, sort of," Marcus go on, "but you already knew *I'd* been seeing Marguerite and I know youve been seeing her, and—well—I thought you might want to know that theyre splitting up."

"What you say?"

"Yes, he's off in Switzerland with some young woman he met there. According to him, theyre going to get married. Marguerite's taking it pretty hard. To compound problems, I may very well be out of a job if he persists in allowing his personal life to get in the way of the project we've been assigned to."

"Gotcha," I register as he wink at me wobbly-like and move on back to the scene and the eats.

Squirrel layin up there in her cream-colored turtleneck, got the lamplight so low I cant hardly tell it's her.

"Know what I been thinkin bout?" I tell her after we go thru the peck-on-the-cheek thing all over again.

"Something good, I hope."

"The time we took the kids campin down there near Monterey, remember that?"

"How can I forget? Pfeifer State Park."

"Yep, and Cornelia fooled around and got poison oak. Aristotle cut his foot wide open runnin round barefoot where it was some sharp stones. You got a bad crook in your neck from bein all scrooched up in the sleepinbag, and I came down with a cold it taken me yeahbout a month to shake. Aw, that was a mess, wasnt it?"

"It was pretty bad all right," she say, smilin kinda. "But you forget. That doggone crook in my neck wasnt anything compared to the way my right eye swoll up there from that insect bite. I thought I was going blind."

"Listen, dont laugh. The same thing happened to me a coupla years ago right there at the hotel. I woke up and couldnt even get open my left eye, think it was, and I was shonuff figgerin it was time for me to quit foolin round with that old Ripple and mess and, tell you, that's exactly what I done. Went runnin to the doctor. He go to yankin on my eyelid, take one look and say, 'Looks like a nasty insect bite to me, Mr. Prettymon.' I was ready to move out the Blue Jay which I presume got chinches and bedbugs and things. Two days later tho, I'm back functionin OK—but I betcha one thing. Betcha I aint never touched another dropa that stuff."

"Didn't have any business touching it in the first place," Squirrel bat her tired eyes and say.

My main idea's to make the woman forget about things and just groove along on light conversation, but I can tell from in front she on a serious kick.

"You prayed for me, didnt you, Sidney?"

"Sure did."

"Do you know I can tell?"

"How?"

"Just by the way things've been going. I think a lotta people must be pulling for me spiritually. I can feel a power flowing my way, a certain kinda strength. You get to the place where I'm at now and you can see and feel and sense this sorta thing. I know something or somebody is watching over me. When I was a little girl, my grandmama on my daddy's side would tell me, 'The dark days're gonna come, Sequoia, and theyll blind you at first, blind you something fearful. But you dont pay em no mind. You just stick around close to God and He'll make everything all right. By and by youll live to see the light again.' "

It's that *by and by* part that keep hangin me up. Me, personally, I'm tireda Negroes always yearnin; all the time down on they knees, fumblin and mumblin: *O Lawd, I'mo make it on over one of these old days.* It's plenty white folks and black ones too that go for that image. So long as we stay in bondage, cussin out the white man, or dancin and singin and shootin up the place, rappin bout pussy and watermelon and revolution, and crackin jokes; just so long as we stay in our place, then it's all gon be settled in the Great By and By.

Aint no way in the world you can come out ahead with that type of outlook. You just cant win. If you fail at somethin, people gon say it's on accounta your race. You didnt have the same opportunity as white folks. If you luck up and get somethin worthwhile goin, the first thing they gon say—like Willie G. done already let me know—is that's just because you black and got special privileges. Whatcha gon do? You can stay drunk or go on dope—like a lotta bright people wind up doin —or you can get you a horn or a gun or some kinda act together, or even get rich or get religion, but they still aint gon leave you alone, not these neurotic and psychotic people that's in the world now, meddlin in everything. I grew up with a lot of em and I mean to tell you they really dont mean nobody much good, not even they own selves!

Squirrel check me out while I'm thinkin all this and say, "C'mon now, Sit, speak what's on your mind."

"Dont start me to talkin," I tell her. "I'm like old Sonny Boy Williamson, God rest his soul. I'll tell everything I know."

We run thru subjects we aint never really discussed before —women, men, time, raisin up younguns, how come we couldnt get along, Frazier, money—and we even reminisce about the ocean, our ocean, that fabulous rainy mornin.

"Listen," I say, "since we been on the subject of money. I got somethin to present to you."

"What?"

"Here."

"What's all this?"

Squirrel cant believe what I'm doin—countin out the two thousand dollars from my KRZY money, pilin it right there next to her on the edge of the bed. I still cant hardly believe it myself.

"What's all this?"

"What do it look like?"

"Money, money and more money, but what does it mean? Why are you doing this, Sidney?"

"Means I'm makin a token payment."

"Token payment on what? What's the matter with you? Where'd you get all that from?"

"Got it clean and legitimate, the same as Frazier and Aristotle and Marcus, from professional services rendered, Squirrel."

"But what am I supposed to do with it?"

"Do whatever you want to. Put it in your savins account. Invest it, spend it, sew it in your mattress, whatever you feel like doin with it."

"You mean to say this is what they paid you for being in those television commercials?" She scoop up a handfulla twenties and there Andrew Jackson is, with his ornery self, lookin her dead in her eye. "Youre making me nervous, Sidney. I dont understand."

"Honey, there's nothin to understand. I want you to have this money. I dont really need it."

"Poor as *you* are? What you mean you dont need it?"

"I mean just that. I want you to know I been thinkin bout you and, even tho money aint no true measurement of nothin, it would still do me a lotta good if you'd just accept this gift and forget it."

"Are you losing your mind?"

"How come you say that?"

"Sidney, now, listen, will you?" She place both hands down on the bed longside her and scoot up a notch or two so that the pillow now restin round the middle of her back and she practically talkin to me face to face. "Frazier and I, as you well know, are far from being what's called well-off, but we have managed to make ends meet and, as far as I can see, with insurance and whatnot, we should be able to survive all my medical bills and expenses. I think youre an angel for thinking of me but—now, how can I say this?—I, well, I really cant accept your money." She reach out and pat my cheek and grin for a second. "What is it youre feeling so guilty about anyway that you have to come on so extravagant? All I asked was for you to pray for me. That's all Ive ever asked of anyone in the family."

"Squirrel, I know that. Cant you just take the money and

sock it away someplace and forget we ever had to go thru all these silly changes?"

"Nope."

"No?"

"Forget it, Sit. You need it more than I do. All I want outta life right now is a little of my health back and to serve God by doing right by Frazier and the kids and our grand-children."

Our grandchildren. That's enough. I grab all the bread up, cram it in my jacket pocket and study her peculiar half-grin—buck teeth and all, overbite's what they call it now-days—long enough to just lean over and give her one of them sad, happy, serious you-still-my-woman kisses where your mouths and tongues get mashed up together and you jealous of whoever it was created the world for havin sense enough to put a part for a man and a woman in it.

Izetta come tippin in as I'm steppin out. She look so pretty in her denim pantsuit, I wanna just haul off and hug her. In fact, that's just what I do and half near scare her to death.

"How's Squirrel?" she ask as she let go of me.

"Seems as strong as ever to me."

"How do you mean?"

"Youll see. Go on in. She'll be happy to see you."

I say this, feelin like a failure still, yet knowin Izetta have to go in there and do a little battlin of her own with Squirrel, namely the kind that mamas and daughter-in-laws seem to get they jollies off on.

246

SPRING

38

I think what I like most about joggin—now that I done finally talked myself into keepin it up—is the way your mind work when you be out there doin it.

Like, now that the weather done cleared up some and the mornins is dry and clear, I'm up by six and out there runnin in the fields round Stanford no later'n seven. I really try to do it up right too—put on my little sweatsuit from Sears that come with a hood, along with my Adidas tennis shoes, got my jockstrap on and chuggin away like the Southern Pacific commuter train you can hear comin and goin way back in the distance if you listen hard enough that hour of day.

And when I'm runnin and workin up a sweat, I dont be studyin bout nothin but good stuff. Actually, it's possible to work off tensions and work out problems while I'm makin them rounds, lettin my whole head unwind. I use to get out there a little later—round eight o'clock—but then I'd keep runnin into this young dude name J. J. Moon he call hisself, one of them supercomputerized modern Negroes that's got everything timed and all worked out, or so he think, and cramp anybody's style with all that depressin, undigested talk he carry on bout race and politics, mostly on a superficial basis. Now since I been gettin out earlier, way ahead of the sun sometime, I aint got to put up with no J. J. Moon, plus

I'm happier, losin weight, gettin in shape and cant wait to get home and soak in the tub.

Just how long I can keep this up, I dont know. The first few times I went out, it like to killed me. I'd cramp up in my side and the backa my legs and be all outta wind in no time. But little by little it got to where I could do fifteen, twenty minutes, a whole half hour and finally a good forty-five minutes. Doctor done warned me to hold it down to thirty.

Aristotle want me to move into a condominium not far from theirs up there in Oakland. He say I could walk over to Lake Merritt mornins and do my joggin. Archie Moore the fighter use to work out round there in the old days, way before they dug all that dirt out and pumped in the lake. But, like I say, I still dont know.

I'm still speculatin bout a whole lotta possibilities that's done cropped up here recent. It's another kinda life I'm bout to go up against and I aint too sure I'm ready for it yet.

You see, use to be you could count on old friends and all the prestige and seniority you be done built up after bein in a particular place goin on so many years. Nowdays, my friend, you can plain forget it! Grandfolks and oldsters dont seem to count for too much no more. You out there on your own with just yourself and your younguns if you got any. And if you *really* gettin old, too bad. Unless you got a little bread, a little dust to thump around, you can yeahbout count on both hands the number of old folks that's relaxed and thrivin and still gettin a charge outta this thing called life, lemme tell you.

My children and grandchildren—I worry about em. I mean, it's to the place where they got old-timers that can afford it cooped up in so-call adult communities. They got the young marrieds hemmed up someplace else with other folks that's in the same boat as them. Now the singles thing is goin over big, gettin bigger and bigger in fact. Marriage goin outta style. People just aint got the time. They too busy doin they own thing to be foolin with wives or husbands or kids, much less they own fathers and mothers. What's it all comin to? Scares me a little. Like, when I read in the *National Enquirer* bout how they busy now tryna create life in test tubes—workin hard at it too—plus on topa that they wanna control what type of person gets born, it kinda got me to wonderin what's the point of it all in the long run.

Now, I ain't nobody to talk. I got enough guilt rattlin round inside me to make up for stuff I aint even pulled yet. If my life was only a tape like the one playin now on this cassette machine I'm recordin all this on, I would rewind back to the parts I wasnt happy with and just retell em, you know, make em over again. But what's done gone down is for real and cant be erased. I aint about to lie to come out lookin respectable. When all this is wrote up, I want it to be wrote up right, straightforward, *down,* so my kids and they kids'll know I came down this path once, done a lotta trippin, and taken the time out to tell all about it.

All such as this is what be runnin thru my mind when I'm out there tryna exercise the fat from round my heart.

When I saw Broadway's picture in the Palo Alto *Times—* PENINSULA SUSPECT SEIZED IN EAST BAY DRUG ARREST—I figgered out it musta happened at his girlfriend's apartment, the same one he'd been watchin me on television that night with. Cocaine was what it was all about, what else? A hundred thousand dollars' worth which, from what I'm told, aint all that much, but Broadway, accordin to the write-up I clipped out, was parta some regional network. His favorite tune he use to punch up on the jukebox at the Ocean Cafe was a thing by a group, Chairmen of the Board, about how if you danced to the music, dont you know, you got to pay to the piper, ask your mama.

Much as I hate to say it—and yall know aint no love lost between me and Broadway—I catch myself missin him, the same way I miss Miz Duchess who finally got in touch with her son. He sent her the money to fly up to Vancouver for a reunion, a kinda test run. "I'll go up there, Sit," she wanted me to know, "but if it isnt to my liking, youll be seeing me back at the Blue Jay fast." I slipped her a coupla twenties, figgerin she'd be back in a week, but it's been some time now. The other day I got a card from her that say:

Greetings, Sit. Well I guess you can see that I'm still here.
All it does is rain all the time and my arthritis is acting up.

251

*It is good being around my grandchildren and their par-
ents. So far we are all getting along okay. Miss everybody
there in good old sunny P.A. My boy is going to pay for
my junk to be sent up. I'll send a longer letter when I have
more to say. Love to you and all the folks.*

Ms. Duchess

So the Duchess is gone too, bless her heart. Willie G. back
workin at another wreckin yard, this one in San Francisco
over round Army Street. I decided to let bygones be bygones
and dropped by to see him one afternoon after I'd got thru
posin for JoJo at her place up on Portrero Hill. He was settin
in the shed chompin on a cheeseburger, got grease and grime
all over his hands and it's seepin all in the bun, look so nasty!

"How come you quit the museum?" I ask him.

"It was a sweet little gig, Sit, but I couldnt make no money
at it and the junk business aint too bad to be connected with
now that the money done got so funny. People tryna fix those
old cars up a little insteada rushin out and buyin new ones,
and *we* got the best used parts, you know? How you and JoJo
gettin along? I was by the club night before last and she told
me you subject to move up here too."

"Aw, we doin all right. She a pretty good woman, a helluva
artist too—got that paintin so it favor me more'n I do myself.
It's like lookin in a mirror, only more innerestin."

What I aint about to tell Willie G. is how JoJo—who know
everybody that's anybody, look like—done put me on to some
kids that's startin up a brand-new advertizin agency to make
TV commercials. They crazy bout them ads I was in for
KRZY and want me to sign with em. Already they done
landed they first account to do a pet food commercial. Miz
Duchess would flip. I'mo play this chauffeur that's drivin this
Airedale and this Siamese cat around in a Rolls-Royce. Am I
gon take em up on it? You better believe it! Five thousand
dollars aint nothin to sneeze at.

"Well," Willie say, "when you move out the Blue Jay, thatll
just leave your old pal the Professor, hunh?"

"Naw, you mean you aint heard?"

"Heard what?"

"The Professor got married."

"You jokin."

"Nope, I'm dead serious. Married that cute little Stanford gal he was goin with—Karen. And he aint no fool neither."

"I never thought he was."

"Her daddy got some money, live up there in Los Altos Hills. They sent me one of they fancy wedding invitations and for a while I was even thinkin bout attendin the reception. But then I got to picturin myself standin up there makin all them overeducated people nervous, aint got no servin tray in my hand or chef's hat on my head. What I look like? So I just bought em a present and wished em the besta luck."

"Yeah, I know how it is," Willie say. "The first thing you know theyll go to talkin sports with you or the race problem, prejudiced as they can be and dont even know you know cause they dont even know it theyselves. You think youll move to San Francisco or cross the Bay or where?"

"Been thinkin bout Oakland. Let's face it, Willie. Sixty is sneakin up on me fast."

"Sneakin up on you?" Willie G. laugh. "Look to me like old Father Time done taken his sickle and been hackin you *all cross* your face and upside the head."

"OK, man, you got me on that one. Anyway, I'mo try my best to get along with my kids and be round my grandkids more. It aint too much else I got goin for me."

"The question is do they want *you* to be hangin round *them?* Hey! Are you losin weight or couldnt you find the right size jacket at the Goodwill?"

"You dont ever let up, do you?"

"Glad to see you gettin your sense of humor back, Sit. I was worried for you there. You got a new job lined up over there in the East Bay?"

"I'm tryna get somethin goin. I can go on unemployment for a while, just long enough to get relocated, you understand. Something'll come thru."

"I'll cross my fingers for you. Wish the hell something'd come thru for *me*. I got a new woman I been jivin round here lately, a social worker, older woman. You right about these young women and girls and things. I'm switchin over to the ones that's got a little mileage on em. They got more goin for em, specially in the finance department. Romance without finance dont be gettin it no more. Nothin from nothin—you know what that leave. A few wrinkles and crow's feet dont bother me none. That's gon be my new thing, Sit."

This new thing I'm fixin to tiptoe into might work out and then again it might not. I figger I aint got nothin to lose. At least my grandchildren got a savins account goin for em now with close to two thousand dollars in it, steady gatherin innerest.

Squirrel still thin and sickly-lookin but she up and gettin around and goin strong for the time bein. How long it's gon last, dont nobody know. She couldna picked a better man than Frazier to hook up with. That joker got patience on topa patience. We even went out a coupla weeks back, just me and him, and had a few drinks, hard liquor, which I probly wont tell the doctor about. Squirrel just might end up outlastin both of us in the long haul. But, hey, if this was to happen, I dont reckon it'd faze anybody, least of all yours truly.

I know it's gon always be some hurdles to be gotten over, somethin aggravatin to test you out every incha the way. I'm just gon try to take it in my stride—like I been doin with this joggin—a little at a time and do the best I can. When you come right down to it—aint much else I *can* do, you wanna know the truth.